continued . . .

"A promising new series . . . Entertaining and vivacious characters."
—*Romantic Times*

"I cannot imagine a cozier setting than Renaissance Faire Village, a closed community of rather eccentric—and very interesting—characters, [with] lots of potential . . . A great start to a new series by a veteran duo of mystery authors."
—*Cozy Library*

Praise for the Peggy Lee Garden Mysteries

Poisoned Petals

"A delightful botany mystery."
—*The Best Reviews*

"A top-notch, over-the-fence mystery read with beloved characters, a fast-paced storyline, and a wallop of an ending."
—*Midwest Book Review*

"Enjoy this pleasurable read!"
—*Mystery Morgue*

Fruit of the Poisoned Tree

"I cannot recommend this work highly enough. It has everything: mystery, wonderful characters, sinister plot, humor, and even romance."
—*Midwest Book Review*

"Well-crafted with a satisfying end that will leave readers wanting more!"
—*Fresh Fiction*

Pretty Poison

"With a touch of romance added to this delightful mystery, one can only hope many more Peggy Lee Mysteries will be hitting shelves soon!"
—*Roundtable Reviews*

"A fantastic amateur-sleuth mystery."
—*The Best Reviews*

DEADLY DAGGERS

Joyce and Jim Lavene

BERKLEY PRIME CRIME, NEW YORK

THE BERKLEY PUBLISHING GROUP
Published by the Penguin Group
Penguin Group (USA) Inc.
375 Hudson Street, New York, New York 10014, USA
Penguin Group (Canada), 90 Eglinton Avenue East, Suite 700, Toronto, Ontario M4P 2Y3, Canada
(a division of Pearson Penguin Canada Inc.)
Penguin Books Ltd., 80 Strand, London WC2R 0RL, England
Penguin Group Ireland, 25 St. Stephen's Green, Dublin 2, Ireland (a division of Penguin Books Ltd.)
Penguin Group (Australia), 250 Camberwell Road, Camberwell, Victoria 3124, Australia
(a division of Pearson Australia Group Pty. Ltd.)
Penguin Books India Pvt. Ltd., 11 Community Centre, Panchsheel Park, New Delhi—110 017, India
Penguin Group (NZ), 67 Apollo Drive, Rosedale, North Shore 0632, New Zealand
(a division of Pearson New Zealand Ltd.)
Penguin Books (South Africa) (Pty.) Ltd., 24 Sturdee Avenue, Rosebank, Johannesburg 2196,
South Africa

Penguin Books Ltd., Registered Offices: 80 Strand, London WC2R 0RL, England

DEADLY DAGGERS

A Berkley Prime Crime Book / published by arrangement with the author

PRINTING HISTORY
Berkley Prime Crime mass-market edition / September 2010

Copyright © 2010 by Joyce Lavene and Jim Lavene.
Cover illustration and logo by Ben Perini.
Cover design by Lesley Worrell.
Interior text design by Laura K. Corless.

ISBN: 978-0-425-23644-4

BERKLEY® PRIME CRIME
Berkley Prime Crime Books are published by The Berkley Publishing Group,
a division of Penguin Group (USA) Inc.,
375 Hudson Street, New York, New York 10014.
BERKLEY® PRIME CRIME and the PRIME CRIME logo are trademarks of Penguin Group
(USA) Inc.

PRINTED IN THE UNITED STATES OF AMERICA

10 9 8 7 6 5 4 3 2 1

One

It was June 20, summer solstice, the longest day of the year. The sun was shining clear and hot in Myrtle Beach. A man dressed as the Pied Piper was leading a group of children to the Mother Goose Pavilion for story hour. And across the King's Highway, William Shakespeare was making three maidens in jewel-colored gowns laugh at his odes.

It was good to be back!

I'm talking about my triumphant return to Renaissance Faire Village and Market Place, of course. The sights, sounds, and smells had called me home. My life as an assistant professor of history at the University of South Carolina at Columbia was a world away, except for the work on my dissertation, "Proliferation of Renaissance Crafts in Modern Times."

I felt like a spy with two identities. The assistant professor had closed up her apartment for the summer and sneaked down here today. The other part of me is always here, at least in spirit.

"Jessie!" Chase Manhattan, my main man and the bailiff of the Village, scooped me up and swung me around. "I thought you'd never get here!"

Life was good. Everything was going to be perfect this summer. I could tell by the way it was starting. No clouds on the horizon for me.

"You're not going to believe who's coming tomorrow." Chase took my only bag from me as we started walking toward his apartment in the dungeon.

Every bailiff has to have someplace to administer the laws of the Village. Chase's place is the two-story dungeon with fake cells (and prisoners) on the first level and his place (which I share when I'm here) on the second level. Outside are the stocks, of course. Vegetable justice is administered at least twice a day. If no real evildoer can be found (in this case, visitors who want to do something unusual), then Village personnel are recruited to have squishy tomatoes and other soft fruit thrown at them.

It's all in the name of reenacting life in the Renaissance, or a reasonable facsimile. There are a few anomalies in the Village. Some of them include living storybook characters, like Mother Goose and Bo Peep. Some take the form of historical inaccuracies, such as King Arthur being alive at the same time as Robin Hood and William Shakespeare.

The thousands of visitors who fill the cobblestone streets each day are enough to keep Adventure Land, the parent company of Renaissance Faire Village, happy and wealthy. That means all of the drama students and otherwise crazy inhabitants who live here full- and part-time get to continue hiding from the real world in colored tights and doublets.

"Who's coming tomorrow?" I waved to Fred the Red Dragon, and he saluted back with his big claw.

"Alastair the Great! He's going to be here for one night

to put on a show! Can you believe it? All the years I've been here and he's never made it this far south. Usually he spends all his time at the really big Ren Faires out west."

I recognized the name right away. I mean, who wouldn't? Alastair is one of the best-known swordsmen in the modern-day Renaissance world. Every Rennie knows him. "He's coming *here*? That's amazing! Do you know what he's doing yet?"

"Are you ready for this? He's dueling Daisy."

"Daisy?" A picture of Master Armorer Daisy Reynolds flashed into my mind. Daisy was a large woman with big, muscled arms. She always wore a breastplate with a phoenix on it. Her badly dyed blond hair made me want to drag her to the nearest salon. The unnatural shade actually made my eyes ache. But she was formidable with a sword or a dagger. No one, not even the legendary Alastair, could take her down. I planned to put good money on that fact.

I was apprenticing with her this summer. She was going to show me everything about sword making as they did it during the Renaissance. We had bonded during my stays here. There was something between us now, almost like a mother-daughter tie. It would probably never be broken, at least not until my apprenticeship was finished.

"She'll mop the floor with him." I smiled smugly as we passed the Monastery Bakery where the Brotherhood of the Sheaf make bread at least three times a day.

"You don't get it." Chase clued me in. "Alastair doesn't lose. It's all planned, like everything else around here. It would be like King Arthur not being able to draw Excalibur from the stone."

"That's not fair. Daisy has spent years as one of the best armorers and sword fighters in Ren Faire history. She can't roll over for Alastair."

"She will if she wants to keep her job," Chase snickered.

"Relax. It's not real. It's not like it matters who wins or loses. As long as the customers are happy and Adventure Land keeps sending out the paychecks."

"You don't *really* feel that way. If you did, you'd be working all the time on your patent attorney job." I stared at him, wondering what was wrong. "Is something bothering you?"

"Let's duck into Peter's Pub for a minute. I suddenly need a beer more than life itself."

I followed him into the crowded pub that was darkened to help keep it cooler. The smell of stale beer and some kind of food cooking wasn't very appealing. I put it down to the fact that I was still wearing my street clothes. When I'm fully acclimated, this is one of my favorite places.

"Hey, Jessie! Good to have you back!" Peter Greenwalt, the longtime proprietor of the establishment, hailed me. He sloshed down a tankard of ale on the table. "Here's a free one for you. Where are you apprenticing this summer?"

"Thanks! I'll be with Daisy all summer."

There was a significant pause during which I noticed a few knaves and varlets who had obviously stopped in for something cool. They all looked up at me silently for a few seconds, then looked away.

Peter rubbed his thick brown muttonchops. They went well with the long hair that was pulled away from his long face in a ponytail. "Good luck with that."

I knew better than to ask him or try to solicit answers from the knaves and varlets. Instead, I leaned closer to Chase as he stared into his tankard. "What's up with everyone? What's going on?"

"It's nothing. I told you about Alastair. Everyone is acting stranger than usual because of the duel."

I took his word for it. My Renaissance Village home

away from home is a delicate balance of insanity and drama. On any given day, twenty madmen (all part of a guild) are at work on the cobblestone streets beside jugglers, walking trees, and fair maidens. It doesn't take much to upset the applecart.

I noticed that Chase was still looking kind of gloomy. "Are you that upset about this thing with Daisy?"

"Thing with Daisy?" He glanced up at me. "Oh, yeah. The duel. I'm not worried about her, Jessie. She'll get by. Adventure Land loves her, and so do the king and queen. I'm sure she'll get a nice bonus for her trouble."

I sighed. This was like prying nails out of wood. "Then what *are* you upset about?"

"My brother."

"Did something happen to him?" I didn't even know Chase *had* a brother. That bothered me a lot.

"No. He's coming here." Chase polished off his beer in a single swig.

"And that's bad because . . . ?"

"Remember me telling you about the family business back in Scottsdale? Morgan only comes to visit when they've all decided to pressure me about going home."

I absorbed this information and realized how terrible it was. No wonder he was depressed. Leave Renaissance Faire Village forever? It was unthinkable. "Is he your older brother?"

"No. He's my evil younger brother. He's unscrupulous, conniving, and manipulative. Much more like our father than I am. I don't think he's ever worn anything except a suit and tie. I seem to remember him being born in one."

I laughed. Chase's frown told me right away that laughing was not the desired response. He didn't think it was funny. "We'll have to think of something to keep him busy while he's here. It won't be that hard. By the time we're finished with him, he'll want to stay here instead of taking you back."

Chase groaned. "Not exactly what I had in mind."

"Don't worry. We'll get through this. Morgan doesn't stand a chance." I tested the name Morgan Manhattan in my thoughts. At least he wasn't named after a bank, like Chase. Their parents must have come to their senses after their firstborn.

"You don't know Morgan." He shuddered and drank more beer. "He'll be here tomorrow. Between that and the extra security for Alastair's visit, I don't know what I'm doing."

"Let me help. I know Daisy will understand. I probably don't have to worry about doing much tomorrow anyway if she's getting ready to meet Alastair. Let me take care of Morgan for you. I'll show him around the Village."

"He's been here before."

"I'll show him around again. Really. I can do this. You concentrate on what you have to do. I'll handle Morgan."

Chase's dark brown eyes met mine with a faint glimmer of hope. "If anyone can take him on, it's you. Promise me no swims in Mirror Lake off the pirate ship."

"I promise."

"And no locking him in a privy and having it taken away."

I finished the last of my ale. "You know, those things are once-in-a-lifetime experiences. I'll come up with something fresh for Morgan."

"Now I'm worried." But he looked happier anyway. He paid Peter for our drinks and picked up my bag again.

It was fun to watch a few of the highborn ladies and one or two pesky fairies ogle Chase's tall, muscular form when he bent over. No doubt he was a fine hunk of man from his long brown braid to his leather-clad legs. And he was mine. Morgan sure wasn't going to take him back to Arizona without a fight.

"Why didn't your parents name Morgan something financial like they did you?" I asked as we emerged back out into the blazing sunshine.

"What do you mean?" Chase nodded to a passing knight who wore his chainmail even in the heat.

"I mean they named you Chase Manhattan. Why didn't they name him something to do with money?"

He smiled and kissed me right there on the street. "His full name is Morgan Stanley Manhattan. My mom made some serious cash with her investor the year he was born."

"Oh." What would I know about investing after all? My brother Tony and I came from poor stock that never had more than whatever it took to get by. Still didn't. "Speaking of brothers, have you seen my evil twin recently?"

"He's actually working at the castle right now. Queen Olivia was looking for a personal assistant. *You know?*"

"*Eww!* I don't want to think about Tony and Livy. Why would he do that?"

He shrugged his broad shoulders beneath his dark green tunic. "I believe it's probably easier than being a knight and jousting all day. Besides, she liked his demon dancing last fall and demanded a command performance. He's been up there ever since. Usually he's with her when she takes her stroll."

"I thought Livy and Harry were back together again."

"I think they are." He opened the door to the dungeon. "But you know how that goes. Harry has a personal assistant, too."

I held the dungeon door open as Chase passed through. The Village reveled around us with music, dancing, and plenty of food, the smell of which was beginning to appeal to me now. I wouldn't let my brother, or Chase's brother, mess up my perfect time here this summer. Everything was going to be exactly like I wanted it to be.

Chase and I hadn't seen each other in a week or so, since his last visit to Columbia. There was only one thing on our minds when we got upstairs and looked at each other. He smiled his cute smile. I laughed and threw myself into his waiting arms. We kissed, nice and long, for a few minutes.

Then his two-way radio went off. There was trouble at the hatchet-throwing game. They needed him right away.

"Sorry." He kissed me one last time, then started out the door. "I'll see you later. Are you going to check in with Daisy?"

"As soon as I put my stuff away." It didn't surprise me that something had come up. Chase wasn't merely a figure-head at the Village, like the king and queen. He actually had some police and paramedic training, which made him more like a constable. He resolved disputes, held shoplift-ers for the police, and generally kept the Village running.

It meant we were interrupted from time to time, but I knew we'd come back together later. I'd only recently adopted this more mature way of looking at his role in the Village. I was more secure as his girlfriend now. I wasn't worried about him fooling around with one of the fairies, or that I'd come back and find him here with Princess Isabel.

We'd been a couple for about a year, but we'd been friends first, and that's what made me confident in our rela-tionship. I knew I was needed, wanted, possibly even loved, although we didn't go into that on a regular basis.

So the new, more mature me put my few things into the drawers Chase always left open for me. I hadn't brought much, just a few cute nighties and some underwear. I'd trade in my jeans and T-shirt for Village garb this afternoon after talking to Daisy. That was another plus about spending time here: my own wardrobe lasted longer. I'd worn the clothes of a kitchen servant, craft apprentice, a wench, and a pirate, to name a few. My first few years were random jobs. This summer's attire would probably be something simple, like short pants and a tunic.

I looked through Chase's stuff, like I always do. What kind of girlfriend would I be if I didn't snoop around some?

He collected a lot of little things from around the Village: horses, knights, flags, and pirate paraphernalia. His clothes were always carefully folded and tucked away, not like mine, which were usually shoved in and wrinkled.

I looked at the pictures of him with his family, noticing his brother beside him for the first time. Maybe I only had eyes for Chase before, I don't know. I suddenly felt as though I were in some kind of science fiction movie where relatives are mysteriously added to pictures.

But Morgan had probably always been there. He was a head shorter than Chase, with short, brown banker hair. He wore a suit in all three adult photos and a cowboy outfit in a picture of the two of them as kids.

There was one photo with a tall, thin blond woman who was standing almost on top of Chase, between him and Morgan. I couldn't tell for sure which brother she was with, but she definitely wasn't their sister, even though she looked really comfortable with them.

Maybe she was Morgan's wife. I hummed a little as I thought about it and put Chase's pictures away. That was it. She belonged to proper, button-down Morgan.

Of course, my old insecure self would've immediately demanded to know who she was as soon as I saw Chase again. But not my new and improved self. I was with Chase. We were a couple. Even if she had been his girlfriend back in Scottsdale, that was a long time ago. I have plenty of men in my past. For years, I had been with someone new each summer while I was here. There was no point in dredging up old flames. Chase and I were together. That was all that mattered.

I left the dungeon and wandered back out to the Village. There were teenagers fooling around on the tree swing next door. I passed the Caravan Stage where twenty girls were dancing in their colorful harem costumes while eager men watched and tired mothers caught a breather with their interested children.

I waved to Sam Da Vinci, who winked at me as he worked on a pretty maiden's portrait. Then I headed to Armorer's Alley where Daisy had her sword shop.

The Alley is made up of three arms makers: Swords and Such, Splendid Shields, and Enchanted Armor. There are other arms sellers in the Village, of course, but these three are the official Village armorers. That means they make armor, swords, and shields for the king and queen as well as many of the nobility. Basically, it makes them top of the food chain in their guild.

Daisy, at Swords and Such, is probably the most successful. She's been here since the Village opened and is the head of the Weapons Guild. She's very influential, and I love her vitality, her reckless I-don't-give-a-damn attitude, and her arms. No, really. Her *real* arms. This woman could probably lift a horse without any problem. I'd love to have the kind of commitment it takes to have muscles like that. I envy her spirit of not caring what anyone thinks about her and living her life exactly as she wants to.

I pushed open the door to Swords and Such and nodded to the handsome young guy with great hair at the counter. "I'm here to see Daisy. I'm Jessie, her apprentice for the summer."

Sir Great Hair swung his loose, flowing, chestnut brown

hair (exactly like a model in a TV commercial) and smiled at me, showing his perfect white teeth. I remembered seeing him here before in visits past. Daisy had good taste in men. "She's in back. Let me know if there's anything else I can do for you."

I smiled but kept my distance. Sir Great Hair was good-looking, but he didn't hold an oil lamp to Chase. When you've got the best at home, why take the leftovers while you're out?

"I'm Ethan, by the way. I'll be happy to show you around the Village when we're finished this evening."

I was about to put the word on him that I was taken, despite my lack of visible ring, but there was a shout from the back of the shop, and I ran toward it. "Daisy?"

She looked up at me, half caught in a light blue silk gown. Her usually frizzy, strangely colored hair was smooth and a normal blond shade. There was also a mass of curls around her robust face. For the first time since I'd met her, Daisy Reynolds, armorer to nobility, was wearing makeup.

And not light makeup. She looked like she had spiders on her eyes. The huge false eyelashes had to make it hard for her to lift her eyelids. She was wearing so much blush, it was as if she'd been out in the sun all day with only her cheeks exposed. Her lips were red and drawn into a bow shape. The overall effect was one of a giant, muscular Kewpie doll.

"Help me get out of this damn thing," she snarled. "How do women wear these anyway?"

I ran to her side, and so did Ethan. He didn't blink as we helped her out of the gown. Maybe he was gay. Most men look no matter what, in my experience.

Then I realized he knew more than I did. Daisy was still wearing her armored breastplate and shoulder padding. On her hefty legs was light chain mail, like the knights wore beneath their armor during the joust. Ethan glanced at me and shrugged.

"You can't wear so much gear under these dresses," I explained. "They're only made for a corset or a petticoat or two."

Ethan swung his hair perfectly. "I tried to tell her that. I told her if she wants to wear chain mail, it has to be *over* the dress, not under."

Daisy sat down hard on a crude wood footstool. "Who knew dressing up was so stupid? I give up. Alastair will have to like who I am now, not who I used to be twenty years and forty pounds ago."

Was this my idol primping for a *man*? A man who was destined to beat her in a showy mock battle? I couldn't believe it. "Do you *know* Alastair?"

"*Knew him* would be more like it." She glanced up at Ethan. "Fetch me some ale from the pub, and be quick about it. Dressing up has given me a major thirst."

Ethan nodded and left without a word. I sat down on another roughly made bench and straightened out the beautiful gown she'd almost clawed her way through.

"Alastair and I were a hot ticket a while back," Daisy confessed with a heavy sigh. "I thought I might be able to rekindle that magic while he's here. Nothing permanent, you understand. I was thinking about a quick tumble in the blacksmith's hay."

"This is a beautiful dress." I completely understood what she meant by keeping her life free of encumbrances. Until last year when Chase and I got together, I'd felt the same way. "Maybe we could still make it work."

Her blue eyes (I'd never noticed before what a gorgeous shade of blue they were) looked up into mine with hope. "You think so? I'm not so good at this girly stuff. I think I used to be better. But I don't know. Maybe I'm only making a fool of myself. Alastair travels with a buttload of girls wherever he goes. Why would he even look at me?"

"Because you have something they don't have," I explained. "You're probably the *only* woman in the Ren world that could kick his ass. Men find that strangely attractive. I think you might be surprised by his reaction when he sees you here."

Daisy got to her feet, amazingly agile for a woman her size. She slapped me so hard on the back, I nearly fell on the floor. "Well, what are we waiting for? I'm supping at the castle tonight with him, Livy, and Harry. I'm glad you're my apprentice this summer, Jessie. I'm gonna need all the help you can give me."

Two

Accompanied by a chorus of grunts and groans, the occasional curse, and a few whiny complaints, I managed to help Daisy unbuckle and remove her breastplate. That was the easy part. Apparently, she hadn't gone out without her full-body chain mail in years.

"The dress won't fit with the chain mail under it," I told her finally. "You have to take it off."

"I'd feel naked without it," she complained. "Look at how thin that dress is. A good, stiff sneeze could penetrate it. How am I supposed to be protected?"

"I think that's the idea." I tried to be patient. "I'm sure the last time you saw Alastair twenty years ago, you two weren't wearing much between you."

Daisy sighed, her big blue eyes gazing skyward. "Only some really good chain mail. You know, the kind you hear them talking about that's light but strong. I haven't had anything that good since then."

I realized then that I couldn't reason with her in her

current, besotted state. "You want to wear the gown to impress Alastair, right? Then you have to take off the undergarment."

She finally agreed, and with several moments of tugging and cursing, I managed to help her get the chain mail off. Beneath it, she was as smooth and pink as a baby. I looked at the chain mail in my hands. Maybe she had the right idea.

At that moment, Ethan came in with the tankard of ale. Without any sign of ill ease, he strode forward and handed it to her. Daisy (again, no embarrassment whatsoever) drank it down in one thirsty gulp and handed the tankard back to him. "By God, I needed that," she said, then let loose with a large belch.

I picked up the light blue silk gown and pushed it over her head, mindful of the curls and lipstick. Ethan watched as though I were dressing a doll. His blasé observation seemed a little weird to me, but obviously it was part of their relationship. I didn't want to get involved in that.

The gown flowed over her, a perfect fit except for the length. Daisy was stout and muscular, a good six inches shorter than my six feet in height. And she had the smallest little feet. I envied her those tiny digits. I could imagine stuffing them into petite glass slippers, not like my size-twelve gunboats.

The gown's extra length pooled around her ankles. There was no way to tuck all of it up into the sash at the waist. My skill with a needle and thread was only good enough to mend small tears in my clothes. I couldn't repair what needed to be done on the dress.

Ethan smiled and took a needle from a pincushion on a table next to him. He swung his hair out of his face and helped her stand on the little bench where I'd been sitting. "Lucky for you one of my foster mothers taught me how to make a dress when I was in kindergarten. You stand right there, and we'll have you ready in a few minutes."

"Do I look all right?" Daisy's voice was gruff and her eyes were a little tearful. "Twenty years is a long time. You can't even imagine, Jessie. You were a kid when Alastair and I were together. Time changes a person. And not just physically. I hope he'll be willing to overlook my flaws."

"He will if he loves you," I quoted that time-honored phrase mothers have been telling their daughters for thousands of years.

Ethan stared at me from his spot on the floor, and Daisy bit her lip. "I hope it's better than that," she said. "Alastair and I didn't part on good terms twenty years ago. It wasn't easy being young and ambitious. We were both so beautiful and talented. We both wanted the world at the end of a sword. Alastair has that now. But it kind of passed me by."

I started to remind her that people who didn't go to Ren Faires had no idea who Alastair was, but quickly reconsidered. Telling her that wouldn't help her feelings of inadequacy, so I kept my mouth shut while Ethan scooted around in his tights on the wood floor.

"I'm supposed to duel him tomorrow night at the castle," Daisy said. "And I'm supposed to lose. He's Alastair, the greatest swordsman of our time. Of course I'm supposed to lose."

I smiled. "I bet you could take him, though."

She grinned back at me. "In a fair fight? You bet! I've watched his videos. He favors his right leg because of an old wound I inflicted once when we were practicing together." She stared off with a those-were-the-days look on her face as I helped her with her makeup. "It doesn't matter. Sure, I could beat him, but they're paying him big money to be here and the crowd wants to see him win. We'll give them the show they want."

It was beautiful in a sad and pathetic way. This place and other places like it around the world created their own heroes and legends. I wouldn't want it any different.

Ethan sewed for a few more minutes in silence before pronouncing that the gown was ready to go. "You look like a queen!"

Daisy took his hand and stepped down from the bench. "I feel like a queen. Thanks, you guys. Let's hope Alastair feels the same. Now, where's my sword and scabbard?"

We tried to convince Daisy that she didn't need her sword to have dinner at the castle. Ethan tried to coax her into thinking of herself as nobility for the night. "You aren't Daisy Reynolds the sword maker. You're Queen Daisy of Swords and Such. Think about being mysterious, beautiful, and enticing. You don't have to stab him with a sword to get his attention."

Daisy patted his arm. "My sword goes with me, my friend. Let me find my boots and go to the castle to woo my oldest love while the day is still fresh."

"About the boots," I began, hoping she'd change her mind and wear something more appropriate.

She laughed at me. "I know. Just jerking your chain, Jessie. Have you checked in yet? If not, take the rest of the day and enjoy yourself. Report back day after tomorrow for apprentice duty. And make sure that pasty-faced Portia gives you something better to wear than a fairy costume or some nursery-rhyme character. I work my apprentices. I'll see you then."

I was already enjoying being Daisy's apprentice. I knew this was going to be the best summer ever!

"I'll see you later, Jessie," Ethan said with a little head bow that threw his gorgeous hair forward.

"Until then, sir." I did the appropriate half-head bow that showed respect but not the full-head bow one would do for the nobility.

My short, kind of choppy brown hair could never measure up to Ethan's elegant tresses. I was wondering what kind of woman would date a man with hair like that when two beautiful wenches came in and called his name. They both belonged to the same gorgeous hair club Ethan obviously was part of. As I walked out the door, I briefly mused about what a child born of Ethan and one these women would look like.

I took Daisy's advice and strolled through the Village, talking with people. I had some maple fudge at Frenchy's Fudge Shoppe. I'm not sure if fudge even existed during the Renaissance, but in this case, I'm willing to let it go. There are too many other anomalies that the Society for Creative Anachronism, or SCA, wouldn't approve of. Fudge is surely the least of our sins.

I followed the King's Highway up past William Shakespeare's spot and Brewster's Tavern. A little ways up from there, Galileo was showing teenagers where to look for stars in the summer sky. The smell of barbecue pork swept down from the Three Pigs Barbecue, battling it out with pizza smells from Polo's Pasta.

Between them, the Lovely Laundry Ladies were putting on their performances as they washed clothes at the well (showing plenty of cleavage) and told bawdy jokes. The Green Man was taking a stroll down the cobblestones while children danced around him. The Green Man (sometimes a woman) is a treelike figure (human on stilts) that moves slowly around the Village all day. Visitors like to have their pictures taken with it.

I was surprised to see it still following me as I neared Mirror Lake. That was some fast moving for a figure on stilts. I waited as it came nearer, ignoring Pan playing his pipe as he danced around a fountain. Something about the tree's lumbering movements caught my attention. Usually the tree moves stiffly, for obvious reasons. This tree's movements gave me the impression there might be a bear inside rather than someone on stilts.

A small window at the base of the tree crown opened, and a familiar face smiled at me. "Hello, lady. It's good to see you. You were gone too long."

I smiled back, realizing this human tree didn't need stilts to tower above most visitors. "Hello, Bart. I see you decided to stay on."

"You never know what's going to happen here. One day, I'm Death, or at least the personification of Death. The next day, I'm a walking tree. I like the tree better."

"I don't blame you. You make a very good tree."

"You really think so? I try my best to make it real for everyone."

"I really think so." I laughed. "I'm sure everyone enjoys seeing you."

He moved his leafy branch arms to give me a big tree hug. "What are you doing now?"

I told him about my apprenticeship with Daisy. "It's going to be a great summer."

Bart's large features, framed by green tree leaves, looked sad. "I hope Daisy doesn't take losing to the Great Alastair too personally. I hear she has to lose or he won't ever come back again."

"That's what I hear. Good thing for him, or Daisy would send him packing."

We were descended on by what appeared to be an entire busload of children all wearing the same red Camp Watogame T-shirts. There wasn't any more time to talk, but I knew we'd run into each other later after the Village closed for the night. I saluted him as the camp advisors started taking pictures and he closed the face hole.

That was a surprise. But working at the Village always

is. I never know who I'll meet here or who will be gone from summer to summer. I watched the pirate ship, *Queen's Revenge*, sail majestically across Mirror Lake in front of the castle. It was a sight that never failed to stir my senses. I'd been a pirate for a summer. Maybe pirate blood never really leaves you.

I skirted my way around the edge of the lake while workers began putting up posters advertising the duel between Alastair and Daisy. It was to be a battle royale between two iconic figures, an event sure to draw a huge crowd. There would probably be standing room only in the Great Hall tomorrow night. I noticed, too, that ticket prices reflected that thought. They were twenty dollars higher than for a normal event.

I passed Stylish Frocks, where many of the costumes for the Village were made. Next door was the costume rental for visitors, which doubled as the free costume shop for the Village residents. This is where fairies, wenches, pirates, and wizards were made. It was a never-ending job for the dozen or so seamstresses behind the costume changes to keep up with Village folk.

Surprisingly, there was no line, despite the crowd of visitors traipsing through the main gate just beyond the shop. Usually you had to wait at least thirty minutes to get a costume, whether it was one you wanted or not.

Portia, the pale-faced mistress of costume control, was at her usual spot in the open window from which she dispensed boots, belts, doublets, and hose. She was leaning her head on one hand, sighing as usual, staring out at the Village before her.

"Hey, Portia!" I thought I'd go with a happy greeting and see where that got me. "I like the way you're wearing your hair this summer. It looks really good on you."

Portia and I don't always see eye to eye or britches to

gowns, as the case would be. Many times we've growled and snarled over a costume she wanted me to wear that I wouldn't wear. I've lost count of how many times we've argued over colors and materials. Not that I *want* to give her a hard time, but whatever you take, you're usually stuck with for your time at the Village. Wearing the same basic outfit for eight weeks, especially one that's too big or too stupid, makes for a rough summer.

To my surprise, she smoothed her dark hair back with a hand and smiled. "You think so, Jessie? I've been working on my appearance for a while. There's a man I'd like to impress."

Bart could've knocked me down with one of his beefy arms and I wouldn't have been more surprised than to hear Portia's response. What was it with everyone? First Daisy with Alastair, now Portia with whomever the lucky lord or serf was who'd caught her attention.

"Anyone I know?"

She nodded toward someone in the street behind me. I turned and saw Ethan, of all people (not in Swords and Such, as he should be), sporting the two perfect-hair women on his arms. The three of them looked like an ad for Renaissance plastic surgery. *Wouldst thou not adore to looketh this way?*

I wanted to offer her some encouragement, but what could I say? Portia was older, plainer, and just this side of dowdy. Why would she even *consider* someone like Ethan? Why not someone like Bart, who was more her speed? "Oh, *him*. You know, I think he's gay. Maybe you should look for someone else."

She sighed. "There won't ever be anyone else for me." Her beady little eyes focused back on me. "Who are you apprenticing with this summer, Jessie?"

She remembered my name twice in a conversation. I

was amazed, since she'd called me everything from Janie to Jezebel in past encounters. Like she didn't know the answer before she asked. "Daisy, at Swords and Such. I hope you have some nice common-young-man-type outfit for me. Boots would be great."

Like a personal fairy godmother, Portia quickly assembled the requested clothes from her stock of costumes; as if by magic, the outfit I wanted—including a really nice pair of boots—soon lay on the counter between us.

"I was thinking you might be able to do me a good turn with Ethan," she almost purred from her side of the counter. "Since you'll be seeing him every day, you could point him in my direction."

I was flattered. Really. But it wasn't possible. I'd put together some good matches in my day and mended some problems between couples who never thought they'd be together again. But I knew this particular pairing was simply *not* going to happen. "I'll see what I can do," I told her as I carefully moved the clothes I coveted away from her.

"I'll see to it that you wear whatever you want this year," Portia promised. "But I want him, Jessie. Make it happen."

I smiled at her, wondering what she'd say if I told her the truth. It was too ugly to imagine, so I lied. "It'll be my pleasure." But all the while, I was thinking about Bart and Portia. I'd never seen Bart with a woman, be it fairy, witch, or sprite. Why not get the two of them together? Portia needed someone. So did Bart. Ethan didn't. It made perfect sense to me. Portia and Bart would never know what hit them.

"I'll be expecting to see some progress soon," Portia said with an evil smile.

"I'll let you know." On second thought, maybe Bart was too nice to get mixed up with her. I might have to think of someone else. Maybe whoever was playing the Black Knight this summer.

I walked away from the costume keeper feeling a little less optimistic about my perfect summer. But I told myself these weren't storm clouds threatening to rain on my Renaissance Parade. These were simply obstacles to get around. I already had the clothes in my possession. Maybe I could rinse them out for the next eight weeks and not worry about Portia's love life.

I waved to Robin Hood and Maid Marion as they came out of Sherwood Forest. The forest was almost a separate theme park of bandits who lived in trees, made up their own rules for survival, and took toaster ovens from unwary residents. It was also one of the most popular parts of the Village, at least as far as visitors were concerned.

"Good day to you, Mistress Jessie." Robin doffed his cap and swept me a low bow.

He was one of my summers in the past. I'd stayed with him in Sherwood Forest, feeding the band of hungry Merry Men and sharpening arrows. "Good day, Robin. Marion."

Marion nodded (small head bow) and smiled. "It is good to see you here again. Where are you staying this summer?"

And so it went as I reacquainted myself with all my former Village friends, and sometimes lovers. Toby Gates, who'd been Robin Hood for several years (including during my time in Sherwood Forest as Maid Marion) was still a good-looking bandit. There was a rakish air to his good-guy charm.

I continued across to the Village Square where a group of troubadours were singing and playing to a rapt crowd of visitors. I came through Squires' Lane and stopped to see

Mrs. Potts at the Honey and Herb Shoppe. She was looking well and knew all the latest gossip about the players in the Village. She told me everything, from Galileo dating Sarah from Sarah's Scarves to my brother's latest conquest, a barmaid from the Peasant's Pub who was there for the summer from the University of California at Berkley.

"It's always something," she said as I munched her fabulous honey cookies and washed them down with chamomile tea. "I've even heard a few tales about Crystal the Pirate Queen getting back together with her husband, the straight-laced accountant from Georgetown. They say she may give up the Village for good. Probably just as well for that baby of hers. No self-respecting mother would raise her child with a bunch of pirates, that's for sure."

"Have you heard anything about Bart dating anyone in the Village?" I thought this might be a good time to find out if he was attached to someone already. I didn't want to break someone else's heart to make Portia feel better, even if she had given me my awesome boots.

Mrs. Potts wrinkled her normally smooth brow beneath her white mobcap. "Why, no. I haven't heard anything about Bart since he put on the tree suit. It's hard to make time with the ladies when you're dressed like a tree. Do you have someone in mind for him?"

I didn't want to give away my idea. It needed time to incubate before I hatched it. I told her I was only wondering about him and thanked her for the tea and cookies. With a promise to come back soon, I left her shop and started back toward the dungeon. The day was waning, and even though there was a long night ahead (the Village closes at midnight on Saturdays), I thought Chase and I might be able to have dinner together.

The Dutchman's Stage was full of comedians doing their routines, which frequently included hysterical jokes about body-function sounds and female anatomy. What always amazed me was how they got women of all ages to join them on stage. Had they never seen this kind of show before? One thing for sure, most of them went back to their seats with red faces.

I didn't see any sign of Chase as I approached the dungeon and the stocks outside. A man and woman were standing close to the door, their heads bent together as they spoke. He was broad shouldered, good-looking, and had a familiarity to his face that told me right away he was Chase's brother. The woman was a little harder to figure out until she faced me as I walked toward them. She was the woman from the picture in Chase's drawer.

She's got to be Morgan's wife or girlfriend. Maybe she came with him for moral support while he tried to convince Chase to go home to Arizona. My heart was pounding and my mouth was dry as I reached them. They were both in street clothes, very nice, expensive street clothes. The kind normal people would never wear to the Village. *They want to show Chase that they won't sink to his level.* I hated them already.

Even as I formulated some wonderful rhetorical remarks, one of the queen's pages raced by shouting his news to everyone in the Village. "Daisy challenged Alastair to a duel on the Village Green!"

"I thought that was tomorrow night at the castle," I shouted back.

"Not that one," he yelled as he reached the tree swing. "She punched him in the face, then demanded the duel. It's gonna be a massacre!"

Three

People started hurrying past, trying to reach the Village Green for the duel. I heard the mystery woman by the dungeon door ask her companion, "What's going on, Morgan? Where's Chase?"

I was wondering the same thing myself but realized he would probably be at the Village Green, since something was going on there. If Daisy was about to demolish Alastair in an unrehearsed duel, I wanted to see it, too. Chase's gorgeous brother, and whoever his equally gorgeous counterpart was, would have to get along without me. Better in the long run anyway, since I already regretted knowing they were there.

"Excuse me!" Morgan tapped me on the shoulder. "Can you tell us where we can find Chase Manhattan?"

Rats! Hoisted on my own petard! I should've moved faster.

They were suddenly both staring at me. I wanted to pick up a cross and hold it up to them. They had to be vampires. They looked too perfect to be human.

"I know *you*!" Morgan said in a triumphant tone. "Chase sent us a picture of the two of you. You're Jenny, his girlfriend, right?"

Okay. I had no choice. It was either take the time to indulge in polite but meaningless conversation with them or watch Daisy duel. No way was I going to miss the duel. "Come with me quickly," I yelled. "Chase will be at the duel."

I started running, holding on to my costume and boots for dear life, hoping they wouldn't dirty themselves by following me. I was wrong. "What do you mean duel?" the woman asked. "Is Chase dueling with someone?"

I had to admire her strappy pumps and wished I could afford a pair. But they would no doubt represent my food budget for the year. And here she was running alongside me, abusing them on the cobblestones. Sacrilege.

"Chase isn't dueling," I promised her. "But he'll be there. He's the bailiff. He goes wherever he's needed. He'll be needed at the duel."

"Thanks, Jenny." Morgan loped along beside me.

"Jessie. The name is Jessie."

He grinned. "Sorry. I guess Chase misspelled it when he sent his note with the picture."

As if. I was onto his game. I knew what he wanted. If he thought he could make trouble between Chase and me, he'd do it like the Village monks make bread (multiple times a day, always perfect loaves). I still couldn't bring myself to ask who *she* was. It was as if a sixth (or seventh) sense was telling me to leave it alone. It would break my heart soon enough.

When we reached the Village Green, we saw that a huge crowd had encircled the grassy area. Musicians had fled from the spot, leaving Daisy and Alastair facing each other.

Daisy's beautiful gown was torn and dirty. I wondered what had happened to it. What had caused this premature duel? Maybe it was a publicity stunt for tomorrow night's command performance. But if so, where was the media?

Visitors pressed in close to see what was happening, but they did that each day when Tom, Tom the Piper's Son stole a piglet, too. They had no idea what was going on. It was another event at the Village for them, no different than any other.

I looked at the faces of the other Village residents and realized they all seemed scared and worried. Everyone was wondering what was going on. There's plenty of theater in Renaissance Faire Village, but this wasn't part of it.

Alastair was certainly not up to my expectations. I'd never met the man, but I had seen plenty of pictures of him. Obviously they'd been taken when he was much younger. Unlike the promotional posters and website photos showing a twentysomething, handsome, dark-haired man, the in-person Alastair looked closer to fifty and had a balding head and a good-sized stomach. He was not much taller than Daisy. They seemed the perfect couple, physically. But looks were deceiving in this case.

I maneuvered myself closer to the corner where Daisy was standing, conscious of the two bad angels who'd followed me there. Morgan and Mystery Woman were right at my back and not in a good way.

I could see Daisy had been crying. Her eyes were red, makeup smeared. I tried to envision what could've happened and failed. This emotional side of her was something I had never seen. My sword-wielding idol seemed to have lost her way. No matter. That's what friends, and sometimes fans, are for.

"Let me be your second!" I shouted over the gossiping, funnel-cake-eating crowd that separated us. I could see

Alastair had a young man at his side who was holding his sword before the duel. Behind him were his famous groupies, a bevy of pretty young men and women who reportedly fawned over him and did his bidding. He never traveled without them. That's why he'd had to stay at the castle. There wasn't enough room for him and his entourage in Village housing.

Daisy lifted her head and looked around. I waved and jumped up and down to get her attention. She shoved back her curls and beckoned to me. I didn't hesitate to push my way through security to her.

Morgan and Mystery Woman stayed behind this time. I realized why when I looked back and saw Chase with them. I didn't have time to worry about it. I had other things on my mind.

"You don't have to do this," Daisy said. "I don't need a second. I can handle it by myself."

Her breathless weeping between words told me otherwise. I threw my clothes and boots on the ground and snatched up her sword, glaring at her opponents across the Green. "I know you don't need me. But I want to be here with you, if you'll let me."

She nodded and followed my line of vision to Alastair. "He hates me, you know. He did this to me in front of his followers. I wish I could *really* run him through instead of this pretense."

I wanted to ask what happened. It sounded bad. But there wasn't time. King Harold and Queen Olivia decided to grace this auspicious occasion with their royal presence. That meant trumpeters and courtiers. Lights suddenly winked on around the Green, turned on by unseen hands and hidden in bushes and trees. The resulting soft glow was supposed to give the impression of lantern light rather than non-Renaissance electricity.

"We are pleased and excited to see these two champions on the field," King Harold proclaimed in his most ringing voice.

"Yes, my dear," Queen Olivia joined him, not to be outdone by his words. "We welcome our visitors to this magnificent display of swordplay. Duelers, attend your swords!"

I had to admit Livy and Harry were up for the part. They both wore matching gold lamé with full regalia of paste jewels and crowns. Livy's gown was cut low across her ample bosom, as was proper for the time. Harry's tights were a little saggy, but he was too dashing above them to find fault.

The trumpeters sounded their horns again as the king and queen ascended the small stage and were seated in makeshift thrones. The beautiful Princess Isabel was with them, dressed in blue velvet with a small rhinestone tiara on her head. She was forced to stand behind them while someone scampered back to the castle for another chair. There would be hell to pay in the castle later for that slight.

"This is it." Daisy wiped her tears with her hands again.

"Here. Use this instead." I handed her the apprentice shirt Portia had given me, knowing a little makeup wouldn't matter compared to what I'd get on it later.

She wiped away most of the makeup and tears, then handed it back to me. "Thank you for being here, Jessie. It means a lot to me. We shall triumph, forsooth, for our cause is righteous."

There wasn't enough language in Ren speech for me to express what I was feeling. "Go over there and kick that jerk's ass!"

She smiled at me, then ripped the rest of her gown away from her legs. A swordswoman wouldn't want to get caught up in blue silk while she was fighting. It was a waste of a truly great costume. I could feel Portia cringing somewhere in the crowd. It would be a long time before she'd have something like that for Daisy again.

Alastair took his sword from his second. The light that surrounded us caught on the blade and reflected back at us. It was very impressive.

Daisy took her sword from me and saluted him by waving it once to the side then bringing it to her face. There was no plastic safety tip on either sword as there usually is during duels in the Village. The metal blade made a whooshing sound as it went by a few inches from my nose. I touched my face to make sure it was all still there. Duels could sometimes be a messy business for the seconds, too.

They advanced on each other across the grass. The crowd realized the moment was upon them, and they immediately quieted down. The air was still and hot around us, even though it was nearly nine P.M. It wouldn't really cool off until after midnight, a fact those of us who'd lived without air-conditioning were well aware of.

Alastair took wide, masterful steps and was the first to charge into the duel. Daisy only defended momentarily before she pushed into his assault. The swords rang in the silence. It was only a few minutes before both duelers were sweating and grunting in the heat. Swordplay is best in cooler climates. That's why our early ancestors knew they needed guns as soon as possible.

"I will flay the flesh from your bones, harlot!" Alastair called out in grand dramatic fashion typical of most Village duels.

Hearing his Ren speech made me feel a little better. Usually there was no real tension in these mock battles. Alastair seemed to consider this an opportunity to impress his fans.

But Daisy didn't return his banter. Her eyes were fixed on his face. Her movements seemed directed at wearing

him down. I'd seen her duel many times before. She was
never this intent. This was the real thing for her, which
was kind of scary, considering she had a few hundred
witnesses and an unprotected blade.

She brought her sword down like a sledgehammer on
his. I could see the tremors as metal hitting metal caused
his arm to shake. At that instant, she pressed her advantage
and had him down on his knees fending off her assault. I
had a twinge of concern about the murderous look on her
face. What if she really meant to kill him?

While a cold chill went through me, the crowd let out a
loud "Huzzah!" The triumph was short lived when Alastair
used his heavier blade to beat Daisy back. He was up from
the ground with a bounce in his step as he held his arms out
in triumph. The crowd that had approved Daisy's apparent
victory now roared for him. Fickle Ren folk! They only
love the winner.

Daisy didn't waste any time. She went back on the
attack, though I could tell her sword arm was tiring. The
thrust and parry between them ranged across the Green
with no end in sight. I'd never seen Alastair duel before,
so I couldn't tell if he was losing power. I knew if Daisy
couldn't defeat him soon, she'd have to give in. I didn't
like that idea, and from the look on her face, neither
did she.

"Ha-ha!" Alastair crowed after a particularly good
riposte. "Surrender and I will be merciful. You need only
kiss my boot and clean my sword, wench!"

Daisy paused for a moment, sweat dripping down the
sides of her face. It was one of those out-of-time experiences
where everything seems to stop. I saw her move but didn't
realize she'd used her foot to sweep the back of his leg until
he fell hard on the grass, arms and legs outstretched. She'd
taken advantage of his secret weakness, his old wound that

she'd inflicted. His sword dropped from his hand and rolled out of his reach.

Daisy put the tip of her sword to his throat above the chain mail that covered his chest. "Yield, dog, or I shall run you through!"

She was breathing hard, covered in sweat that matted what was left of the blue silk to her skin. But she made her point. Alastair nodded in agreement, then his head dropped back on the grass.

"Huzzah!" The crowd shouted over and over until the thick night air was full of it. Daisy had won over the supposedly unbeatable foe. I thought my chest would burst, I was so proud.

As is proper, the victor laid her sword at the feet of the Royal Court on the platform. Daisy knelt beside it, awaiting the official word from their majesties.

I was so busy watching her that I didn't notice Alastair sneak to his feet and pick up his sword until I heard booing from the crowd. He ignored the hisses and advanced on Daisy's prostrate form. The crowd began throwing popcorn, pretzels, and other food items at him to show their anger at his actions. But Daisy remained as she was in front of the king and queen.

I argued with myself that she would get up and turn against him. Then I thought she might not be able to get up and fight again. She was clearly exhausted. What if she couldn't get up and Alastair got carried away?

There was a spare sword at my feet. I snatched it up and ran to the space between them. I held the lightweight blade against him and dared him to approach our champion. "As the Master Armorer's chosen second, I demand you retreat, coward! You were fairly beaten. Lay down your weapon before King Harold and Queen Olivia. Do not bring greater shame to yourself with this action."

The crowd went wild. I could see Chase out of the corner of my eye. He'd cleared the crowd but paused before joining the fray. I appreciated his vote of confidence. By not coming forward, he showed he believed I could handle the situation. It was so *hot*!

Alastair had a crazed look in his eyes as he continued closer to me, blade outstretched. My insides felt like Jell-O, but I didn't waiver. I faced him down while Daisy got to her feet and picked up her blade to stand beside me. The two of us waited for him, swords at the ready. I didn't know about her, but I was praying I wouldn't have to use mine.

"Sir Alastair!" King Harold got to his feet. His voice rang out above the boos and hisses of the crowd. "You do yourself a disservice with this action. Put your sword down or face our Village justice."

An inch or so before he met our swords, Alastair gave a loud shout and drove the point of his sword into the ground. He glared at Daisy, then stalked off through the crowd, toward the castle.

I heard the boos and hisses change to *huzzahs* again. I knew it was over. The sword sagged down with my arms, and I joined them on the grass. My knees felt weak, and I was afraid I was going to barf in front of everyone.

"You are a superior apprentice, young Jessie!" Daisy smacked me hard on the back and gave a loud guffaw. "I knew you were exceptional. We shall feast this eventide with the joy of victory added to our ale!"

Queen Olivia stood, joining King Harold, and urged Princess Isabel to do the same. Together the royal personages commended Daisy and me for our bravery and skill. Finally, the queen ended with, "We are certain you will be victorious at the King's Feast tomorrow evening at the castle, six P.M. Tickets are still available for the event at the main gate and the Great Hall. Huzzah!"

The crowd lifted Daisy off her feet and surfed her through them. I stayed on the ground, too depleted to get up. That was okay because Chase found me and lifted me up against him. "You are the heroine of the day!" He laughed and kissed me hard while I put my arms around his neck.

"You know how I always complain when you pick me up like this?" I snuggled in close to him, clutching my abused costume.

"Yeah?"

"I'm not complaining tonight. Take me home, Sir Bailiff. My legs need your support, and the rest of me could use some attention, too."

He kissed me again and had begun walking away from the crowd toward the dungeon when a whiny female voice rang out, "Chase Manhattan! Don't you *dare* walk away without even acknowledging me and your brother!"

Chase stopped and turned back to face Mystery Woman and his brother. "Hi, Morgan. Hi, Brooke. See ya."

Morgan stopped his brother from proceeding away from them with a hand on his arm. "Is this all we get after we came all this way to see you, Chase?"

"I'm sure you'll be back tomorrow. For now, that's about all."

Brooke wasn't satisfied with that. She sidled up to him and put her hand on his chest in the only spot I wasn't covering. "Is that any way to treat the woman you almost married?"

I glanced at Chase, knowing they were playing us, but still intent on getting down. Despite the fact that I didn't think my legs would hold me, I pushed until he let me go. I couldn't face this pair without standing up and looking down on both of them. "I hope that wasn't meant for me, Brooke. Because as far as lethal barbs are concerned, that one was truly pathetic. You'll have to work harder if you want to break us up and take Chase back to Arizona. Right, Chase?"

Chase didn't respond for a minute. He stared at Morgan before saying, "Excuse us for a while, Jessie. It seems we have something to discuss right now. I'll meet you back at the dungeon."

Brooke looked so smug and superior, I wished I still had the sword and could smack her with it a few times. Then I was angry with Chase for dismissing me like some little kid he didn't want to overhear his conversation. All in all, not a good moment.

"There you are!" Daisy came upon us with several young men and women in tow. "Let's go get that feast, my young apprentice. The night is still young."

So I went with them and didn't look back. If Chase had some startling revelations for his brother and ex-fiancé, I wasn't going to hear them. I might as well go eat and drink too much with Daisy and confront Chase later.

I remember going into one of the pubs, probably the Pleasant Pheasant. The room was full of after-hours Village residents, like always. There was something to eat and plenty to drink. I wasn't sure when we left the pub and headed out into the Village, but when Sunday morning broke across the castle, the sunlight reflecting off Mirror Lake, I found myself sleeping on a bed of straw in the back of the blacksmith's shop.

My mouth tasted like someone's old boot, and I smelled like stale ale. Not a pleasant scent. I was still in my street clothes and had fallen asleep using my Ren garments as a pillow. I realized slowly that I'd never made it back to the dungeon. The mean-spirited part of me was glad and hoped Chase had been out looking for me all night. The other, much smaller part was worried about what had happened with Brooke and Morgan. Maybe they were gone. Maybe Chase had pushed them out the main gate himself.

As usual in the early morning hours, especially on Sunday after the late close on Saturday, there were very few Village residents out on the streets. The shops and restaurants were closed up tight. I could hear some sheep baaing from around Bo Peeps's place. This was eventually accompanied by the whinny of horses and then the trumpeting of an elephant. It was like being in a zoo, not great with a pounding headache.

"Jessie?" Ethan, looking as perfect as ever as he rested against the hay, smiled up at me. "What a night, huh? Daisy really knows how to throw a party!"

I looked around the blacksmith shop, but there was no sign of our new celebrity armorer. "I wonder where she slept last night." It seemed as though only Ethan and I were in the straw, luckily several yards away from each other.

As I was collecting my costume and thinking about heading toward the dungeon to yell at Chase and take a hot shower, a Village crier came by, ringing an annoying bell as he broadcasted his news across the cool morning air.

"Alastair the Great is dead! He has been smote by his own sword at the castle. Hear ye! Hear ye!"

I sat back down in the straw. "Oh, *great!*"

Four

Admittedly, my brain was a little fuzzy. The first thing I thought after hearing the crier's news was, *It's a publicity stunt for the duel tonight. Of course Alastair isn't really dead. That's ridiculous.*

It took me a few minutes to get to my feet again and pick all the little pieces of hay out of my clothes and hair. It took me another few minutes to realize I wasn't the only one taking straw out of my hair. Ethan was studiously assisting me from behind. I stepped away from him and clutched my costume to me.

"I'm going to look for Chase now." I smiled at him to make sure his feelings weren't hurt. After all, I was going to have to work with him over the summer. "He's my boyfriend."

Ethan slipped his arm around my shoulders. I had to admire his really great hair. I wondered if those were natural highlights. "Jessie, don't be so nervous. We can go look for Chase together. I have a feeling he'll be at the castle, if Alastair is really dead."

I started walking, glad that being six feet tall gives me a wide stride. Ethan was shorter (especially from waist to ankle) and kind of had to run a little to keep up with me. "You know Alastair isn't *really* dead. This is another stunt to sell tickets. They'll do or say anything to make it more interesting."

Ethan shrugged (panting a little). "Why bother doing it now? The Village is closed. All of us are a captive audience. They don't need to make it interesting. Could you slow down a little?"

We were headed very quickly for a confrontation with a knight on horseback who was cantering toward the castle. It seemed we were all going in the same direction. I felt dizzy just thinking about it.

Several distressed-looking flower girls were whispering about Alastair being dead as we passed them near the three manor houses that make up Squires' Lane. Jugglers, fools, and knaves, some in costume, some in street clothes, were following the familiar path toward the castle.

The smells from the Monastery Bakery almost made me stop before joining the masses thronging to see what was going on. The scents of cinnamon rolls, freshly baked bread, and heavenly coffee emanated from the familiar place. I probably would've moved off the cobblestones and ended up there, but a surge of Village folk intervened, pushing me away toward Mirror Lake and the supposed site of Alastair's death.

"I'm going to be angry if he's not *really* dead. And good riddance if he is," Mother Goose told me as we were pushed together in the crowd. "If this is some stupid stunt to sell tickets, I might give all of them a good ear pull!"

Mother Goose is rarely in such a temper, but I felt the same way. I mean, how much were we supposed to care if they hadn't sold their quota of tickets for the show? And what were we supposed to do about it?

Unless, of course, they had the media ready to see our startled faces when we reached the castle. They'd done it before. There was nothing stopping them from exploiting us this time. We needed a union instead of our stupid guilds. Maybe I needed to form the Renaissance Faire Village Residents Union. I'd have to think about that.

But the closer we got to the castle gate on the far side of the Village near Merlin's Apothecary, the more I began to wonder. I certainly agreed with Mother Goose that the report of Alastair's death seemed fake, but there were a lot of police cars parked near the castle. It would be a stretch of the imagination (even mine) to think Adventure Land would involve them in their scam for publicity.

Unless the police cars weren't real. It was early in the morning and I couldn't be sure. It's sometimes hard to tell what's real and what's part of the show in the Village. True, the costumes and props would have to come from outside, but that had happened before, too. I wasn't sure what would convince me this whole thing was real.

"Those are police cars," Ethan acknowledged.

"There are *always* police cars around here somewhere," a varlet dressed in brown cotton said. "They all work together."

"No, I'm afraid it's all true." Merlin joined us as we passed the apothecary. "Alastair was found early this morning with his sword protruding from his chest. Not a good way to start the day."

"And you're sure it's the real thing?" a juggler dressed in red and green asked. "You know how they are."

"I do indeed." Merlin acknowledged with a wink in my direction.

He winked (I hoped) because I'm one of the privileged few who know his secret. Merlin is the CEO of Adventure Land. He lives here most of the time, as I understand it from Chase. His gold-starred purple robes hide an astute businessman.

He's also a part-time flasher. This I know through personal experience. He tends not to bother wearing anything under the robe.

"I don't know," Mother Goose said with a sneer. "It looks real enough. Maybe they didn't get us up for nothing. Maybe the old fake is really dead."

"Fake?" the juggler demanded. "What do you mean? He was received by royalty at hundreds of Ren Faires around the world. I heard he dueled a real duke in front of a real queen in some European country."

"Well he couldn't beat Daisy last night," Mother Goose reminded him. She looked a little rumpled in her white apron and mobcap. Maybe that's why her temper was sour. "Daisy trounced him good and fair. He was going to cheat and get her when her back was turned. Coward! Good thing that girl was there to stop him. Was that the new Lady Godiva? I know I've seen her before."

I didn't want to blow my own horn, but I could hardly stay quiet on the matter. "That was Daisy's new apprentice."

"That's right. She used to work at the Lady of the Lake Tavern. They kicked her out for getting into fights." Mother Goose was very convinced of my identity.

"No," I corrected with a calm demeanor. "It was me. Jessie Morton. I've apprenticed for Master Archer Simmons, Roger Trent at the Glass Gryphon, and Mary Shift at Wicked Weaves. You know me. I brought you a glass of iced tea one summer when you had a cold."

She studied me carefully, then waved her hand in dismissal. "That's right. Sorry, Jessie. You looked taller and thinner last night. Putting on a little weight with age, are we?"

As put out as I was by both her memory and her obviously bad eyesight, I was entranced to see Chase near the castle gate with Police Detective Donald Almond of the Myrtle Beach PD. I stopped thinking about why I looked thin last night but fat this morning when I realized Alastair's death *had* to be real. Chase wouldn't be there with Detective Almond unless something bad happened.

"It wouldn't surprise me if Daisy ran him through after he went to bed last night," Mother Goose said. "It would serve him right for being such a deceitful dog!"

She spat on the ground to show her disdain. This was a mistake because it led to everyone in the group around us to start spitting, too. It's some kind of Village ritual that I've never gotten into. I mean, don't they realize we have to walk around in that stuff? It's bad enough that there are droppings from every animal in the Village.

When everyone was done spitting, Merlin wiped his mouth, white beard, and mustache on his sleeve. "Why would you say such a thing, dear lady? Our master armorer is a courageous fighter and a loyal resident of the Village. She would do no harm to a sleeping man who could not defend himself, dog that he was."

Merlin spit first this time, and another ten or twelve people joined in, including a few of the pirates who'd left the *Queen's Revenge* to see what was going on.

"I'm only saying that it would serve him right," Mother Goose replied defensively. "I'm not saying she did it, mind you. Though the dastardly devil deserved it." She spit liberally on the ground, and a whole new wave of spitters joined her.

"Okay! Enough!" I'd had it with the spitting and people saying Daisy would kill anyone. At least not for real. "Daisy is too honorable to do something like this and slink away in the night. If she'd wanted to kill him, she would've done it last night on the dueling field. She wouldn't do something like this. I know her better."

"Even against that cowardly cur?" One of the pirates posed the question, then spit again.

While everyone else was spitting, I leveraged my elbow into his side and got out of the heart of the group. Sometimes these spitting contests went on for hours. There were enough Village residents here that they could continue coming up with names to call Alastair until they couldn't spit anymore.

I saw Chase talking to Detective Almond and pushed my way through the crowd toward them. There were fewer people once I made it past the Feather Shaft and the Lady of the Lake Tavern, but a ring of uniformed police officers were blocking those of us who'd come this far from getting any closer to the castle. As determined as I was, they were a little more daunting than a bunch of half-awake Village residents, even when the residents were spitting.

I waited until Chase looked my way, then jumped up and down and waved, calling his name. The police officers looked at me a little strangely, but considering that I was standing between Romeo and a man in half a toad suit, I supposed they looked at us all that way.

Chase turned back toward the castle without noticing me. It was depressing. And without coffee or a cinnamon roll for comfort, I couldn't let it stand, so I darted between the police officers and ran toward the entrance to the Great Hall where Chase and Detective Almond had disappeared.

I really didn't expect to outrun the officers who took off after me, but I managed to elude them (probably because I know the castle so well) until I was within a few yards of Chase. I yelled his name as the officer closest to me took me down. I dropped my costume, boots and all, and fell, sprawled under the weight of my assailant. "Get off of me! I'm with the bailiff."

"Jessie?"

I looked up into Chase's beautiful face, forgetting my anger (at least temporarily) about last night. He seemed a little perplexed to see me, but I didn't care. I was happy to see him. "Will you tell him to get off of me?"

Chase glanced back at Detective Almond, who rolled his eyes but said, "Let her up, Sanborn. I thought I could get through this without any added problems. I guess I was wrong."

Sanborn got up and dusted off his uniform. He held out a hand to me, but I refused his help and got up on my own. I rushed for Chase in case Detective Almond changed his mind.

"Why are you here?" Chase whispered out of earshot of the police. "You can't *want* to see this. I don't."

I glanced toward the hall that led to the main living quarters in the castle. The king and queen resided here and occasionally hosted visiting dignitaries. Usually that meant people from Adventure Land. In this case, it was Alastair and his entourage. "Is he *really* dead? It's not a publicity stunt?"

"Not according to Detective Almond." Chase's face changed. "Where were you last night? I searched the whole Village for you. If you weren't going to come to the dungeon, you could've at least called. I know you must have your cell phone with you—even though you didn't answer it when I called you ten thousand times last night."

"You told me to get lost so you could talk to your old girlfriend and your brother, remember? I did what you told me to do, like a good little puppy." Okay, the anger came back kind of fast and unexpected.

"Constable," Detective Almond cut in, reminding Chase of his actual rank, according to the police department. "If you're finished having domestic issues, I'd like you to take a look at the crime scene before we move the body."

Chase glared at me. I smiled with particular sweetness. You know the look. Like a big, fake cinnamon roll on top of several fake chocolate bars. It's all you can do not to throw up. "We're finished," he said to Detective Almond, then whispered back at me, "*for now.*"

That was fine with me. I was dying for a knockdown, drag-out. Hopefully not before I had some caffeine but definitely sometime this morning before we made up.

I followed behind Chase as he walked with Detective Almond down the long hall. This was where the good stuff was kept. Livy and Harry had been the top sales people for Adventure Land before they took their positions here as king and queen. They had traveled the world and brought back amazing tapestries, paintings, and sculptures. All of these were kept in the main living quarters, displayed up and down the halls, well out of the reach of visitors.

Outside the area, which was blocked off to common foot traffic, the entranceway to the Great Hall, where the King's Feast is held every Sunday evening, was covered in fake tapestries, art, and sculptures. Many of these had absolutely no place in a Renaissance castle, but they looked good. They could also be easily and cheaply replaced. A good thing, too, since once in a while they managed to go home with some lucky visitor.

I'd spent one summer in the castle as a kitchen servant (not quite as good as a wench), so I knew the structure well. Harry and Livy and their guests ordered snacks, wine, and various other things all day and night. In the Village, they really were treated like royalty. In the castle, their word was law. Not to obey them meant instant dismissal. Every Village resident knew it, too.

The guest quarters weren't as elaborate as the private quarters, but they were still very posh. There was fabric on the walls, expensive carpet underfoot. The furniture was faux Renaissance, most of it from Europe. Every comfort had been seen to as well as a few extraordinary benefits like big flat-panel TVs and cable.

The rest of the Village mucked it out in makeshift residences that usually house several people. You were lucky if you were a shopkeeper or lived in the dungeon where basic comforts (not sharing hot showers) were to be had.

People wanted to live at the Village anyway, despite the inconveniences. There was always a huge waiting list to get in. It was the romance of living in another time, I guess. Kind of like primitive camping next to a scenic waterfall.

Alastair had been given the biggest suite of rooms. There were four bedrooms (each with a bath that had a marble hot tub), a kitchen, and a living area. His groupies, about twenty of them, were huddled into the living area with several police officers. They were crying and moaning (the groupies, not the cops), still wearing their pajamas or something like pajamas.

One young woman, who seemed familiar to me, was wearing a chastity belt, some kind of metal bodice, and a jeweled collar around her throat. I didn't even want to know what that was all about, but I did wonder where I'd seen her before.

Detective Almond led us into the biggest bedroom. Alastair's body was still laid out on the enormous gold four-poster. Red velvet was draped around him. He was clutching the large sword he'd threatened me with last night. It was sticking straight up out of his chest. His eyes were wide open, staring up at the elaborate painting of the Greek gods on the ceiling.

"I found him this way," a grief-stricken young man said. I recognized him as Alastair's second from the duel last night. "He's dead. He's *really* dead. I didn't think he could die."

Detective Almond looked him over. "And your name is?"

"Onslow Chivers. Alastair's personal assistant."

"Make sure someone has your statement and your real-life ID." Detective Almond nodded to an officer who led Onslow away from the bed turned crime scene.

The bed was covered in blood. It had soaked into the expensive-looking white linen sheets, marked the white silk comforter at the side of the bed, and even smudged the huge (no doubt down-filled) pillows.

"Medical examiner puts time of death at around four A.M.," Detective Almond told Chase. "His friends out there said he slept alone, except for Marielle, the one with the . . ." He made diaper-type motions with his hands.

"Chastity belt," Chase filled in.

"Yeah. Sure. Anyway, she says she slept through it and woke up to find him this way. I don't know where she was sleeping, since she didn't have any blood on her."

"She was probably sleeping on the floor," I said in what I hoped was a helpful manner. "You saw the collar around her neck. She probably wasn't allowed to sleep on the bed yet."

Detective Almond looked at me as though he wished the words hadn't come out of my mouth. "Have I ever mentioned how much I hate that they assigned me to this place?"

"More than once," Chase responded as he smiled at me.

I fought against smiling back. It was hard to maintain a stern expression when Chase smiled at me, but I wasn't ready not to be mad at him yet. I admit the corners of my mouth turned up a little, mostly I think I kept him guessing.

"Anyway. We think someone stood over Mr. Alastair

and drove the sword into his chest," Detective Almond continued. "The sword is embedded all the way down to the box spring. The medical examiner said anyone could've done it, even that little girl out there. Standing over the victim would create that kind of momentum."

"Of course, whoever did it would've been covered in blood," I added. "And Alastair had to be asleep; otherwise, he would've fought back." My years of watching *CSI* were paying off.

Detective Almond frowned at me, then looked at Chase. "Any ideas on who might want to take this boy out?"

Chase glanced at me, too, and I wondered if he was thinking what I was thinking: Daisy could be a suspect in Alastair's death.

"I'm sure Alastair had plenty of enemies, any one of whom would be capable of doing this to him, since most of them are master swordsmen," Chase explained. "I could try to get you a list of people he's fought. I couldn't tell you which of them could be here now. They move around a lot."

Good answer! Chase had effectively put a few hundred people on the suspect list. It would take some time for Detective Almond to realize that Daisy would probably be number one on that list. I didn't think she was capable of it, like I'd said outside. But rationally, she had motive, opportunity, and certainly means. *And she wasn't with Ethan and me when we woke up this morning.*

"Yeah. I'd appreciate that list, Manhattan. In the meantime, my men will talk to everyone in the castle and make sure they didn't see or hear anything. You put your feelers out to the people who live here and see what you can come up with." Detective Almond looked at me. "Does that work for you, Princess? What are you supposed to be dressed up like anyway? Were there blue jeans in the days of yore?"

"I'm still in my street clothes," I explained, despite his snickering. "I got here last night and haven't changed yet. But I'm apprenticing with the master armorer this summer."

I didn't mention her name, and I was proud of it. He wouldn't get anything from me that would lead him to Daisy.

"That's fascinating. I'm sure it's better than sleeping on the beach." His gaze wandered away from me and took in the details of the dead man on the bed again.

"If that's all," Chase said, "we're going. I'll get you that information as soon as I can."

"That's it. Let's get this wrapped up, Manhattan."

There was a flurry of activity at the door as Harry and Livy invaded the room with their ruffled and furbelowed nightwear and their attendants. "You won't have to shut down the Village, will you?" Livy sounded hysterical. "After all, this man was only a guest here. Our fine justice should be able to find the culprit responsible."

"That's true," Harry agreed with her. "Probably a personal matter between him and his killer. Something that spilled over into Renaissance Village but not really a part of it."

"I don't see any reason to close down the attraction at this moment," Detective Almond replied. "If I change my mind, you'll be the first to know."

"Of course! And thank you for your consideration," Livy added. "I'm sure the bailiff will have the master armorer delivered for questioning shortly."

Detective Almond looked at me again. "The same one little Jersey here is going to work for this summer? *That* master armorer?"

Harry cleared his throat in a regal way. "Certainly! We assumed you knew about their life-and-death altercation last eventide. Bailiff? Why have you not informed the good detective of that event?"

Chase took a deep breath when everyone turned to look at him. "I'll find Daisy and get her over here."

"Thanks," Detective Almond said. "What the hell is eventide anyway?"

Five

"Please tell me you were with Daisy around four this morning," Chase said as we walked out of the castle.

The Myrtle Beach police had dispersed the residents who'd gathered at the castle gate. Now everyone seemed to be studiously ignoring the area, still surrounded by police from the outside world.

"I'd like to tell you that," I explained, "but I have no idea. I woke up at the blacksmith's shop with Ethan. There was no sign of Daisy. He didn't know where she was either."

"With *Ethan*?" Chase stopped walking and stared at me. "Why him?"

"Because you were busy with other things that didn't include me," I reminded him. "I think I remember seeing Daisy after we left the pub, but I'm not sure."

"So you're telling me you spent the night with Ethan because you were mad at me?"

"No. I'm telling you that I'm mad at you and Ethan was

there when I woke up this morning. We weren't together. He was on the other side of the room."

Chase hugged me fiercely to him. "Don't scare me like that, Jessie. I'm sorry about last night, but I knew if I didn't handle it right away, Brooke and Morgan would be the biggest pains in the butt since the Inquisition."

When he stepped back a little, I tried to maintain my anger at being summarily dismissed, but it was no use. He was trying to get rid of his ex-fiancé, not cuddling up with her. "I didn't like the way you did it, but I guess I understand."

"I bet you could understand a lot better with some caffeine in your brain. I know I could. Let's hie to yon bakery for our repast and a few triple-shot lattes."

I agreed, and we were about to head in that direction when a bone-thin woman in a gray business suit stopped us. Her hair was very blond, almost white, but it looked natural, since her eyelashes and brows were the same color. Her ponytail was pulled back from her pale, sharp face and narrow glasses hung on the edge of her nose. "You're the local law, right?" She held out her hand to Chase. "Tavin Hartley. I'm Alastair's business manager and attorney. I know you'll need some information from me to help you find his killer. I want to set that up right now."

"Chase Manhattan." He shook her hand. "Village bailiff. This is Jessie Morton."

She nodded to me but focused on Chase. "I don't understand this place. I never understood Alastair's obsession with this era of history. But I want his killer brought to justice."

"We all do, Ms. Hartley," he assured her. "I know the Village. The police know what they're doing. We'll find out what happened."

"What about this Daisy person who cheated in the

match against Alastair last night? Does she have an alibi for the time he was killed?"

"Wait a minute!" I objected. "Daisy didn't cheat in the duel. Alastair did. If anybody had a reason to kill someone for what happened, it would be Alastair, not Daisy. She made him look like an idiot."

Ms. Hartley glanced at me as if I were a pesky mosquito. "I'm sure there are people here who are loyal to this woman, but believe me there are thousands who are loyal to Alastair, and they'll demand justice."

"Don't worry," I assured her. "They'll have justice, but not at Daisy's expense."

She adjusted her tiny glasses and half smiled at me, her eyes a pale blue. "I'm sure we all want the same thing. If there's anything you need from me, don't hesitate to call."

She handed us each a business card with three cell numbers on it plus an e-mail address. Chase and I watched her walk back toward the castle. It was painful watching anyone in six-inch heels walking on cobblestones.

"Where does she get off telling us what to do?" I demanded as we set out again for the Monastery Bakery.

"I guess since she's Alastair's lawyer, that gives her the right to say whatever she wants. Back to what happened to Daisy last night . . ."

"I don't know. I can look for her if you want. Does she have to turn herself in or something?"

"They'll want to question her for sure." Chase held open the door to the bakery. "Make sure she talks to me first. Then I'll go with her to see Detective Almond."

The wonderful aromas coming from inside the bakery made my stomach growl and my head feel dizzy. "I'll do that. Caffeine and food now, please."

I sat down at one of the crudely made tables and let Chase order breakfast and coffee. What a morning! This wasn't the wonderful beginning of my time here that I'd been expecting. Alastair being killed was bad enough, but everyone suspecting Daisy was much worse. It didn't make any sense to me: why would anyone suspect Daisy of killing Alastair? Even if she couldn't account for her whereabouts early this morning, she had no reason to murder her ex-lover.

I was horrified to realize I'd given her the best motive of all. After all the primping we'd done yesterday, Alastair had rejected and humiliated her in front of his groupies at the castle. She'd retaliated by dueling him into the dirt. I remembered that much from my evening at the pub with her after the duel was over. He'd made fun of the way she looked and even used his sword to tear her beautiful gown.

She'd gotten him back, at least as far as I was concerned. She'd beat him like an egg in front of everyone. After that duel, no one was going to look at him the same way. At least not once word got out to the Rennies who made up our world. I'd known last night that today there would be blogs, tweets, and camera-phone pictures posted all over the Internet documenting Alastair's defeat.

"Here we are." Chase put coffee and a cinnamon roll in front of me. "This should get you up and thinking again."

"You better hope not," I warned. "I think I'm still mad about last night. I haven't been able to muster the energy to show it, but that could change."

He sat beside me and sipped his coffee. "Let's get this all out in the open before it goes any further. Yes, I was engaged to marry Brooke. That was a few years ago, before I went renegade from the homestead and wound up here. She has no claim on me. I haven't thought about her in a long time. You shouldn't even ask me how I feel about her. Have I ever acted like you aren't the fire in my hearth?"

I drank some coffee and ate a few bites of my cinnamon roll. My brain was beginning to clear. "I wasn't worried about her or Morgan until you dismissed me last night. That's what I was mad about. And I'm still mad."

"I apologize for that. They get me so frustrated sometimes. You're lucky you weren't here before Christmas when my mother flew out to grill me on my future."

"I saw you Christmas Day. You didn't even mention it."

"I was over it by then. I didn't want you to know how my family really is."

"You know my brother." I laughed. "I think it's fair for me to know about your family skeletons."

"I guess that's true." He kissed my hand. "I'm sorry we got off to such a bad start this summer. Can we move forward now?"

How could I say no? I kissed his lips, and we clung together for a few long minutes until Brother John (spiritual leader of the monks who run the bakery) told us to take it outside. I couldn't fault him, I guess. Their passion for bread is the monks' only outlet. They're supposed to be celibate.

Chase and I stopped kissing long enough to eat and finish our coffee before getting ready to head back out into the Village. "I'll piece together everything I can without talking to Daisy," Chase said as he gathered up the remains of our meal.

"I'll find her and bring her to you. You might want to give me a two-way radio in case I need to call you and set up a meet." I picked up my clothes and boots again. It would be good to finally change out of my street clothes.

"Oh, no. Let's not start *that* again! You always want me to give you a radio, but then you abuse the privilege. The radios are for emergencies only." Chase got up and threw away our coffee cups. "No radio. You know better. I'll check in with you at Swords and Such in a while, after I have time to make my rounds and talk to a few people."

"Fine. I was only trying to make it easier for you. I don't know why you don't trust me with a radio. I've been a big help before." I made my best pathetic face, but he wasn't falling for it.

We parted ways at the door to the bakery. Finding Daisy was more important than arguing about a radio anyway. If she didn't already know everyone suspected her of having taken part in Alastair's demise, she needed to be informed. I assumed that was part of being a great apprentice, too.

But what were the chances Daisy wouldn't know what everyone was thinking? Nil. News in the Village travels faster than a speeding cannonball. And sure enough, by the time I got to Swords and Such, Daisy was sitting around talking about it with Ethan and the Village blacksmith, Hans Von Rupp.

"Where have you been?" Daisy asked when she saw me. "And why are you still in your street clothes?"

As the three of them stared at me, I was suddenly aware of my ragged appearance. I still had straw sticking up all over, my clothes looked as though I'd lived in them for the past twenty-four hours (which I had), and my hair was probably a mess. Why hadn't Chase said something?

"I was worried about you." I hoped that made a difference. "I tried to get over here as fast as I could to warn you."

Ethan stretched back his hands behind his head, his glorious hair (why wasn't he a mess?) spilling across his shoulders. He looked like someone on the cover of a romance novel. "We've known about it for hours. We were trying to decide what Daisy's next move should be."

Hans got to his brawny feet. And I mean that literally. Every part of this man is brawny, like Schwarzenegger from the *Conan* movies. I guess it comes from using that heavy hammer when he hits the hot metal. "I think she should lie low and let the cops come for her if they want her. No point in making it easy for them."

"There's no point in *not* making it easy," Ethan argued. "We know Daisy didn't kill Alastair. After the conversation, they'll know it, too."

Daisy looked up at me after digesting their remarks. She was wearing her breastplate again with short black pants. Her makeup was gone, but her hair was still curly. She had it pushed up out of her face with a metal band. "And what do you think, Jessie? Do I give myself up to the cops or let them come here?"

"For right now, Detective Almond would be happy if you went and talked to Chase. They want to know if you have an alibi for the time Alastair was killed, about four this morning."

"That's easy enough," Hans said. "She was with me all night."

"Me, too," Ethan agreed.

Daisy laughed. "I was a busy lady last night! Seriously, folks, I couldn't begin to tell you where I was at that hour. I woke up on the other side of the Village, looking at the fountain with the woman in it, at about eight A.M. I don't know how I got there or when I got there."

"There's no reason you should," Hans said. "If the four of us say we were together all night, who's going to question it?"

"There's only one problem with that." I explained how I'd already told Chase I hadn't seen Daisy since last night. "I can't tell him something else now."

"Fine. That doesn't stop me and Hans from telling him she was with us," Ethan said. "You really should watch your tongue around the bailiff, sweetie. It's gonna get you in trouble."

"But neither one of you was with Daisy early this morning," I argued.

"Are you saying you think I killed Alastair?" Daisy demanded.

"Of course not." I stared back at her. "But if you tell this lie and someone who saw you by yourself next to the fountain this morning tells Chase or Detective Almond different, they'll really start asking questions. And I *know* you don't want that either."

Daisy seemed to consider what I'd said. Then she made a face and shrugged. "Nah. I'll take my chances. The only way Chase will know I wasn't with Ethan and Hans is if *you* tell him."

Of course I swore myself to secrecy on the matter. I went in back and changed into my costume, a little the worse for wear, since it was smeared with makeup and sand. Immediately I felt more relaxed and in tune with the Village. Daisy was right. I knew she hadn't killed Alastair. What difference would it make if Ethan and Hans were her alibi? I wished I hadn't told Chase that I wasn't with her. Then I could lie for her, too.

When I came back out, Ethan was behind the counter and Hans was gone. The Village was about to open, and everyone was getting ready. Sunday was a short day, but it culminated in the King's Feast. Usually the day was crowded, leading into the amusements of the castle in the evening.

I wasn't sure what those were going to be with Alastair's death and all. No doubt they were cooking something up, even if it was only a joust or some other feat of bravery. The crowd would pack in around the Great Hall. The bad guy would be booed, and the good guy would receive Princess Isabel's favor. In between, hundreds of tiny chickens would be devoured, their little bones thrown at the contestants as they battled.

Was I getting jaded? With castle life, surely. I hadn't enjoyed it when I worked there for the summer a few years ago. With the Village, no! All I had to do was look beyond the doors of Swords and Such and see one of the Village idiots trying to swallow a piglet he'd captured to impress one of the pretty fairies. How could anyone get jaded about something like that?

I was looking forward to helping Daisy make swords throughout the day, but she decided she wasn't going to bother. "My head is killing me. I think I'm going to go take a nap. Ethan? Will you get Jessie started polishing those new display swords. I think there are a few knives over there, too." She smiled at me and waved. "That should keep you busy for a while."

Ethan stuck me in a corner with several polishing cloths and a few tins of polish. Then he took some swords and set them at my feet. "Make sure they're bright and shiny. That's the way Daisy likes them."

I looked at the big pile of dull metal and tried not to be discouraged. Of course there had to be some menial labor involved that wouldn't benefit my dissertation interests. There always was. Polishing swords could be rewarding, too, I told myself as I picked up the first sword.

The hilt was intricate and delicately made. A sword for an elf or a militant fairy. I put some polish on my cloth and started rubbing. I knew the time would go by faster if I was busy and didn't feel sorry for myself.

Customers came and went in the shop. I had to admire Ethan's elegant salesmanship. He appealed to all the female customers, ninety percent of the market. They sighed over his good looks, then bought tiny daggers for their garters (which he personally installed) or bought swords for their boyfriends or husbands, which Ethan politely gift wrapped. No wonder Daisy kept him around.

One older woman in a beautiful Renaissance gown made of silk and velvet walked over to my corner as Ethan was wrapping her sword. Her kind blue eyes smiled down on me, and she patted my head. "You are doing a wonderful job, lad. Your swords are breathtaking."

Lad? This was always the problem I had at the Village while I worked on my apprenticeships. True, my hair is short. Women didn't wear their hair short during the Renaissance, unless they had the plague. For some reason, doctors back then thought they'd get well if they cut their hair.

When I first started coming here and dressed like a wench, highborn lady, or washer woman, it wasn't a problem. But put on a pair of pants, even if you're a pirate, and right away people think you're a boy.

She flipped me a quarter and took her sword from Ethan. I pocketed the change and tried not to feel too bad about it. Now if I had a breastplate like Daisy's, no one would have to wonder which sex I was. I could guarantee that, with all modesty.

I went back to polishing without looking up for a while. I was surprised when Daisy came down from her apartment. It was almost three P.M. In an hour, shopkeepers would begin getting ready for the King's Feast. Attendance at the weekly event was mandatory for all Village residents. Shopkeepers dressed in their finest (but not finer than the king or queen), and food vendors brought their wares to be sampled.

I noticed Ethan had been busy getting Daisy's swords ready to take to the feast. Customers were still going in and out, some buying and others looking. Daisy's sword collection was formidable. I wasn't sure if any of it was for sale. Many of the craftspeople had private collections they showed during the feast and other special events.

"Have you been polishing those swords all afternoon?" Daisy asked when she saw me in the corner.

"That's what you told me to do." She looked a lot better after resting. Most of that yellow tinge to her face was gone. I didn't remember much about last night, but it was obvious we'd all had a *very* good time.

"She's slow, mistress." Ethan played it up for the visitors in the shop. "Methinks you would be better off finding a new apprentice."

Daisy laughed. "Don't pay any attention to him." She picked up one of the swords I had polished and examined it. "What ho! You've done an excellent job, apprentice. You deserve some time outside. Have you had lunch yet?"

"No, mistress." I followed their lead. The visitors ate up these little tableaus. "I am quite famished."

"Ease your hunger and thirst, good apprentice." Daisy tossed me some money from the register. "Mayhap you will find some dashing bailiff to enjoy your repast with you."

I put down the sword I was working on and bowed my head to her. "Thank you, mistress. Bless you."

She winked at me as she started showing off her sword moves to the group assembled in the shop. Ethan picked up a sword to fence with her, and I quietly slipped out the door.

It was nice to be out in the sunlight. It was cooler inside with the fans (no air-conditioning), but the fresh air was a welcome change from the shop smells.

I went to the privies to wash my hands, but there was a long line and I didn't want to waste my free time waiting. I was only a few steps from the dungeon, and I decided to go there to get cleaned up. A hot shower was first on my list. I could always look for food, and Chase, later.

Visitors were rambling through the ground floor of the dungeon, remarking on the pathetic figures in the cells. I had my key for the door that led to Chase's apartment and managed to get upstairs before they noticed me. I hated to break the performance for them. The spirit of the Village was important to the people who came here. They didn't want to know that I was hungry and dirty, unless it had something to do with Renaissance entertainment.

Chase wasn't there, but he'd left me some food and a cold drink in the minifridge. He wrote me the cutest little note and even drew a picture of the minifridge to show me where lunch was. He can be very sweet. I found myself eager for the night that would follow the King's Feast. When the lights went out in the Village and everything got quiet, Chase and I would finally be together again.

In anticipation of that, I stripped off my apprentice outfit and jumped in the shower. It was nice to see my bottle of shampoo and conditioner still waiting for me. It made the apartment feel like home.

Clean at last, I put on some sexy red lace underwear for later that night, then replaced my apprentice clothes. I did what I could with my hair. I never expected much from it when I was at the Village. It was hot. It was humid. My short, straight hair responded by sticking up in places it wasn't supposed to. I lived with it.

I watched a little CNN while I ate lunch and reveled in the air-conditioned apartment. There was only a brief mention of Alastair's death. It was after four when I finished. I left Chase a little note he might appreciate and skipped back down the stairs to the first floor of the dungeon.

I was careful opening the door in case visitors were watching, but I didn't notice anyone until I had already closed and locked the door to the apartment. That's when I saw Marielle, Alastair's plaything, standing in the shadows. She came forward when she saw me. She was wearing a cloak, thank goodness, and some really nice red boots I admired.

"I don't know if you remember me, Jessie. We were kitchen wenches together here one summer." She glanced around like she was making sure we were alone. "I have to talk to you. It's a matter of life and death."

Six

That's why she looked familiar! "Let's go outside." I ushered her out the door as a large group of teenage boys came in to inspect the dungeon. If I seemed a little unimpressed by her dramatic statement, I have to blame it on the Village.

I mean, when you've dueled with the devil, helped look for pirate treasure, and faced down Death himself, you tend to get a little sanguine about any theatrics. The Village is filled with high school, college, and adult actors who dramatize everything. It's the way things worked here. A matter of life and death didn't put me into a frenzy.

We went over to the picnic tables in the shade of the Mother Goose Pavilion. I could hear Mother Goose's voice telling the story of the goose that laid the golden eggs. Her goose, Phineas, usually sat close by her as she worked the crowd. The kids loved it.

"I don't think you understand how serious this is."

Marielle attempted to impress me again. "Alastair's collection of daggers was stolen when he was killed."

She paused for effect, and I waited patiently. A sword swallower dressed in royal purple took up a spot close by and put out his brass pot to collect tips while he plied his trade.

When she didn't continue, I said, "Did you tell the police? That could be why he was murdered." Sometimes you have to play along to get the ball rolling.

"I dared not. My lord would not want his magical daggers falling into the hands of nonbelievers."

I glanced up at her, away from the interesting prospect of a man forcing sharp objects down his throat. "Magical daggers?"

Marielle nodded, tears starting to her violet eyes. She was really a beautiful girl: smooth skin, shiny, dark hair. "Alastair entrusted me with his secret. He had collected magical daggers from around the world during his travels. Some of them were cursed. Some were ancient, such as the dagger used by Brutus to kill Julius Caesar."

Okay. Not only magical, but *cursed* daggers. "I don't really know why anyone would want to steal magical, cursed daggers. You'd think that would be bad for you."

Her face grew sullen. "You mock me, Jessie! I came to you because I thought you of all people would understand why this is so important."

I didn't really even remember Marielle from my time as a kitchen wench in the castle. I wasn't sure why she felt she could trust me at all. "I'm sorry. I don't mean to sound like I don't believe you. But you should tell the police, not me. They could actually do something about it."

"I can't tell them." She burst out crying. "My lord bewitched me to prevent me from telling anyone I met *after* him about the daggers. That is why I'm telling you. I recognized you this morning and knew I could trust you."

This was almost as interesting as the sword swallower who had drawn a small crowd as he attempted to put three swords down his throat at the same time. I mean, how do they do something like that? Not that I'd consider an apprenticeship with him to find out. One mistake and you'd be eating baby food the rest of your life.

I didn't know what to say to Marielle. It was apparent to me that this had gone beyond good theater. She was dramatic, and I believed that she believed what she said to be true. Not wanting to sound unsympathetic or cause her any more stress, I promised to tell Chase about the daggers. "I'm not bound by Alastair's magic. I can tell the bailiff about the theft, and he can look into it."

She looked relieved. I *felt* relieved. "That would be a blessing, Jessie. Thank you. I didn't feel I could bear the burden of certain death by myself."

"Certain death?" She'd lost me again.

"My lord's magic was the only thing that kept the daggers in check. Without his influence over the daggers, they will surely kill again."

This was really getting interesting. Magical, deadly daggers that would go around killing people because Alastair was dead. I wasn't sure if anyone else would believe it, but I couldn't wait to tell Chase.

The sword swallower was lighting a sword on fire before he pushed it down his throat. I could feel the apprehension of the crowd that was watching him (and putting plenty of green in his brass pot) as they wondered if he could do it without hurting himself.

I heard a scream from the Mother Goose Pavilion. It sounded like Mother Goose herself. It was followed by lots of kid screams and children running out the door into the street beside us. A few loud cries of "Oh, God!" and "What happened?" made me jump to my feet and run to see what was going on. Marielle ran with me. Even the sword swallower paused right before stuffing the flaming sword down his throat.

With everyone gone from the pavilion, it was easy to find Mother Goose. She was on her knees beside her storytelling chair. Her white mobcap was askew, and her apron was covered in blood. "Phineas! How could someone do this? How could anyone hurt Phineas?"

Marielle and I crouched down beside her and looked at the dead goose. In its throat was lodged a jeweled dagger. "And so it begins, even as my lord foretold."

I ignored her prophecy and looked closer at the goose. "I don't think that's Phineas." I picked up the slain bird. "It's stuffed. Someone put blood all over it, but I'm pretty sure it's not real."

Mother Goose looked closer, too. She threw her mobcap on the ground and swore like an unemployed dockworker. "Someone *pretended* to kill my goose? I'll rip their heads off and stuff 'em down their throats. Call the bailiff! Someone has Phineas!"

We waited fifteen minutes for Chase to arrive. When he got there, he wasn't alone. Brooke and Morgan, dressed in Renaissance clothes, were beside him.

I know I was supposed to be upset about the pretend goose being killed and the real goose being kidnapped, but when I saw the three of them coming down the cobblestones, I was a lot more upset about *that*.

Mother Goose pounced on Chase, telling him everything that had happened from the moment she set foot in the pavilion that afternoon until she screamed when she thought she beheld the dead goose. By that time, at least fifty Village residents had gathered around to hear the story told.

I shuddered to think how many times it would be retold before something else came up to take its place.

In a weird way, we were lucky to have a new incident to discuss; it meant we wouldn't have to hear all the gory details of Alastair's death again and again that night when we all broke for dinner. This meant trauma for Mother Goose, of course, but she would have the sure knowledge that some new bit of excitement would occur to make us all forget her, too.

"And this is where Jessie and Marielle came in?" Chase barely glanced up at us.

"Marielle was explaining to me that the curse put on the daggers would cause them to kill again now that Alastair is gone," I explained.

Marielle looked shocked when I blurted it out. I could hear the collective intake of breath from the crowd around us. But how else could I say it?

"Cursed daggers?" Chase lifted his left brow (he is so cute when he does it) and held my gaze in question. "Maybe we'd better take this inside."

The crowd groaned when they realized they weren't going to hear the good stuff. Talk of cursed daggers set loose upon the Village to kill pretend geese and who knew what else was enough to make any inquisitive person salivate.

As interesting as the daggers were, I really wanted to ask why Brooke and Morgan were still at the Village, dressed in Renaissance gear, no less. What was up with that? They didn't seem like such a threat in their street clothes (especially when they were leaving), but dressed like one of us, they seemed particularly dangerous.

I guess I'd thought their imminent departure was a done deal after I'd talked to Chase and he'd reassured me that Brooke didn't mean anything to him anymore. But evidently I'd read something more into that conversation.

Inside the pavilion, Chase examined the skewered stuffed goose. "There's no sign of Phineas anywhere?"

"No. I didn't pay attention to him when I came in after lunch. I thought he was here, but sleeping. He's quite old, you know. He sleeps and poops a lot," Mother Goose replied.

"When did you see him last that you were sure he was alive?" Chase asked.

"This morning. I fed him and took him around the Village for his walk and his swim. I left him here to go home and change clothes. Then I came back. I guess that was around ten."

Chase put on the evidence gloves he always carried with him, then took the dagger out of the fake goose. He examined it closely, then put it into a plastic bag. He bagged the goose and a dried blood sample from the floor, too. He's very thorough. "Marielle, what can you tell me about this dagger?"

He held out the plastic bag with the dagger in it, and she took a step back. "I'm sorry. I'm not going to touch any of them. And I can't speak of them, except to Jessie."

She whispered her answers to me, and I said, "Alastair told her they were all completely evil. He said they had killed many creatures before his magic enslaved them. With him dead, they will kill again."

"But this is a stuffed, fake goose," Mother Goose argued. "The dagger didn't really kill anything except some polyester and cotton. But where's Phineas?"

"Is this dagger part of Alastair's collection?" Chase asked Marielle.

"It is." Marielle whispered, eyes riveted on the ruby-encrusted dagger. I translated. "This is the dagger used to kill Julius Caesar. Alastair kept all twelve daggers together in a glass traveling case. He could never leave them anywhere for fear something like this might happen. He may have been killed so that the thief could set them free."

"That's all well and good," Mother Goose interrupted. "But where the hell is my Phineas?"

"I hope this evidence will help us find that out." Chase got to his feet. "I'll post some flyers around the Village. I might be able to get Adventure Land to offer a reward for his return. This looks more like a prank to me than cursed daggers. Let's not panic. We'll find Phineas. I'm sure he's fine."

Mother Goose didn't appear to be so sure. She sobbed into her white apron. "I've had that goose for a very long time. He's like the child I never had. Or at least the grandchild, since I had his mother, too, God rest her soul. Whatever you need me to do, Bailiff, don't hesitate to tell me."

"I will, and I'll keep you updated." Chase hugged her, then ushered Marielle and me out of the pavilion.

Most of the crowd had moved on to the more pressing issue of getting to the castle before the King's Feast. Only a few lackeys scurried around for their masters alongside one or two fairies preening their wings.

"I need more information about these daggers," Chase told Marielle. "Why didn't you say something this morning at the castle?"

"I was afraid," she admitted. "I don't know what the consequences will be for me now. My lord told me never to speak of them. I told Jessie in the strictest confidence because I was worried about this kind of thing happening. Now I know it's too late to stop it. You can read all about the evil Alastair had contained for more than twenty years at the terrible cost to him. Look at his website and you'll understand."

"He had a website for them? I thought he didn't want anyone to know?" I looked at Chase to see what he was thinking.

Chase shook his head. "I guess there's a difference between your people blabbing it and selling your product on the Internet." He said to Marielle, "I may have to talk with you again about this. Detective Almond may want to have a word, too. Please don't leave the Village without telling me. I'm sure they can make you comfortable in the castle."

She nodded and dropped him a brief curtsey. It wasn't deep, but as a sign of respect, it was believable. Only the king or queen would've deserved more.

I watched her walk away. Her movements were very graceful, more gliding than walking. She was very elegant even in her day-old clothes. Knowing she wore only the metal chastity belt under her cloak was the only thing that kept me from being jealous of her. Those things are really uncomfortable!

"I hope you were planning to tell me about the missing daggers," Chase said. "This is the first I've heard that there was a theft with Alastair's death."

I looked around. Brooke and Morgan were hanging out by the dungeon door. They were very color coordinated in their pale blue velvet and silk. It made me much angrier to see them waiting for Chase. "I only found out about it a little while ago. She said we were kitchen wenches together at the castle. I don't really remember her. As for the killing daggers held in check by Alastair's magic, I don't know if I would've mentioned them or not. Why? Do you feel like they're the key to Alastair's death?"

"I don't know about the key, but they may be an important piece of the puzzle."

I nodded toward the dungeon. "I thought they were leaving?"

Chase glanced at Morgan and Brooke. "I thought so, too. But it seems they want to experience the Village so they can understand why I want to be here."

I didn't know what to say that wouldn't sound bitchy or whiny. Lucky for me, Daisy and Ethan were starting toward the castle and needed my help. "I guess I'll see you later. I think Daisy has a cot on the floor in her shop where I can sleep tonight."

"Let's talk about this before you get bent again," Chase said. "Wait for me at the Lady of the Lake after the feast."

I didn't confirm or deny that I would wait for him at the tavern. I wasn't sure yet which it would be. My perfect summer was getting a little frayed around the edges. Like the Village, nothing was as it seemed.

"Daisy," Chase said. "I need to talk to you about Alastair."

She smiled and patted his cheek as she walked past him. "I know you do. And I'm sure we can find time for that after the feast. There's not really much to say. I'm sorry Alastair was murdered. I didn't do it."

"I suppose you have someone who can vouch for your whereabouts this morning at four or so."

Daisy continued walking after handing me a bag full of swords. At this point, they were shouting at each other as we moved toward the castle. I wasn't sure why Chase didn't follow us, but I assumed he had to be somewhere else. Maybe with Brooke and Morgan.

"I do," she yelled. "I have Ethan and Hans. They were with me. Isn't that right, my friends?"

Chase was looking me right in the eye as Ethan spouted off a bunch of poetic nonsense about Daisy being innocent and Hans proclaimed Daisy's innocence in no uncertain terms.

He didn't say anything else (we were too far away), and finally the three of us turned away to walk past Squires' Lane and Harriet's Hat House. Already the line to get in the Great Hall was stretched around the lake, past Eve's Garden. Apparently, no one had mentioned that the duel was off. Or the visitors hoped they'd get to see Alastair anyway. It's hard to tell with visitors.

"A goodly number of peasants, my lady," Ethan commented as he shifted his bag of sword paraphernalia from one shoulder to the other. He was dressed in a dark green velvet doublet and matching tights. His hair was perfect, of course. Standing between him and Daisy, I felt like the drab stepchild.

Daisy was resplendent as well in her usual tournament gear, which consisted of her breastplate over a red tunic and matching tights. The grim determination on her face reminded me of how she looked when she was fighting Alastair last night.

When she sent Ethan ahead to find out what entertainment we were providing at the feast, I decided to ask her about what had caused her confrontation with Alastair. She'd been uncharacteristically quiet about the event at the pub last night, at least as far as I could remember.

"What really happened with you and Alastair before the duel last night?" I put down my bundle of swords and rested against the side of the climbing wall near Mirror Lake.

"Nothing happened," she denied. "I went to see him. We fought. That's it."

"I might believe that if I hadn't been on the Green with you. You were crying. Your dress was torn."

She looked at me with troubling anger in her pretty blue eyes. "I don't want to talk about it. Haven't you ever heard that you shouldn't speak ill of the dead?"

"You expected to hook up with him when you left the shop yesterday. Something changed. What did he do?"

"He laughed at me. That's what he did. He pretended he wanted me, too, then he laughed at me. I wanted to kill him last night. I didn't. I guess I'm not as tough as everybody thinks. This breastplate doesn't protect my heart."

I hugged her. "I know you didn't kill him, if that's what you're wondering. I'm not so sure about his intentions last night after you beat him."

"He was a big blowhard. He would've blustered and pretended, but we all knew I beat him. His reputation would never have been the same anyway. Who am I? A two-bit sword maker in a little village most people haven't heard of. But I took out the Great Alastair!"

"I'm sorry I told Chase about you not being there when I woke up. If I'd known you needed an alibi, I would've been there for you. I didn't know."

She gave me a hearty shoulder pat that knocked me against the wall. "Don't worry about it, Jessie. I'll be fine. I didn't do anything wrong. I might've considered it last night while we fought, but afterwards, I could've cared less."

Ethan came back and told us Daisy was still part of the main show in the Great Hall. People had been calling in all day about seeing the woman who'd bested Alastair. The king and queen wanted to play up what was bound to be a short-lived phenomenon.

It bothered me that Daisy had a very real motive for killing Alastair and no alibi, by her own admission. Chase and Detective Almond didn't know about her real-life thwarted romance with the great swordsman. But that, and the manner in which he was killed, would certainly pique their suspicions in her direction if they ever found out.

I liked Daisy and respected her. I didn't believe she'd sneak up on anyone. I wasn't sure how the police (and Chase) would take the information about the long-ago love affair between the pair. I decided they wouldn't hear it from me. If Daisy decided to tell them, that was fine. Otherwise, they would have to find out on their own.

Would I have felt more charitable toward helping Chase in his investigation if Morgan and Brooke weren't still hanging around? I guess we'll never know, since they were the first people I saw once I got in the Great Hall (an hour later) with Daisy and Ethan. Morgan and Brooke were seated at places of honor on the dais where King Harold and Queen Olivia entertained guests and Adventure Land executives.

And where was Brooke getting her clothes? She had on another gown, different from the one she'd been wearing earlier. This one was made of gold material and managed to make her look like a bosomy statue. Morgan wore a matching gold doublet and tights. There was no sign of Chase, but he was bound to be in the castle somewhere.

Already the Great Hall was filled with visitors devouring Cornish hens, baked potatoes, and some kind of green vegetable. The kitchen staff bustled back and forth between the sections that were separated by the dueling/jousting field where Daisy would no doubt duel in good time. Right now, a group of jugglers and acrobats were amusing the crowd. Daisy, Ethan, and I found an empty space under the bleachers in the area reserved for Village staffers.

The knights were urging their squires to ready their horses for the customary joust. The creak of leather and clanging of metal could barely be heard over the shouts of the visitors in the stands. The big horses pawed the ground while the knights checked their lances and chewed breath mints for the after-hours show (not sanctioned by Adventure Land).

"What do they want me to do?" Daisy asked Ethan as we took out a trio of swords for her to choose from during the duel.

"I'm not sure," he admitted. "It looks like a free-for-all. Everyone wants to see you fight. I don't think they care who you fight or how you do it."

She nodded. "I don't much care either. Jessie, get my

helm. I would be ready by the time Lord Dunstable calls my name. Be quick, apprentice. The night approaches."

Everyone was in a good mood after laughing at the acrobats. The jugglers missed a few, but that was funny, too. They came into the waiting area, breathless and dirty from rolling around in the dirt and hay that made up the floor in the arena. All of them wished Daisy good luck and punched fists with a few of the knights.

Seeing the knights reminded me that Chase began at the Village as a knight. He was the most popular of the Queen's Champions for a long time (at least one summer). He had a dashing, rogue style that was very appealing, even though he was the good guy. Usually the crowd liked the Black Knight the best. But not when Chase was jousting.

As if thinking of him conjured his appearance, he ran across the arena toward us. The knights were supposed to go out next, but instead, Lord Dunstable called for Daisy to take the field in an amazing feat of champion swordplay.

I took Daisy's red cloak out of the sword bag and fastened it to her shoulders. As she smiled in thanks, I emptied out the rest of the bag on the floor. In the bottom was a finely crafted gold dagger, obviously old and certainly valuable.

"What's that?" Chase asked.

I sighed. "It looks like an evil dagger to me."

Seven

I picked up the dagger and shoved it back in the bag. "There are always a few extras around."

Daisy took the dagger from the bag as I fussed with her red cloak. "This one isn't mine. I wish it were. It looks like it might be solid gold."

Chase took it from her. "I think this might be one of the missing daggers from Alastair's collection. You don't mind if I keep it, do you?"

She shrugged. "I don't care. But I know what you're thinking, Bailiff. I didn't steal the daggers, and I didn't kill Alastair."

The crowd in the stands above us was going wild, stomping their feet and yelling Daisy's name. They were already throwing little chicken bones into the arena. If she didn't get out there soon, there was no telling what would be next.

"Is there a problem over here?" Lord Dunstable descended from his meritorious spot slightly above the field. "Daisy, are you ready or not?"

She put on her helm. "I'm ready, unless Chase says I can't go."

We all swiveled our eyes to look at Chase. He put the gold dagger in the pouch at his side. "Go ahead. But we have to talk when this is over."

She nodded and strode confidently into the arena. Cheers threatened to bring down the roof as Lord Dunstable announced her opponent, one of the other sword makers from the Village. He didn't have a chance against her, but the crowd didn't know that. Ethan excused himself and went to find dinner in the kitchen. That left Chase and me alone with a few horses in the stalls behind us.

"I need to know everything you know about what happened to Alastair," Chase said.

I didn't look at him. It was easier to lie that way. "You already know everything. I told you about the daggers as soon as Marielle told me and we found the goose."

"Jessie, Ethan said you were with him and Daisy this morning when Alastair was killed. You told me earlier that you didn't know where Daisy was. Which is it?"

I didn't want to lie. I really didn't. But I also didn't want to get Daisy in trouble. I compromised on something between the two. "I didn't get up and look around the whole blacksmith shop to see if anyone else was there. I saw Ethan and then the Village crier came by with the news about Alastair. Maybe she was there. I'm not sure."

One minute I was watching Daisy fighting the young apprentice sword maker in the arena, the next Chase was standing between me and the match. He took my hands and put them on his chest. Those wonderful dark brown eyes looked into mine. "You're not sure?"

"That's what I said." I squirmed away from him, pretending an interest in the match that I didn't feel. "Do you *want* Daisy to be guilty of something?"

"You know I don't. But we have to figure out the truth. Bawdy Betty said she saw Daisy over by the Lady Fountain this morning right before sunrise, about six thirty."

"Like Betty was out that early. She has a hard time getting her bagels done before noon every day!" I knew that wasn't the point. I didn't know what else to say.

"Daisy probably wasn't asleep in the blacksmith's shop. She was asleep by the Lady Fountain. You're protecting her, Jessie."

I summoned all the righteous indignation I felt on Daisy's behalf. "You don't know what she went through with Alastair!"

Realizing I had said something I didn't mean to say, I put my hand over my mouth (before something else stupid could come out) and turned to face the match again.

Releasing my hands, Chase came up behind me and slipped his arms around me. "You can tell me the truth, Jessie. I thought we never lied to each other."

"Don't ask me about this if you don't want me to lie," I said as bluntly as I could. "There might be something about Daisy that could implicate her in all of this, but you won't hear it from me."

He sighed and kissed the side of my head. "That's okay. I'll ask Daisy. You don't have to lie."

I settled back against him, happy to have him there. "Thanks."

Daisy had won the match and was grinning broadly when she returned. "You wanted to talk to me, Sir Bailiff?"

"You know I do."

She tidied his braid with her fingers and stroked his cheek. "I could use some ale. What do you say we go to the kitchen and partake of the feast?"

"That's fine." Chase put his arm around my shoulders, and the three of us darted across the empty arena. Visitors were eating Banbury cakes and were mostly quiet as the king and queen did their feast speeches with plenty of *what-ho* and *odds bodkins* interjected. Most of the visitors didn't know what they were talking about, but it sounded historical and that's what mattered.

The kitchen staff, mostly serfs and wenches, were lounging about, exhausted now that the main part of the meal was over. There were no empty chairs, but we found a few full flour sacks on the floor. The three of us sat there and ate. The food was cold and the ale was warm, but it was good anyway.

Daisy told Chase everything, including the part about her encounter with Alastair before the match on the Green. I tried to caution her a few times to hold back, but she didn't seem to care. "And I wasn't with Jessie or Hans or Ethan when I woke up this morning. I couldn't tell you where I was or what I did after we left the third pub."

"We made it through three pubs?" I asked in complete disbelief.

She laughed. "I'm getting old. I used to make it through ten pubs without having a hangover the next morning. Now I couldn't even tell you which three pubs we were in last night. Ethan might know. He's a little more conservative than I am."

"So you could've been with Alastair and you might not remember," Chase suggested as he washed down chicken with ale. "Detective Almond is probably going to want the clothes you were wearing. He'll need to check them for blood."

Daisy put down the tankard. "I can't help you there. I burned the gown. I never wanted to see it again, and this way I don't have to. I know that looks bad, but you can understand my feelings on the subject."

"Maybe," Chase said. "But I don't think the police will. You're the perfect suspect. I'd expect them to want to talk to you at the station."

"That's fine. I have nothing to hide."

I wanted to tell her that she should've hidden a lot more. Maybe if Ethan had been here instead of me, he'd have convinced her to keep her mouth shut. Chase was right. On the police detective shows I watched on TV, the smart-mouthed homicide cop would have had Daisy holed up in one of those small interrogation rooms, reading her Miranda.

"It's too late tonight to do anything about it," Chase said. "I'll call Detective Almond first thing in the morning."

"Fair enough." Daisy got to her feet. "One last night to have a good time. My thanks, Sir Bailiff. I am at your disposal in the morn."

I was surprised Chase let her leave without asking about the daggers. When she was gone, I said, "She probably knew all about the daggers, since she was his lover for a few years. Don't you think Detective Almond will want to know about them?"

"I'm not telling him about evil, magical daggers," he said. "No one besides your friend Marielle has mentioned that anything was missing. And since she's on the top of the suspect list for Alastair's death, that doesn't make her information very good."

Chase took my hand and pulled me to my feet. "Seriously? Someone thinks Marielle—skinny-armed, good-breeze-would-blow-her-down Marielle—killed Alastair with that big sword? How could that be possible?"

He shrugged. "If he was unconscious on the bed, anyone

could have done it. She wouldn't have to be that strong. Gravity would be on her side. The police like her because everyone knew she was closed in with him for the night. She's saying she slept through whatever happened. They aren't buying it."

"Well that lets Daisy off the hook."

"It did . . . until she told me that she had the best motive for killing someone, unrequited love, not to mention no alibi and superior strength. No one could look at her and doubt that she could kill Alastair if she wanted to."

"But you're not going to tell Detective Almond, right? If he doesn't figure it out on his own, he'll go after Marielle."

"I thought you were friends with Marielle?" Chase mocked me. "Is that the way you treat your friends?"

"I'm trying to protect my friend. I don't know Marielle at all. But I know Daisy, like you do. We both know she didn't kill Alastair."

We walked past Peter's Pub, which was full of after-hours diners. Light and music along with the sounds of conversation and laughter spilled out through the open door. I envied them their casual way to end the day. Mine seemed to be a little more problematic.

"We don't know if Daisy killed Alastair or not. People can be motivated to do anything. It will be up to the police to figure that out. My job is to give them as much information as I can. I can't pretend not to know that Daisy and Alastair had an affair that went sour."

We passed a flirty little fairy who was trying to get Bart's attention. He was half in and half out of the walking-tree costume. It reminded me of my promise to Portia. Although, after thinking about it, I'd decided they didn't seem right for each other. Not that I thought Ethan would have any interest in her. I would have to give the matchmaking matter more thought.

Many of the Village folk were straggling home after the feast. Knights led their horses toward the outdoor stables located near the Field of Honor where the outside jousting tournaments were held. Some pirates I didn't recognize were flirting with a few of the Lovely Laundry Ladies near the darkened Dutchman's Stage. The sword swallower I'd seen earlier was talking to this year's Juliet from the Romeo and Juliet tent near Harriet's Hat House.

"Where's your brother staying?" I decided to change the subject before we reached the dungeon. I wished I'd thought of it sooner. I wasn't too keen on making good on my idea to sleep on the cot at Daisy's shop, but looking for someplace else to sleep would be difficult at this time of night.

"He and Brooke are staying at a hotel on the beach," Chase said. "I didn't want them staying with us."

"Us?" It had a nice ring to it that made me smile. I compensated right away by frowning and acting as if it didn't matter. After all, Chase and I had never said we were a permanent couple. We'd never said we were getting married or anything.

"Of course *us*. What did you expect?"

"I don't know. He *is* your brother." *And she is your ex-fiancé.*

He hugged me closer. "And you're more important to me than either of them, Jessie. I didn't mean for you to sleep in the blacksmith's shop last night. I tried to find you and bring you home."

"It sounds like we were all over the Village. No wonder you couldn't find me."

"I'm sorry your first night here was messed up." He kissed me and smiled. "We'll make up for it tonight."

I agreed, and we went into the dungeon together in one of those love-haze moments. Unfortunately, reality came to burn away the haze before we could get lost in it. Detective Almond called Chase for an update on the Alastair case. I sat in front of Chase's computer, languishing in the air-conditioning while he talked on the phone, and googled Alastair's evil, magical dagger collection.

Marielle was right. There were twelve daggers that each had a bad reputation. The ruby dagger that we found in the faux goose supposedly killed Julius Caesar. It was worth a fortune, according to the website. Since each dagger was linked to a larger photograph, I was able to identify the gold dagger I'd found in Daisy's sword bag.

"Good work!" Chase said when he'd seen what I'd done. "What does it say about the gold dagger?"

"It's preposterous, kind of like Alastair," I explained. "It says the gold dagger belonged to King Midas."

"The guy with the golden touch?"

"Exactly. I can't believe anyone could fall for this magical, evil-dagger stuff. I know this is Renaissance Village, but come on!"

Chase sat beside me. "What about the expensive-looking dagger in faux Phineas this morning?"

I showed him the picture and story about the ruby-studded dagger. "I wonder how Alastair got all those daggers."

"He probably stole them or had them stolen, *if* they're real. He couldn't have afforded them, that's for sure. For all of his mythology, Detective Almond told me he was in a lot of debt. Maybe he took a dagger from the wrong person."

We watched the Myrtle Beach news for a few minutes, then turned out the lights. There was still music coming from the Village, a mandolin playing forlornly in the night. The musician, whoever he or she was, played the instrument beautifully.

"I didn't tell Detective Almond about Daisy," Chase

whispered as we stood very close to each other near the window that overlooked the tree swing.

"But you won't have any choice," I said sadly. "It's your job to take care of the Village. I understand that. I wish Daisy would've kept her mouth shut. She obviously looked into your big brown eyes and forgot who she was talking to."

"Women have told me I have that effect on them." He kissed the side of my neck.

"Not me." I played with his braid until the leather thong he tied it with came loose. "When I look into your eyes, I see you."

"And you, I hope." He kissed me. "I don't want anyone to see me without you."

We listened to the mandolin player for a long time before we finally went to bed. In what seemed like only a few minutes, the alarm went off. Shortly after, Chase flipped on the local news, and, no surprise, the Village was on TV.

"The police are still investigating Alastair's violent and untimely death." Tavin Hartley was speaking to a reporter. "Many of his fans have e-mailed me to ask when his funeral will be held. I can verify that he will be cremated on a funeral pyre, as per his wishes. I don't have a time frame on that as yet, but when I do, it will be posted at his website, www.alastair.com."

"I hope she's not planning on doing that in the Village," Chase said. "There are no permits for funeral pyres."

"What if Marielle is right about the daggers? What if someone killed Alastair to get their hands on them?"

"If that's the case, they're doing a bad job keeping up with them. If each of them is worth the fortune Alastair claimed it was, why wouldn't the thief sell them off instead of sticking one in a fake goose?"

"I suppose that's true." I yawned. "Maybe it's a diversion.

I mean, the goose was stupid, but planting one in Daisy's possession wasn't. If you were trying to cover your tracks, it would be a good way to do it. They seem stupid, but maybe they mean something."

Chase rumpled my hair and nuzzled the side of my neck. "And that's why I keep you around. You know how to think on, or in this case, off your feet. What are you doing today?"

I sighed, wishing I didn't have to do anything but be here all day with him. "If you don't arrest Daisy, I'm hoping to learn something about making swords. If you do arrest her, I guess I'll follow you around and help you find out what happened to Alastair."

"Here's hoping you learn to make swords," he quipped as he got out of bed.

"Hey! You said you liked having me help you!"

"I do. But you may be too close to this one."

"You mean you're mad because I didn't tell you everything about Daisy and Alastair."

"Not mad. Surprised, maybe." He shrugged. "It's okay. I understand that you like her. I hope you don't like her better than me."

I jumped out of bed and kissed him hard, wrapping my arms around his neck. "I don't like anybody better than you. Shower?"

"Anything to save hot water."

I had to approach Portia about a new outfit, and I dreaded it. I knew she'd give me something bad if I didn't have some update on Ethan for her. Chase had been called away to some problem at the Three Pigs Barbecue, so I grabbed breakfast and coffee alone at the Monastery Bakery on the way to the costume shop. It was my experience that enough caffeine and sugar could take the edge off of any problem.

I was surprised and pleased to encounter Bart there. He wasn't in his tree getup yet and looked freshly showered and shaved. Maybe things were going to work out fine after all.

He was tucking into his third cinnamon roll (if empty plates were any indication), and I asked if I could join him at his table. "Sure." He smiled and held out his hand. "Being a big tree is lonely work. People like to see me, but I can't talk to them. I think I might have to ask for another character assignment."

"I can understand that. I was the Black Knight's squire for a summer. I never saw anyone but him, and he wasn't much of a conversationalist. Not like Portia."

"Who?"

"Portia." I took a big gulp of coffee and prepared to sell her. "You know. The costume lady. She loves to talk. She's got a lonely job, too."

Bart considered this information. "But she sees people all day long."

"That's true. But they aren't the *right* people, you know?"

"Are you saying she's looking for someone special?" He looked hopeful. "I'm looking for someone special, too, lady. I was hoping I could talk to you about it."

I was about to commend him for his quick assessment of the situation when a ruckus from the back of the bakery spilled out into the dining area. Brother Carl (former head of the Brotherhood of the Sheaf) and Brother John (present head of the Brotherhood of the Sheaf) were wrestling with each other, both of their black monk's robes covered in flour.

"Looks like trouble," Bart said in another quick assessment of the situation.

"Maybe we should step in before something bad happens," I suggested.

Bart stepped in as only he could (being as tall and broad as an old tree), by putting himself between the two monks and holding each one of them back so they couldn't touch each other. "Be good now. Nothing to fight over."

"He has brought shame and dishonor upon the Brotherhood," Brother Carl accused.

"Brother Carl has dirtied our name and good reputation by putting this into our kitchen." Brother John held up a silver dagger that was adorned with sapphires. "We must put an end to his leadership before we are ruined."

"You dare to accuse me?" Brother Carl demanded, his floury hands in fists.

"Who else is to blame?" Brother John glared at him.

The evil, magical daggers strike again. "Good Brothers!" I addressed the two in Renaissance fashion, since we had attracted a crowd of visitors. "We all know there is only one way to settle a matter of honor that transpires within the Brotherhood."

Immediately both men quit struggling against Bart's hold. They still glowered at one another, but they knew my words were true.

"Midnight bake-off," Brother Carl grunted.

Brother John agreed. "Yea, verily."

Eight

I kept possession of the silver dagger and sent one of the younger monks to find Chase and tell him to meet me at the costume shop. I knew he'd want to see it right away. That was three of the evil daggers. Only nine to go. If they caused as much havoc as the first few, the Village might be in shambles by the time they were accounted for. Maybe Marielle knew what she was talking about.

I left the rest of the monks dusting the flour from their robes and plotting their bake-off that would decide the fate of their order. It had been coming ever since Brother John had usurped Brother Carl's place. The dagger was only a catalyst. But why was it there?

With the drama behind me, I coaxed Bart into accompanying me to the costume shop. If I was lucky, he and Portia would hit it off right away and I'd be in great costumes for the whole summer.

Admittedly, they had to have seen each other around without Cupid zinging an arrow into either one of them.

But that didn't mean they couldn't see each other with fresh eyes if I introduced them. I'd seen it happen before. Cupid has nothing on me.

Portia wasn't busy when we got there, which is always a good sign. Rowdy, impatient Village folk and visitors tend to put her at her worst. "Make sure you smile at her when we get there," I told Bart as we approached the window. "You have a super smile. It's bound to brighten her day."

"Okay." He shrugged. "But she might not like it."

"She'll love it! Trust me on this." I sauntered up to Portia with all the confidence of a tavern wench with a tankard of ale for thirsty pirates. "Portia! Look who I found wandering around the Village all alone."

Bart leaned down a bit so she could see his smile. He wiggled his fingers in a small wave. "Hello, Costume Lady."

Portia gave a little shriek and stepped back from the window, retreating into the costume shop. "I ask you for Ethan and you bring me Godzilla!"

"That wasn't very nice!" I glanced up to see if Bart had heard her, but he appeared to be entranced watching the good ship *Queen's Revenge* leave her berth on this side of the lake. "Bart's a nice guy. You said you were looking for someone."

"I said I wanted to go out with Ethan," she hissed before she tossed a costume on the counter. "Let's see how *this* fits you."

I picked up the generic green costume worn by Village employees who helped people on the elephant ride and handed out hatchets for the hatchet throw. I'd worn it a couple of summers when I hadn't been a definite character. "Hey! I'm an apprentice. We don't wear these costumes."

"You know what I want, Jessie. I know what you want. Leave the old costume in the wash bag when you change.

And don't forget to give back the boots." She slammed the little half door in my face.

"It says it's closed," Bart said. "I guess we should come back some other time."

"Yeah. Whatever." I was not giving back the boots. They would go as well with the green Village costume as the stupid-looking green Village shoes (I left those behind).

"Jessie!" Chase hailed me from the back of a large black horse. "I'm glad I caught up with you. Brother Carl said you found another dagger."

"Nice horse. Are you going to be a knight again?"

"Funny. I'm meeting the vet at the gate. The last time he came into the Village was the day we had the pie-throwing debacle. He got a blueberry pie right in the face. Do you have the dagger?"

I held out the plastic bag with the dagger inside, explaining the circumstances of how it was found. I'm tall, but Chase was sitting on a Percheron, so reaching the bag up high enough wasn't as easy as it looked. I heard Bart sigh as he put his hands on my waist and lifted me straight up.

"That's better!" Chase took the dagger in the bag and quickly kissed me. "Thanks, Bart."

"Don't mention it. Jessie's friend dumped me. It would probably be good to throw something now."

"Whoa!" I put a stop to that thought. "Put me down first and go find a rock. You didn't even know her. How can you be upset?"

"She hated me. You said she'd like me."

Chase laughed. "I told you to stop matchmaking!"

"I know a lot of girls in the Village," I promised Bart quickly as visions of being thrown like a javelin danced through my head. "I'll introduce you. No problem. Put me down, please."

"I have to go. Good work, you two. Sorry about the girl, Bart. But Jessie's right. There are a lot of girls here who would probably like you."

His horse cantered away across the cobblestones while Bart put my feet back on the ground. "Don't worry. I wasn't really going to throw you. You're my go-to apprentice, right? I wouldn't want to hurt you."

"That's right." I stepped back from him, hopefully out of reach. It was hard to tell because he had very long arms. I guess they went with the rest of him. I needed a diversion unless I wanted to spend the whole day looking for a girlfriend for him. It was bad enough I'd promised Portia Ethan. Now I'd promised Bart someone else for him.

Before I had to do anything drastic, Merlin approached with a request. "Bart! I've been searching for you everywhere. King Arthur broke his sword in the stone again. We're going to have to turn it over to check out the wiring on the underside. Would you mind moving it for me?"

Bart rolled his eyes. "That makes the second time this month, Wizard! I think you need to move it like you did Stonehenge. Wave your wand."

Merlin tapped his wand impatiently on his hand. "Power seems to be gone right now, my friend. Besides, mayhap a giant helped me with that move. Who can tell? For now, let's go. I know you don't want to be a walking tree forever."

Bart agreed and went with Merlin while I heaved a sigh of relief. I looked at the green costume in my hands, knowing it was the best I was going to get that day. I had started back toward the dungeon to change clothes when I saw Tavin Hartley. It seemed to me that this might be a good time to get someone else's point of view on the evil, magical daggers.

"Excuse me." I had to tug at her gray suit sleeve to get her attention. "I'd like to ask you a few questions."

She paused and looked at me through her narrow-framed glasses. "Yes . . . Jessie, right?"

"Right. I heard about the missing daggers. Actually, I've seen a few of them. I was wondering if you had any idea who took them."

She pushed back an imaginary strand of pale hair. "You mean Alastair's dagger collection?"

"That would be it. I understand they were very valuable."

"They were fake."

I was too surprised to speak for a second, then I choked out, "What do you mean they're fake? I saw them on the Internet. Each of them has some historical significance."

"Do you believe everything you read on the Internet?" We sat down on a bench outside Eve's Garden. "Look, Alastair's reputation was part real-life exploits and part make-believe. You live here. You understand."

I *did* understand, watching as the *Queen's Revenge* began her daily assault on the Lady of the Lake Tavern. "Marielle seems to think they're real."

"Yes." She sighed. "They always believed anything he said, did anything he wanted. If the daggers had any *real* magical power, it was helping Alastair get his way with people. It was like he mesmerized them. I never saw anything like it."

That made me think. "Was there anyone Alastair couldn't charm? Someone who benefited by his death?"

She smiled the first genuine smile I'd seen on her thin face. "You know the police asked these questions, right? What's your interest, Jessie?"

I told her about Daisy. "I don't think she killed him, but I can't prove she didn't."

"I don't know what to tell you. There were plenty of people who didn't like Alastair. Some of them might be here in Renaissance Village. But your friend, Daisy, is probably top on the list, no matter what the police think about Marielle. She's only a child who was infatuated with him. Do you *really* think she could kill anyone?"

I had to admit that I couldn't picture it, and she said she had to get back to the castle. She was in charge of all the media information as well as settling Alastair's estate. I watched her continue on her path to the castle, wondering why Alastair hired someone who didn't fit into the pack of his followers. Maybe he needed someone to be outside the Ren life he led.

I darted into the dungeon and changed clothes. It was well after nine when I ducked inside Swords and Such to take on my responsibilities as Daisy's apprentice.

Ethan tagged me as soon as I stepped inside. "There you are! We were wondering if you were working today."

Daisy looked up from sharpening a long, wicked-looking knife. "Jessie, I need you to be here. Ethan is going to need your help."

"You're not being arrested, are you?" I glanced from one to the other, concerned. "Did the police ask you to come in?"

"No," she admitted. "But it's only a matter of time, since Chase saw the dagger fall out of the sword bag last night."

"Too bad we couldn't have sold it to raise money for your bail," Ethan said.

"It wouldn't matter. Alastair's manager said it was worthless," I explained.

"Balderdash!" Daisy thundered. "I've worked with metal all my life. That dagger was real gold. That witch probably wants it for her own. She doesn't care that Alastair's dead."

"But why tell *me* it wasn't worth anything? She must know I'm not important around here."

Ethan laughed. "Because you look kind of gullible in

that outfit. I don't know if I should give you my ticket to get into the joust or ask you for a turkey leg."

Daisy laughed, too, and I felt conspicuous in my awful green outfit. "I'm sorry I'm late. I'm really looking forward to working with the swords. Tell me what to do and I'll do it."

"That's my girl!" Daisy smacked me on the back, and I thought about Bart. These two would be perfect together. "Come on out back. I think we can overlook your outfit for today. I'll have a word with Portia. I expect my apprentice to command some respect in the Village. Ethan, watch the counter."

Ethan looked so unhappy at being left behind that I started to poke my tongue out at him. Not all beautiful people with great hair get to participate in everything.

In Renaissance times (I knew this from my research) it would take many different people to make a sword, as it does today. Despite movies that show the swordsmith forging away at the blade and hilt, this never happened. But most historical fiction is wrong anyway. Then, as now, it took an ironmaster to make the steel that would become the blade. A cutler forged and ground the blade. The hiltsmith made the grip and handle. A scabbard maker made the scabbard. A gift or display sword would go to an engraver or jeweler for ornamentation.

"This is where you'll be starting, Jessie." Daisy held up something that looked like a sword but was made of wood.

"A play sword?" I hadn't signed up to make play swords. What was she thinking?

"Think of it as a practice weapon. This isn't play anything. But like all good apprentices, you have to start somewhere. No one starts with the expensive stuff. You complete the wooden sword, and we'll work on steel next."

This wasn't what I wanted, but I could see her logic. I

knew from my research that swordsmen frequently practiced with wooden blades, especially when they were starting out. "Okay. Is it like a puzzle and I put it together?"

"Kind of." She handed me the pieces. "These are hard maple, which should make a sturdy practice sword. No point in making a sword if you can't use one."

"You must remember that I already know how to use a sword." We were starting to draw a small crowd behind the shop. Everything is up for perusal in the Village. If you want to do something private, you better do it somewhere else.

"Really?" She drew her ever-present sword from its scabbard on her back. "There's a sword inside the doorway. Get it, and show me your stuff."

I barely made it to the door when Ethan tossed me the sword. "Good luck with that." He smirked and tossed his hair for good measure. Where was a barber when you needed one?

I turned back around with the sword in my hand and realized the enormity of what I was undertaking. I hadn't meant that I wanted to spar with Daisy. She was the best. I'd had some training at the Village, but it was rudimentary and basically meant to be showy for the crowd. "I don't want to fight you," I told her as she began circling me.

"It looks like you don't have any choice." She glanced toward the thickening crowd. I recalled that a survey of Village visitors once said they liked swordplay better than anything, and this was especially true of males under the age of thirty. The crowd around us was dominated by them.

"Daisy, I can't fight you. I know what they taught me to get by. I only meant that I know how to use a sword in a very, very basic way."

She laughed, the wind that smelled like the ocean only a few miles away, caught at her blond curls. "Pick up your sword, apprentice, and let's have at it! You do us both a disservice by standing there like yon wooden post."

I sighed, knowing she was right. I held out my sword and gritted my teeth. "I will honor you with my performance, Master."

The thing about sword fighting, which they never talk about in books and movies, is that your arm starts feeling like it's going to fall off after a few hits with your opponent's sword. I have no arm muscles to speak of, so my taking on Daisy was like using marshmallows to stave off an army. I'd fought several people during my time at the Village, but no one who took it as seriously as Daisy.

"You have skill, apprentice," she called out after a few thrusts and parries. "You could be quite talented in this field."

"Thank you, Master. I try my best." Our swords rang out in the morning air as the crowd around us alternately held their breaths and applauded. I was already working up a sweat (not very attractive in my green outfit), but I noticed Daisy was, too. There was a sheen to her muscled arms and her round face.

We continued circling each other, occasionally adding a thrust or two. I wasn't sure how this was supposed to end, since it wasn't a real duel. I never know unless someone sets out the rules beforehand. Was I supposed to let Daisy win? Should I throw down my sword and beg for mercy? What would a new apprentice do in my position?

I didn't have to wait for long to find out. Daisy came at me with a flurry of thrusts that left my right arm crying out for release. I lifted the sword one more time to rally against her, but she hit it out of my hand. I sank to my knees in defeat, glad it was over. The crowd erupted with applause. All I could think about was that I might not be able to use my arm again that day.

Daisy held out her arms, sword high, like a prizefighter

after a battle. The crowd loved her, but the duel was over and there were other things to do, pretzels to eat.

"Let me help you up." She put her hand on my arm. "You did fine, Jessie. I can't believe you lasted as long as you did. With these scrawny little arms, I'm surprised you could hold a sword at all."

I wasn't sure whether to be offended or pleased. I settled for the latter, since I didn't have enough energy for the former. "Thanks. Do you have directions for putting the wooden sword together?"

Of course she didn't. She gave me the pieces and told me to work on it in the back courtyard at Swords and Such. She went inside for a cold ale. Ethan brought me some water a little later. Oh, the life of a Renaissance apprentice.

If it weren't for my dissertation, I could be a wench or a camel caretaker. But I'm determined to get my PhD so I can make enough money to really be secure in life, maybe buy a little house. Right now, I have a crappy little apartment where the plumbing hardly ever works and a car at least ten years old in the same condition.

I wasn't brought up to expect much from life. My twin brother, Tony, and I were raised by our grandmother after our parents were killed in a car accident. Grandma didn't have much, and taking on the responsibility for two children made what she did have even less.

My determination to make something of myself is the only thing keeping me from living at Renaissance Village permanently and taking on some more distinguished role like Lady Godiva or Little Bo Peep. There are always possibilities.

I looked at my sword pieces and wondered how I would fit them together. There seemed to be two pieces for the handle and two pieces for the blade. There were no screws, glue, or any other way to make all the pieces work. Unlike a jigsaw puzzle, this had to be three-dimensional, up and ready to defend me, if only in a mock way.

It was a test. If I could figure out how to do it, Daisy would show me how to make a real sword. If not, I'd spend the rest of the summer polishing swords and trying to put this one together.

"How's it going?" Daisy came out to check on me. "An hour, and you're still trying to figure it out?"

I glanced at the sundial (learning to read sundials is important Renaissance instruction) and found out she was right. "Sorry. I guess my mind isn't on the task."

"Focus, apprentice. You have to stay sharp."

"Could I ask you something, Daisy? Who do *you* think killed Alastair?"

She slapped her hefty thigh. "Damned if I know. He had so many enemies, they were too numerous to mention. Maybe he caught whoever took his daggers in the act. Maybe he couldn't fight them off. I was surprised when I beat him in the duel on the Green. He'd lost all his strength and speed, Jessie. Anybody could've beaten him, even you."

"Thanks, I guess. The police think it was Marielle, since she was in the bedroom with him."

She nodded, watching the visitors go by in their costumes and jeans. "I can understand that. The girl slept through Alastair being killed. But no way could she ram a sword through a man. You have to have muscles to do that. Even if he didn't put up a struggle, there are muscles and such to go through. Have you ever tried to put a sword through a cow carcass? I don't know all the details, but I know that much. Whoever killed him had to be strong enough to do it. Like me, I suppose. That's why I told Chase everything. Everyone knows everything around here anyway. It's no good trying to keep secrets. I hugged my secret about Alastair close for too long. Look where it got me."

Ethan poked his head out the back door and hissed, "There's a police detective here to see you, Daisy. I think he wants to talk about Alastair."

She got to her feet. "Well, maybe this is it. You work on putting that sword together, Jessie. If I'm not here, give it to Ethan. He'll know what to do after that. He learned the same way."

"Good luck." I felt like hugging her, but I couldn't lift my right arm up that high.

I worked in the little bit of shade afforded by the shop for a few minutes until my curiosity got the better of me. I thought I could go inside with the sword parts and pretend I needed to ask a question so I could hear what was going on. From the doorway, I could hear Daisy and Detective Almond talking, but couldn't quite make out what the detective was saying. Daisy's big, booming voice came in loud and clear, though.

I sneaked in the back and kept to the shadows created by scabbards and swords hanging from the walls and ceiling. Chase was with them, too. His handsome face was serious, his muscular arms crossed against his chest.

Detective Almond was asking the questions. "You have no alibi for the time of your ex-lover's death. You have the physical strength and knowledge of weapons to have done the deed. You burned your clothes. And one of the missing daggers from Mr. Alastair's collection was in your possession. I'm afraid I'm going to need you to come to the station with me, Ms. Reynolds."

I started to rush out with a dramatic protest, but Chase saw me. The look on his face kept me in the shadows.

"Am I under arrest?" Daisy asked.

"No. Not yet. We need to figure a few things out. It would go a long way on your behalf if you came along with me now." Detective Almond hadn't taken out handcuffs or anything. Maybe he really only wanted to talk.

"Okay." Daisy raised her chin and prepared to walk out with him. "Take care of the shop, Ethan."

"You'll have to leave the sword here, please." Detective Almond looked as though saying the words was like eating sour lemons. He was probably used to stripping people of their guns. Swords were another matter.

Daisy removed her sword and scabbard and handed it to Ethan. "Take care of this, too. See you later."

Chase walked out with Detective Almond and Daisy. I was about to run after them, but when the shop door closed behind them, Ethan put on Daisy's sword and thrust his fist into the air, yelling, *"Yes!"*

That kept me in the shadows.

Nine

I slipped back outside and sat down in the shade with my sword pieces. There was more than one puzzle to sort through here. Why would Ethan have had that reaction to Daisy being questioned by the police? I thought he worshipped her.

I thought of hundreds of reasons why Ethan would want Daisy out of the picture. Maybe he wanted Swords and Such. He could want her position as master armorer to the Village. There were always machinations going on behind the scenes—the situation with the monks a case in point.

Ethan and Daisy *seemed* close, but he knew Daisy's background with Alastair. Maybe he was involved in setting her up for the police. He could've planted the gold dagger in her sword bag to get her out of the way, for whatever reason.

The back door to the shop opened, and Ethan slithered out. He seemed more like a snake to me now. He slung his hair out of his face and smiled at me. "Having a hard time with that, young apprentice? I could give you a few hints."

"That's okay. I'll figure it out." I smiled back, even though it made my teeth hurt to do it. "I suppose you had to do this when you first started."

He winked at me (*gag!*) and sidled over to sit by me. "No. Daisy was harder on me. She found me when I was fifteen, after one of my many foster parents left me. That meant I owed her. You're lucky to get by making a sword."

Aha! Maybe this was the root of his evil. He had a grudge against Daisy. "So you two don't really get along?"

"We get along, I suppose." He shrugged. "As long as she doesn't meet some interesting new man. Then I'm extra baggage until she gets tired of him. Ask your boyfriend about it. He needed a sword when he was jousting and couldn't afford the one he wanted. They worked out a deal. Then she dumped him when she got tired of him. Daisy is only interested in men for one reason. I'm sure I don't have to spell that out for you."

"I guess you must've been worried she might get back together with Alastair for good this time." I hoped he might inadvertently admit something. If he wanted Swords and Such, that could be a reason for him to set Daisy up.

"Not really. I think he might be the only man she ever cared about. That doesn't bother me. Daisy is Daisy. We all know and love her."

"I don't know. She might've closed the shop or told you to find another job." I looked at my sword pieces while I spoke, hoping to throw him off the meaning behind my words.

"I'm sure I could find someone else in the Village to hire me."

"Probably."

He grinned. "Besides, I don't plan to be Daisy's full-time apprentice forever. I was supposed to be her partner. That never worked out. I have some things planned on my own."

He suddenly got to his feet and swung his hair around. "I'm going to have some lunch. You can watch the shop, apprentice. When I get back, you can take a break."

"Thank you, kind sir." I refused to call him master. Not unless it was followed by *snake*.

I waited until he'd disappeared into the crowds that were headed toward the noon joust. It was an excellent time to search for other daggers or something else that might give him away. He might have planted more than one piece of evidence.

Upstairs was a mass of clothes and weaponry. The bed was littered with swords and underwear. It would be hard to say which was dominant. There were more killing utensils up here than in the shop below. What did Daisy do with all of these anyway? You can only carry one sword at a time.

I could hardly find the floor with everything piled up on it. Daisy might be a disciplined swordswoman, but she was a slob. I didn't love her any less for it, but it would've been easier to search if she were a little neater.

I heard the door to the shop open, and rushed downstairs, hoping it wasn't Ethan coming back already. I started thinking of all the excuses I could to impress him, but I didn't need to bother. It was someone much worse: Chase's brother.

I slowed my pace on the stairs (no point in ending up at his feet) and acted for all the world like I was glad to see him. "Morgan! What a surprise! What brings you to Armorer's Alley? Are you in need of a sword to go with your wonderful doublet?"

He ran one hand down the dark purple overshirt and smiled. "It's amazing to me that anything like this existed during the Renaissance. I would've thought men wore animal skins and that kind of thing."

That would be a caveman, idiot! "No. They actually wore real clothes. They were quite sophisticated."

"Jessie, I'm not here to buy a sword."

I feigned surprise. "Really? Why are you here, Morgan?"

"I'm here to ask a favor of you, on behalf of my entire family."

I tensed but didn't allow it to show. I'd learned some good acting skills in my time here. "Please continue."

"We want Chase back home. My parents are older and not able to keep up with the family business like they used to. We, I guess I should say I, need Chase back home. It's more than I can handle by myself."

I looked into his eyes that were so like Chase's and yet so different. Obviously one of them favored the mother and the other, the father. I hadn't seen recent pictures of their parents, so I couldn't decide which. "Have you talked with Chase?"

"I have. He won't leave here, at least not while *you're* here."

I pretended to mull over the deep, hidden meaning in his words. Not that there really was one, but I wanted to make him wait. "Are you asking me to leave the Village?"

He smiled and gave a sigh of relief. "You know, I told Brooke you seemed like a practical girl, even though you were here in this place. Yes. Leaving the Village would help. But we'd also need you to cut all ties to Chase. I realize you're an assistant history professor and that could mean a financial burden for you. We're prepared to adequately compensate you for your loss. I don't know how much Chase gives you, but—"

"He's never given me money, except for the occasional Coke or pretzel," I said, insulted. He handed me a check. There were more zeroes on it than I made in five years at the university. If I looked astonished, it wasn't pretend. As soon as astonishment passed (about five seconds), I got angry. "And you thought you could buy me away from Chase?"

It was his turn to look surprised. "We know this will cause you some heartache, Jessie. But I think you'll do the right thing."

I looked at the check again. Chase had obviously been holding out on me. I knew his family was well-to-do. I knew he played around at his quasi career of patent attorney, yet he drove a new BMW. There was some money behind him. *Serious money.* I was glad my brother Tony wasn't here. He would've already had the check cashed.

"You know, I think I'll talk this over with Chase, if that's okay with you. I bet he'll know what to do with this." I folded the check neatly and put it in my apprentice pouch.

Morgan's expression turned ugly. I'd never seen Chase look that way. "You aren't as smart as I thought. But go ahead. Tell Chase I offered to buy you off. It won't matter. We're still family, honey. Blood ties, get it? Eventually, Chase will get over this and come home. He'll marry Brooke and live a normal life. And you'll be scraping by because you made a mistake today. It's your choice."

With that well-calculated speech, Morgan left the shop. I felt like crying because part of me knew he was right. Not everyone is like Merlin, who can live at the Village forever. Most of the older residents (people over thirty) who had been here my first summer were gone now. Someday, Chase would be gone, too, back to Scottsdale and his wealthy family. Not to mention Brooke.

Knowing that, was I a fool not to take the money and run? I took the check out again and looked at it. It would buy a house and still leave me a nice nest egg. I could help Tony get started in a small business or go back to school.

This money could ease both of our lives. And that terrible ache where my heart was told me I was a fool to believe I would be on that plane back to Scottsdale with Chase when he got tired of living in the Village.

I took a deep breath and impatiently wiped the stupid tears from my eyes. Maybe someday I'd be sorry, but not today. I put the check back in the pouch and greeted the next person through the door.

I was surprised (and very pleased) to see Chase in the shop after Ethan came back from lunch. I ran and jumped on him, hugging and kissing him like I hadn't seen him for weeks.

"Hey! I'm glad to see you, too. How about lunch?" Chase looked at Ethan. "Does your apprentice get a lunch break?"

Ethan nodded, playing with a toothpick in his teeth (bad habit). "Sure. Have her back in twenty minutes. I need to straighten some things out in case Daisy doesn't make it back tonight."

Chase put his arm around me and smiled. "We'll be back in an hour. I'm sure you can manage."

And that was that. There wasn't much Ethan could say, since technically it wasn't his shop and I wasn't apprenticed to him. Chase and I walked out together, mixing in with the jousting crowd leaving the Field of Honor.

"Let's eat some real food," he said. "I'm tired of pretzels and corndogs. I don't know how we can even sell corndogs as Renaissance fare."

"Okay. I have an hour and nothing better to do." I grinned at him, loving the differences between him and his evil brother.

He studied my face in the sunlight. "Are you telling me you'd rather not use the whole hour for lunch?"

I waggled my eyebrows and grabbed his butt. "The dungeon is right over there, m'lord. No walk a'tall. I believe we could manage a *little* less time for food."

"Your wish is my command."

"So you think Ethan planted that dagger to make Daisy look guilty?" Chase asked while we were spending our last twenty minutes together eating lunch.

"It worked," I reminded him. "She told you the truth, and now she's at the police station."

"I can't help that she didn't have an alibi for when Alastair was killed. I'm surprised she wasn't with someone. Daisy has had a thing with almost every man in the Village, at one time or another."

I watched him finish his mutton pie (really, chicken) and smiled a little, wondering if I should mention that I knew about him and Daisy.

"Ethan told you about me and Daisy, right?" He frowned as he looked across at me. "I'm not surprised. He was Daisy's apprentice at the time. But it was only one night, Jessie. And it was a long time ago."

"And you needed a sword." I laughed. "Guilty conscience? I think he was trying to cause trouble between us. Don't worry. I didn't buy into it."

"Well, enough of that then."

"Exactly!" I swallowed the last of my warm ale and considered telling him about Morgan's proposition. The check felt hot and heavy in the pouch at my side. I wanted to tell him, but I kept my mouth shut. There was no way of knowing what the consequences would be if I told him. It might even hasten that inevitable end between us that I had envisioned earlier at the shop.

"I don't know what we can do about Ethan." Chase

changed the subject. "Unless you have something material, Daisy is on her own. Whether Ethan planted evidence or not, she was still Alastair's lover and can't account for her whereabouts."

"But he might have stolen the daggers."

"That's true." He sat back in his chair with his hands behind his head. "I gave the daggers to Detective Almond. He'll check them for fingerprints and such. I could suggest that he check out Ethan, too."

"That sounds like a plan." I told him what Tavin had said about the daggers being worthless. "What do you think?"

He shrugged. "I think we'll know that, too, when they examine them. In the meantime, believing her isn't any better than believing the Internet, as far as I'm concerned. She might want to keep them. Who knows?"

"If we could find the rest of the missing daggers at Ethan's place, we could at least prove he's a thief."

"*We?* When did I get involved in searching Ethan's place?" Chase paid the serving wench (who showed a little too much cleavage when she bent over to smile at him).

"You're the Village law, Sir Bailiff," I reminded him. "It's your job."

He mulled it over as we walked outside. Finally, as I wrapped my arms around him and kissed his neck, he said, "Okay. I'll find out where he's staying to keep you out of trouble. I think there's some ancient Village law about hanging people you find messing around with your stuff."

"You check that out. We'll talk later. Thanks for lunch, both parts."

"You're welcome, milady." He made a gallant, deep bow, the kind that would normally be reserved for royalty. "I quite enjoyed the sport myself."

We parted ways, with Chase going toward the castle and me going back to Swords and Such. I heard an odd hissing sound coming from the area around the privies. I looked over to the side and saw Marielle beckoning to me.

It was a weird moment. I wasn't sure that I wanted to have some secret tryst with her behind the bathroom. But her hissing grew louder, frightening away a woman and her daughter in matching green harem outfits. For most people, any costume is a Renaissance costume.

"Have you heard about the evil, magical dagger they found in Sherwood Forest?" Marielle darted nervous glances at the backs of the privies.

"No. I was busy working this morning. Was anyone hurt?"

"Not as far as I know." She looked around again. "This has to stop before someone else dies. Don't you see? The daggers are toying with us for their own nefarious purposes. When the time is right, they'll strike, and someone will pay the price."

This conversation had gone beyond even the unusual Village standards. Not only were the daggers evil and magical, but apparently they also had an agenda. My first thought was that Marielle seriously needed help. She was still dressed in that same cloak with nothing much beneath it. Her hair was matted and dirty. She needed someplace to sleep for a while and hopefully regain some level of sanity.

"How long has it been since you slept?" I tried to sound compassionate without sounding condescending. "You need to have a break from all of this and let other people take care of it."

The look in her eyes was full of horror. "I thought you understood, Jessie. No one else can take care of this. The daggers will strike again. Mind my words. I hope neither one of us is their victim."

With those words of doom, she ran off behind the Caravan Stage. I thought about following her but realized it would be better to alert someone else, like Chase. Marielle needed help. Help I didn't think I knew how to give her.

What could Alastair have said or done that made her snap? I wondered as I continued toward Armorer's Alley. The man deserved to die. There was no doubt of it.

I was beginning to wonder if Marielle had killed him. Maybe she lost it and drove that sword into him while he slept, despite what Daisy said. Desperate people did desperate things. All of this evil, magical dagger stuff could be to relieve some of her guilt.

"You took your time getting back," Ethan remarked when I walked through the shop door. "Apprentices could be whipped for that kind of transgression."

Was everyone totally insane today? Why were they all at my end of the Village? "Don't get your hopes up. I'm going in back to put that sword together. I don't want to use it on you right away."

His eyebrows went up, and he tossed his luxuriant hair. "Methinks the girl has spirit! Carry on, apprentice. I shall alert you if you are needed within."

I was beginning to like Ethan less and less. If he planned on taking Daisy's place, I was planning to do without an apprenticeship this summer. Making pretzels or filling ale tankards would be preferable to being here with him.

The pieces of the wooden sword waited for me on the table outside, mocking me with their uncooperative spirit. The only way I would ever get to make a metal sword, even with Daisy here, was if I first put this thing together. But without a drill and some screws, a hammer and some nails or even some Krazy Glue, I couldn't see any way to do it.

Yet somehow it could be done. Other people had done it. I could do it, too. I just had to figure out how.

It was then that I noticed grooves in the wood. There seemed to be a coordinated placement of the grooves that might be the clue to putting them together. I took the two pieces of wood that were supposed to be the blade and slid them together along the grooves. But that wasn't the answer.

I tried sliding them together and then turning them. The two pieces locked together with a faint snap. I lifted them up and they stayed in one piece. *Huzzah!* I'd found the answer.

Of course, the blade was the easy part. The handle refused to do the same thing. I pushed and pulled for an hour before I finally found the trick to snapping the pieces into place. I lifted my complete (albeit wooden) sword and felt ready to go into battle. I had passed the test. *Bring on the metal swords!*

A single hand clap alerted me to the fact that I wasn't alone. "You did it," Ethan said. "I told Daisy I didn't think you'd get it. She thought you were smarter than that. I guess she was right."

"Thanks for that insight." I put my sword down on the table, but I felt ready to take him on if he came any closer. Fortunately, the shop door chime rang and we both had to go inside and help customers. I spent the next hour sliding Lady Visa and Sir MasterCard into place instead of sword parts.

It was hard to believe how much money these thirty-somethings (mostly men) were willing to put down on the really expensive swords. I wondered what they did with them, besides wearing them to Ren Faires. Of course, that could be enough if you spent a lot of time here and at other places like this.

The day flew after that until it was time to close up. No sign of Daisy yet, but I had hopes she'd be back by morning so I could show her my sword. I took it back to the dungeon with me. I didn't trust Ethan not to sabotage my efforts.

Who knew that the next wooden sword puzzle wouldn't be harder?

Visitors were steadily moving toward the main gate, many tired and sunburned from their day outside. Children were crying in strollers, and women were complaining that their feet hurt. It was all part of the experience. No one ever said living during the Renaissance was easy.

I was thinking about Chase and when he'd be finished with his duties around the Village, wondering which pub we'd hit for supper. I was congratulating myself for getting through the day with Ethan when a gloved hand snaked out from behind the big tree that held the tree swing. The hand dragged me off the cobblestones and held me in place against the back of the tree.

I bit down hard, even though there was a glove protecting the hand, and brought my big, booted foot down on my attacker's instep. His response was predictable. He let go of me and started yelling and hopping around on his uninjured foot.

"What the hell, Jessie?" my brother Tony shouted. "I was only trying to help. Now I may never dance again."

Ten

"What the hell are *you* doing, grabbing me like that? Are you crazy?" I didn't regret that I'd hurt him. Sometimes my twin gets out of control. And speaking of that, why was he dressed in Sherwood Forest garb? I thought he was working at the castle with Queen Olivia.

"I'm working with Robin." He continued nursing his sore foot, testing it a little and limping like a little kid.

"I thought you and Toby hated each other? Remember that other time you were one of the Merry Men? Somebody had to pull the two of you apart. I still have scars from the bruises where both of you kicked me."

"We have an agreement. I'm helping him with his blog tour."

"His *what*?"

"His blog tour. Robin felt like he needed some new PR, and he hired me to work on it." He smiled, his brown hair almost the same length as mine, the two of us staring eye-to-eye while visitors passed on their way to the main gate.

I was familiar with Internet blogging. We are required to blog a bit at the university. Maybe it was a good idea, like Alastair's dagger website. Or maybe this was some scam Toby, er, Robin Hood, had cooked up to get even with Tony. Whatever, I knew it was a mistake for Tony to get mixed up with him again. "I've been in the Village for a while already. Why didn't you come find me so we could have lunch or something?"

Tony and I don't have the closest relationship, despite our genetic link. He frequently criticizes me for working too hard and not knowing how to have a good time. In response, I gently remind him that he isn't getting any younger and needs to settle down with a real job. As much as I love the Village, I know it's only temporary. And definitely not real.

Tony bypassed all the normal rhetoric and told me Robin had sent him to find me. "Some crazy chick has been telling us about the evil daggers let loose on the Village. She said you know all about it. Robin didn't take her seriously until we found one of them. Now he's holding her in the forest until you come and vouch for her."

"Why me?" I was impatient to see Chase and didn't want to spend time with the losers hanging out in the forest stealing toaster ovens and flying on ropes from tree to tree. Believe me, as awesome as that sounds, it wears thin the first time you have to use the back of a tree as an outhouse because you can't make it to a privy.

"I told you, this chick said you know her. Robin knows you and trusts you." He shrugged in his forest green costume, the movement slightly repositioning the little Merry Man hat on his head.

I stared into his eyes, which were brown like our wastrel father's instead of blue like our mother's (and mine). "If you're lying to me and this is some stupid trick to hang me upside down from a tree or anything like that, you'll be sorry."

"I'm not lying. I swear I'm telling you what Robin told me. Are you coming or not? It doesn't matter to me, but you might be able to persuade Robin to set the crazy chick loose. I'm kind of worried somebody might miss her and figure we've got her. This is a sweet gig, Jessie. I don't want Robin going to jail or something."

He seemed sincere. Of course, there'd been plenty of other times he'd seemed sincere but it was all a ruse to get money. I couldn't figure out his angle on this, so I agreed to go. "All right. Let me change clothes and grab a shower. I'll meet you over there."

"Okay. I'll tell Robin to keep a lookout for you. You know the Merry Men can get kind of protective if they think you wandered in uninvited."

I didn't remind him that I'd dated Robin and Alex (his right-hand man) before Tony ever came to the Village. I probably knew my way around Sherwood Forest better than he did. As far as knowing how strange the Merry Men were, after dating a couple of them, I knew there were no words to express their weirdness.

A hot shower in the dungeon felt good after the day's ninety-degree temperatures. I changed for the evening into a long, thin cotton skirt and a halter top. I rummaged around and found my sandals from last year. The boots were good while I was working, but I wanted to dress up a little for Chase. The fairies always had the advantage, since there wasn't much to their costumes, so I had to shine when I could.

I left my clothes on the dresser. I'd turn them back in later. Maybe Portia would take pity on me and give me something decent to wear. Probably not, but it wouldn't hurt to ask. I knew I was going to have to break it to her that Ethan was not a good choice for a mate. I couldn't tell her that I suspected him of evildoing, since she was the biggest gossip in the Village, but I could protect her from her own mad desires.

As I walked toward Sherwood Forest, a slight breeze stirred the evening heat, swirling across the cobblestones and bringing with it the smell of dinner. I could hear people talking and laughing in Peter's Pub. My interaction with Robin had better be over fast, I decided. I was hungry and ready to spend some quality time with Chase.

Sherwood Forest is five acres of pine, oak, and magnolias that somehow managed to survive when this whole area was an Air Force base. These are the only naturally occurring trees in the Village. Everything else was planted after the base closed and the Village took over.

The thing is that the size of Sherwood Forest is deceptive. The visitor's map doesn't indicate how big it is. And standing outside the forest entrance located near the main gate, you can see only that there are a lot of trees going off to the right side of the Village. More than one visitor has gotten lost among those trees and had to be recovered either by Chase or Village security.

Once you're inside the forest, you fall prey to Robin's men (and women dressed as men) who greet you by laughingly telling you they want your purse to help them in their fight against Prince John and the evil Sheriff of Nottingham. Sometimes, if the visitors seem like they're willing to play along, the Merry Men will actually take their purses or wallets and swing them up into the trees where their housing is located. On more than one occasion Chase has found out that visitors spent the night in the forest. This is strictly forbidden by Adventure Land.

It's all part of the fun and excitement, but it can get a little crazy, too. The Merry Men take their mission to rob the rich and give to the poor a little too seriously. Toaster ovens, an important cooking commodity for residents, are only a small portion of what disappears into the trees every day. Lucky for them the forest is very popular with the visitors, so no one bothers them, for the most part.

"Hello!" I called out after officially entering the forest. "It's me, Jessie. I'm here to see Robin. He wanted me to come and see him. Anyone out there?"

The trees are close together along the designated path through the forest. It ends in a clearing where the tree houses are built. Robin (sometimes Maid Marion) and the Merry Men live there.

"Hello? I'm not walking through the whole forest looking for you guys. If Robin wants to see me, he'd better get his butt out here. I have a few other things I'd like to do tonight."

There was still no answer, although a few birds flew up from the underbrush. I could imagine all the Merry Men grinning and high-fiving each other over this really funny game of watching me look for them. Have I mentioned the level of maturity it takes to be a Merry Man?

"Okay. That's it for me. I'm out of here. See you guys later."

Again, no one answered, but as I turned to follow the path back to the entrance and from there, the cobblestone road that would lead back to the dungeon, a soft, swishing sound caught my ear. I knew that sound from my time in the forest. I should've been able to avoid what was coming, but I was one step off. The big net came up, trapping me inside it, as it continued on until it was about ten feet off the path.

"Yo ho!" Robin Hood himself stood beneath me laughing and making stupid faces at me. "Methinks you have forgotten much, Maid Jessie! Forsooth, we would not have caught you so unawares when you were younger."

"Let me down." I had already lost my sense of humor about the whole situation.

"Oh? But you have not paid the toll for your transgression into Sherwood Forest," Robin told me. "To me, my Merry Men! Let us decide the fate of yon wench!"

A whole group, maybe twenty of them, all dressed in forest green tights and doublets, joined Robin in his laughter. I *knew* they were out there. And if Robin thought I was going to help him with anything after this, he was sadly mistaken. My days of thinking it was exciting to be snared in a net were long past.

"Decide fast before this wench calls for backup," I threatened. "I know none of you want the wrath of the bailiff to come down on your heads." They couldn't know that I didn't have any way to summon Chase. I could at least *pretend* to have a two-way radio.

"Oh!" Robin put his hands on his hips and laughed. "The wench threatens us, men. What shall we make of this?"

"Make something fast," I hissed. "If I'm not out of this net in thirty seconds, you're going to think Prince John is a Merry Mynstrel compared to me. Let me down. *Now!*"

I saw Robin move, and a second later I was on the ground. The heavy net was covering me, but it didn't protect me from dirt, leaves, and probably a few squished bugs. Two of the Merry Men helped me get out of the net while Robin stood with his hands on his hips laughing. I wanted to smack that laugh off of his face, but I held back. An action like that would mean spending the night here, and I wasn't into that anymore.

I got up with as much dignity as I could and demanded, "You asked me to come here, Toby. Where is Marielle?"

He shushed me as he put his arm around my shoulders and started walking down the path toward the tree camp. "Hey! Let's not spoil the image for all the newbies, huh?

Besides, you know I had my name legally changed to Robin Hood. Why can't people respect that?"

"Maybe because you ask for their help, then catch them in nets. And that's when you're not stealing their toaster ovens. Honestly, they should make you guys Peter Pan and the Lost Boys instead of Robin Hood and the Merry Men."

"That doesn't make any sense. Peter Pan wasn't a real person. It would be historically inaccurate."

"I hate to break it to you, but Little Bo Peep wasn't a real person either."

"You don't know that," he argued. "Most fairy tales and mythologies are based on real people and events."

"Yeah, whatever." I shrugged off his arm while I picked leaves out of my hair and tried to make sure there weren't any bugs on me. "Let's get to what's happening out here. Tony said you found one of the missing daggers."

He laughed. It was an annoying laugh because he always had to do the whole throwing-his-head-back-and-guffawing thing. I'm all for the occasional good guffaw, but his constant guffawing irritated me, especially right now. "I have so much more than a single dagger to show you, my good lady. You are looking particularly lovely this evening, by the way. Is that perchance a new garment you are wearing?"

"Save it. Don't make me call you Toby again." I lowered my voice. "Really don't make me tell the new Merry Men that you were an accountant before you came here."

He put his hand to his heart and staggered off the path. "You wound me deeply, my lady. Forsooth you have put your dagger of words into my chest."

"Don't make me twist it while it's in there," I snarled back. "Where's Marielle?"

At that moment we reached the clearing in the forest. The trees in which Robin and his men had their houses surrounded the clearing, a huge circular area where a big bonfire usually burned. It was too hot for that tonight, I guessed, since there was neatly arranged wood in the fire ring, but no fire. The lights in the trees around us were picturesque. The smell of cooking food came from all of the toaster ovens, no doubt. The Merry Men could live without bathrooms but not without power.

Marielle came running into the clearing, still wearing the same cloak and very little else. Tony followed her (where there were half-naked women, there was Tony) and smiled when he reached me.

"Thank the Goddess you're here!" Marielle threw herself against me and hugged me tight. "I knew you would take care of this before the evil spreads."

I didn't know what gave her that idea, and I really didn't want to be here. Tony kind of patted my shoulder in a manly way, probably too embarrassed to hug me. "We have to get you out of here, Marielle, and find you some new clothes. You can't walk around like this forever."

She stood up straight and wiped her eyes. "I have sworn to neither eat nor drink until the evil daggers are collected and put under another sorcerer's control. Why would I bother worrying about what I'm wearing? All of us will die, or worse, if the daggers are not found and managed."

"After death, there isn't much worse," I reminded her. "In the meantime, where's the new dagger?"

Robin nodded and one of the Merry Men brought forth the slain toaster oven with the dagger still in it. This new dagger had to be made of something more substantial than gold. It had pierced through the toaster oven, probably leaving it inoperable.

"What fiend could do something like this?" Robin's voice dripped with scorn.

I took the toaster oven, handling it as little as possible

and being careful not to touch the dagger in case there were fingerprints or some other traces of evidence Detective Almond could collect. "Thank you, good Merry Men. The bailiff will hear word of your valor in this."

Robin did his annoying guffaw. "But you have not seen the best part yet, lady." He nodded to another Merry Man, and that one (they all look alike) brought a squawking goose forward. "As I said, we are a boon to the Village! Besides the bailiff, we do more to keep the Village working than any other guild."

"I didn't know there was a contest." I couldn't hold both the goose and the toaster oven, so I asked Marielle to take the goose. "I'm sure Mother Goose will be happy to see Phineas again. I give you the thanks of the whole Village for your help in this matter."

A rousing chorus of "Huzzah!" echoed through the forest. Some of the Merry Men began playing music on lutes and mandolins. Apparently, the wood in the fire ring needed only the quick touch of a torch to light. The fire came to life and added to the charm of the campsite.

I saw a few visitors' faces peering out from the tree houses, but that wasn't my problem. I could see how people would want to spend the night here, even though there were no bathrooms to speak of.

Robin pressed me to stay for supper. They were roasting some large animal. I thanked him but let him know that the bailiff was waiting for me. He bowed low to me (a royal bow) and said good night.

It was really dark by this time and finding the path was difficult. I hoped we wouldn't run into any more traps. I was ready to eat supper and go home. Finding Phineas was a good thing and another dagger was a plus, but this day needed to be over.

"I recognize the dagger in yon toaster oven," Marielle confided as we kept up a brisk pace out of the forest.

"I take it that it's one of Alastair's?"

"Aye. It is the iron dagger that killed Conan."

"The barbarian?"

"The very same. It came to pass that a crown weighed heavily on his head and a usurper thrust a dagger of iron into his heart."

"You've got to be kidding me! That's not even mythology! You know that, right? Conan the Barbarian was a modern-day character invented by Robert E. Howard. I don't know where that dagger came from, but its reputation is bogus."

"Not many know of the legend," she said with conviction in her voice. "The faithful know that Conan lived and later died with this cursed dagger in his heart."

"Oh brother!" Maybe Tavin was right after all. How much could this dagger be worth, except to Alastair's followers? There was no point in arguing with die-hard fanatics (many of them in the Village) who believed in their own fairy tales. "I see some lights. We must be almost to the end of the forest."

By the time we reached the cobblestones and the sign that welcomed visitors to Sherwood Forest, the Village was quiet. The main gate was closed and locked for the night. Maintenance workers were out in force taking care of everything from the grass on the Village Green to cleaning windows and power washing the castle. Residents ignored these signs of modern life as they went about creating their crafts to sell and otherwise getting ready for their part the following day.

Fred the Red Dragon waved as he somehow managed to ride by on a bicycle. The fairies were practicing their flitting and flirting techniques. The Lovely Laundry Ladies were arguing over who would wash the men's underwear the next day. It was a common sight in the evening.

"You must take this creature from me so I might wander the Village in search of the remaining daggers." Marielle tried to foist the goose on me.

"This toaster oven could be important to figuring out who killed Alastair," I told her. "Bring the goose and we'll figure out what to do next."

"But I must wander alone."

"Save it. I'm hungry and this toaster oven weighs a ton. You're coming with me until we find Chase. Got it?"

She nodded meekly and followed me down the cobblestones. I asked everyone we met, from William Shakespeare to Mrs. Potts at the Honey and Herb Shoppe, but no one had seen Chase for at least an hour.

I gritted my teeth, took a deep breath, and headed toward Mother Goose's place. She lived behind the pavilion where she told stories. I was reasonably sure there was nothing the police could get from Phineas, but I didn't want to leave the toaster oven and dagger with anyone but Chase.

Mother Goose was home when we got there. She meticulously examined the goose before proclaiming it as her own. I couldn't see the telltale signs she was looking for, but if she was happy, I was happy. "Where did you find him?" she asked while she hugged him and he squawked.

"I'd rather not say," I hedged.

"The men of Sherwood Forest had him," Marielle supplied.

"I see!" Mother Goose said. "I guess I'll have to rally the Entertainment Guild to respond to the Forest Guild's act of kidnapping. Phineas is a member of the Entertainment Guild, too. I hope Robin Hood is ready for my wrath."

Exactly the thing I was trying to avoid. "I don't think they *took* Phineas. Someone left him there at the same time they left this dagger in the toaster oven. Robin Hood isn't to blame for what's happening, Mother Goose. Whoever is responsible for this is trying to lead us all away from the fact that he or she killed Alastair."

Mother Goose eyed me suspiciously. "Is that what Chase says?"

"Yes." Apparently, it wasn't enough that I'd said it.

She nodded. "All right. I'll wait to see what happens. Thank you for bringing Phineas home, Jessie."

As we left Mother Goose, Marielle started to wander away again. I stopped her. "Stay with me until we find Chase. He should talk to you."

"I already spoke with the bailiff. I have nothing more to say to him. He is a nonbeliever. He cannot help with my quest."

"Jessie!" Chase hailed me from the direction of the Pleasant Pheasant. "I've been looking everywhere for you."

I was really happy to see him, and not only because he was my boyfriend. "You didn't look in Sherwood Forest, I suppose. Marielle and I escaped out of there with Phineas and this strange metaphor for the sword in the stone." I held up the toaster oven for him to see.

"Marielle?" he questioned.

We both looked around, but Alastair's half-dressed, crazy lover seemed to have melted into the darkness.

"Damn, Chase, we have to find her. She's totally whacked out. She claims she won't eat or sleep until she finds all the daggers. She's still wearing the same clothes she had on the night Alastair was killed. I'm afraid she's going to hurt herself or someone else. She may have even been the one who killed Alastair. I have a theory about it."

"I'll call security." He nodded. "Let me get a plastic bag to put that toaster oven in. They don't need my fingerprints on it, too. Did Robin give you a hard time about getting this?"

"Let's not talk about it right now. I'm hungry, tired, and ready to be upstairs in the dungeon with you for the night."

Sam Da Vinci came up quickly, not running exactly, but kind of loping. "Chase! You have to come right away. There's trouble at the bake-off!"

Eleven

I dragged my exhausted body back down the cobblestones with Chase and Sam to find out what was going on at the Monastery bake-off. Normally (and I use that word loosely) the monks use the bake-off process to elect a new leader. Brother John had used the process to oust Brother Carl. The Brotherhood of the Sheaf lived by very strict guidelines.

I knew there had been trouble in the Brotherhood since Brother John took over. Some of the monks had sided with Brother Carl, but they had remained loyal to their guild. The dagger they'd found in the sacred flour was only a catalyst to start the process of selecting a new leader. If Brother Carl won the bake-off, it would mean the brotherhood would have their old leader back.

It didn't matter so much to me which brother was in charge. There'd been several times when Brother John had been a little self-righteous and abused his power over Brother Carl. But basically, if you knew one monk, you knew them all. I didn't base that assessment on the fact that they all wore the same black robes either.

When we reached the Monastery Bakery, there was chaos outside the building. Though it was a little after midnight, all of the monks seemed to be brawling in the street. A large crowd of residents watched, probably exchanging money from time to time on who was going to win.

Tom, Tom the Piper's Son and King Arthur moved aside quickly when they saw Chase. Sam and I darted in behind him.

There was flour everywhere. The monks were covered in it. It wasn't like there was a spill or something. They were hitting each other with open bags of the stuff. The powdery cloud surrounding them made me sneeze.

"Bless you." Brother Carl was close to me when an unnamed monk hit him with another sack of flour.

I didn't have time to thank him before Chase yelled for them to stop. It took more than one shout, but eventually they all stood there looking at him, some still holding empty flour sacks.

"What the hell are you guys doing out here?" Chase demanded in his heavy-handed bailiff's voice that he did so well. Just listening to him gave me chills.

"We were going through the bake-off process," Brother Carl began to explain.

"When *he* cheated," Brother John joined in. "We could not allow this transgression to go unanswered."

At that, all the monks started up again. Flour sacks and their contents flew everywhere. The spectators backed away, but it was too late for most. Coated in flour, we all looked like ghosts in the modest Village streetlights.

Chase yelled again and finally got their attention. "Okay, Carl, John. Inside. The rest of you stop throwing flour and calm down until we get this sorted out. If I have to come out here because I see another flour fight going on, all of you are going to spend the rest of the night in the dungeon. And I'm not talking about the *good* part of the dungeon."

The monks seemed to take him seriously because they stopped hitting each other with flour sacks and most of them sat down on the cobblestones. I went into the bakery behind Chase, Carl, and John, not bothering to ask permission. If I had to be out here for this, I was at least going to hear what caused it.

"We're all going to sit down and talk this over." Chase took a seat at one of the crude wooden benches.

"I shall not sit beside this cheater," Brother John stated. "You can put me in the dungeon for the rest of the week, if you like. I'm not sitting with him."

Chase took a deep breath. "Fine. You sit over there. Carl, you're with me."

When both monks were seated (scowling at each other over the mess they'd left behind in the bakery before taking the fight to the cobblestones), Chase tried again to make some sense out of what was happening. "So, if I understand this correctly, you decided to have the bake-off because you found one of the missing daggers in your flour."

Brother Carl nodded. "This would never have happened under my watch. I challenged Brother John to the bake-off to prove I am the better leader for our Brotherhood."

"And I won the bake-off because he cheated," Brother John added smugly. "That's what happened. The fighting erupted after that. As far as I'm concerned, I am still the leader of the Brotherhood of the Sheaf."

"How did Carl cheat?" Chase asked.

"He used the wrong flour." Brother John sniffed as he said it with an air of regal disdain.

"I did not. I used the blessed flour we always use," Brother Carl said, defending himself.

Brother John jumped to his feet and picked up a flour sack from the ruined floor. "You see this? This is not our flour. I'm sure even the bailiff recognizes that."

Chase checked the bag. It didn't take long to realize what he said was true. Even I knew that all of the monks' flour came from a tiny mill in the mountains of South Carolina where other monks ground it.

This bag was clearly marked by a regional grocery store. The monks would never use this flour. We all looked at Brother Carl.

"I didn't inspect the bag before the bake-off," Carl said. "The new monk, Brother Onslow, gave me the bag right before we got started."

Chase and I exchanged glances. There couldn't be two men in the Village with that name. Alastair's right-hand man, Onslow Chivers, was obviously into wearing robes. No wonder one of the daggers had ended up here. That seemed to shoot down my theory about Ethan stealing them, unless the two men were working together.

"I'm sure this was a mistake." Chase tried to smooth over the situation. "Why not consider holding the bake-off again with all of the ingredients in clear sight, exactly what you're supposed to have?"

"I will never agree to that!" Brother John shot to his sandaled feet again. "I am clearly the winner."

"*I* won," Brother Carl reminded him. "But I am willing to agree to the bailiff's compromise. I was tricked. You lost. Holding the bake-off again is the only fair thing to do. Otherwise this senseless violence will continue until the Brotherhood is ripped apart."

It was a good speech, as speeches go. I looked at Brother John to see whether he was going to go for it. I thought at first he wouldn't, but then he nodded and agreed that they would redo the contest.

"But there must be a judge to let us know if anything is wrong," Brother John said.

"I am in complete agreement." Brother Carl nodded. "I think we should ask the bailiff to be that judge."

"Done!" Brother John agreed readily. "This way, the outcome will be fair and unbiased."

They set the day and time for tomorrow at six P.M., right after the main gate was closed for the night. I was glad they'd moved away from the midnight-contest routine. They were messing with my personal life.

Chase and I left the bakery as Brothers John and Carl were announcing their plans to the rest of the monks. Chase was headed in the wrong direction, toward the castle instead of the dungeon.

"Where are we going now?" I kept pace with him as he walked. "Please tell me we're going to get something to eat at the Lady of the Lake Tavern and that we're not on our way to the castle to question Onslow about what happened with the monks."

"You should go home and get something to eat. This might take a while."

"I'd rather be with you." I smiled, but I realized it was too dark for him to see me.

"I'd rather be with you, too, Jessie, but the sooner we get this whole thing with Alastair taken care of, the sooner my life will be easier. I have to go see Onslow and try to get some answers. I hope he hasn't left the Village already. I don't know if Detective Almond did any more than a cursory questioning of him. He wasn't exactly on the suspect list like Marielle, even though he found the body."

"And Daisy," I reminded him. "And now, Ethan and maybe Marielle."

"One suspect at a time, huh? They don't pay me enough to investigate murders."

Master at Arms Gus Fletcher, a huge hunk of a man, was standing in front of the castle door as always. He was an ex-pro wrestler who obviously took his responsibility to the king and queen too seriously.

"Gus, don't you ever sleep?" Chase greeted him as they did the arm clasp that was the Village's version of a handshake.

Gus laughed, a low rumble from his throat. "I could ask you the same thing, Sir Bailiff. What brings you to the castle at this time of night?"

Chase told him he wanted to question Onslow and asked if he'd seen him recently. Gus nodded, "Yeah. When he came out to get the pizza he ordered about an hour ago. I didn't know Polo's delivered."

"Me either," Chase agreed. "I guess this means I don't go home yet."

"Too bad." Gus nodded at me. "I'll be glad to keep Jessie company while you're busy."

That was not going to happen, even if Chase agreed—which wasn't very likely. Surely he'd noticed Gus's romantic interest in me. I started to find a nice way of objecting when Chase put his arm around me and said, "Sorry, I need my scribe. But you can keep an eye on this toaster oven until I get back. Don't touch it. See you later."

Inside, the castle was darker than usual. The Great Hall was blocked off and had been cleaned long before. The dimly glowing lamps in the sconces on the walls created more shadows than light as we made our way down the hall to the royal living quarters. Lucky it was a straight shot to the interior of the castle. The suites went out from that vantage point.

"He should still be in the guest quarters." Chase kept his voice low. "I don't want to startle him and create some kind of situation. Let's act normal."

We went over to the big doors that opened into one of the

guest suites, and Chase knocked on the wood. I recognized one of Alastair's groupie girls when she answered the door. Chase asked for Onslow, and she let us in with a smile. She said he was sleeping but she would go and get him.

It was odd being in the castle this late. Even when I worked here that first summer, I'd stayed outside in Village housing. I'd never heard it so quiet. Usually, either Livy was yelling about something or minstrels were playing. Something was always happening within these walls.

This was the heart of the castle. It probably would've been the keep if it were a real castle. Instead, this was the original structure of the Air Force base control tower where they had guided planes down from the sky. The rest of the castle had been built around it, the whole thing covered over in stone and mortar to give it a real-life effect. The Main Hall was added on later.

Realizing I'd had enough time to think about how the castle was built made me aware that we'd been standing here for a while. "Maybe somebody should check on them."

"Yeah. I was thinking the same thing. You stay here in case he's naked or something." He started walking into the dark areas of the suite and then looked back at me. "And don't get into any trouble while I'm gone."

I didn't bother to ask him what he meant by that remark. Obviously he was confusing me with someone else who didn't help him solve his biggest problems. I yawned as I leaned against the heavy door and wondered if the night was ever going to be over. I was beyond hunger, thirst, and exhaustion. Probably a lot like Renaissance knights who made pilgrimages to holy lands to prove themselves.

As I leaned there, thinking of pasta and ale, a fast-moving shadow ran right at me from one of the rooms that made up the suite. I was half asleep and unable to react one way or another. If I'd moved six inches to the left, it would've passed me by and headed out the door.

Instead, Onslow ran right into me. He must've been running with his head down because he butted me right in the stomach. Who knew I had abs of steel? Right after our close encounter, he fell on the floor right before I did.

I couldn't catch my breath to call for Chase, and I was worried Onslow would escape, so I held on to his doublet (or whatever he was wearing). He wasn't going anywhere, at least not fully dressed. He struggled, but I held him there. Just when I thought I couldn't hold him anymore, Chase came out of the dark and slammed him against the door behind us.

"Are you okay?" he asked me.

I had to nod and mouth that I was fine. I still didn't have enough breath to speak.

"Now, you and I are going to have the conversation I planned before you hit me over the head with that stupid shield," Chase told the struggling groupie before he pushed him into a chair.

"You aren't the real law," Onslow said. "You can't do anything to me."

"I'm a fully deputized police officer here," Chase said. "But if it would make you feel better, I have a homicide detective on my speed dial."

Onslow fidgeted in his mock Renaissance chair. "What do you want from me, man? I haven't done anything."

"Then why were you in such a hurry to get out of here?"

"When the police come knocking this late, you know you better get out of here." He kind of calmed down and stared at Chase.

By this time, several other groupies were sitting in the shadows watching us. I noticed Marielle wasn't with them. I didn't know if she was still wandering the Village or had finally crashed in one of the back rooms.

"You dressed up like a monk and sabotaged the bake-off, didn't you?" Chase shook Onslow a little to get his attention. "You stole Alastair's daggers and you've been hiding them in the Village."

"What? No, man!" Onslow looked uncomfortable. "I messed with their flour, but come on, who wouldn't? They're crazy! I only wanted to see what they'd do."

Chase glared at him. "And while you were there, you left a dagger."

He looked at the floor. "I didn't steal the daggers. I mean, I borrowed one from the case. But that was before Alastair died. I tried to put it back, but the daggers were gone. The case was empty. I left the dagger I took with the monks because I was afraid someone would catch me with it here. Somebody else took the daggers, man. I might be the one who killed him, but I didn't steal the daggers."

I felt like singing "I Shot the Sheriff," but I was as surprised as anyone else that he'd just confessed.

"What do you mean you *might* be the one who killed him?" Chase asked.

Onslow shrugged, then lowered his head and started crying like a baby. "I wanted to know, man. I just wanted to know if it was true."

"If what was true?" I couldn't wait for Chase.

"If Alastair was immortal." He looked around at the other groupies, who had moved in close. "Come on! We all talked about it. We all wanted to know. There was only one way to find out. I did what had to be done."

"You shoved a sword through him," Chase said.

"No." Onslow grinned. "I fed him rat poison. I could never have killed him with a sword, man. He was too good. But he keeled over right after he ate the baklava. He wasn't immortal after all. He lied to us."

I wasn't sure whether he was telling the truth or not. I

don't know how the police get a sense for these things. He sounded sincere and scared. But he could've been lying, too. Chase glanced at me, and I shrugged. It could go either way.

There didn't seem to be any hesitation on Detective Almond's part when he arrived a few minutes later. Onslow confessed again for him, and he seemed satisfied with it. "I guess this means the sword maker didn't do it," he told Chase while his officers took Onslow from the room. "We'll have to wait for the autopsy results to get back before we can confirm that this boy is telling the truth. They had us send them on to Columbia, so it could be a while yet."

"What about whoever put the sword into Alastair?" Chase asked.

"I don't know. One thing is for sure, Alastair wasn't dead before the sword went through him, even if he was on his way. He wouldn't have bled out like that. But my money is on that boy finishing the job."

Tavin Hartley walked in looking like it wasn't almost two A.M. Her gray suit jacket and pencil skirt were sharply pressed, definitely not slept in. Her hair didn't have a strand out of place. Had she been up, dressed, and ready to go on a moment's notice in case something like this happened? "Have you found Alastair's killer?"

"Mr. Chivers has confessed to poisoning Alastair," Detective Almond told her. "But I'm sure he'll tell us about the rest of it before the night is over."

I yawned, and Chase put his arm around me. It seemed almost anticlimactic to think that the whole thing was over. But I'd be glad to have Daisy back, even though it probably meant Ethan the snake would get away with whatever it was he did.

Tavin took off her narrow-framed glasses. "I didn't realize that Onslow was disturbed, Detective. I can't believe he killed Alastair to find out if he was mortal. What a tragedy."

"I appreciate how hard this has been for all of you," Detective Almond said. "I'm very sorry for your loss, Ms. Hartley. We'll check this story out and let you know what we find."

Tavin looked even paler as she turned to go. "If you have any other questions, you have my card. Good night, Detective." She kind of nodded at me and Chase but didn't acknowledge the groupies at all.

"We're going, too," Chase told him. "Myrtle Beach PD is going to have to start supplementing my salary if I have to catch *all* the bad guys for them."

Detective Almond laughed and whacked his shoulder in a manly fashion. "Welcome to the joys of police work, Manhattan. I'll give you a call when I know something else about this guy."

Chase and I walked out of the castle into the cool, dark night. He presented the toaster oven to one of the police officers who was smoking outside. Gus winked at me as we went by (lucky I wasn't close enough to pinch), and Chase said good night to all of them.

"You know nothing's open this late," I whined, still starving and near dehydration.

"That's why I always keep a couple of frozen dinners and cold ales in the fridge." He smiled and kissed me as we started past the police car where Onslow sat in the backseat.

"I love men who are prepared for what their women need." I kissed him back, and we would've been out of there if the cops hadn't left the window of the police car rolled down slightly. Onslow called out to us as we passed him.

"He should've lived," he said to Chase. "I loved him like a brother. He told us he couldn't die."

"Maybe you shouldn't have taken him so literally," Chase said.

"I didn't put the sword into him," Onslow whispered. "But I think I might know who did."

Chase stopped walking, and I groaned. "Who?" he asked.

"Ask the guy who made that sword, man. Long hair, pretty face. He argued with Alastair. Ask him how his sword got into him."

One of the police officers ended our brief conversation. We walked away from the castle, past Mirror Lake shimmering with the reflected light from the Village.

"He has to be talking about Ethan," I said.

"Let's go home," Chase said. "I've had enough of this day."

"I don't know how to tell you this, but *this* day has barely begun. Ethan could still be guilty of something. There might be another dagger out there to find, and no matter what, we have to find Marielle and get her some help. Speaking of which, is your head okay?"

"I think so." He felt the back of his head. "How about you?"

"I'll be fine with an ale and a frozen dinner."

We both heard the footsteps coming up behind us on the cobblestones. Chase kind of turned and crouched down a little as though expecting another personal attack.

Instead, it was Merlin, his pointed hat askew on his white hair, starred robe flying out around him. "Mind if I walk a ways with you, Bailiff? I have a thought or two about this dagger situation."

Twelve

We were inside the dungeon, where Merlin insisted we had to be, before he stopped rambling about the daggers and came to the point. "Some of the daggers are fake, of course." He pulled a dagger from under his robe. "Except this one. This is the one I was worried about. I took it to make sure it was safe."

The dagger was plainer than the others but had a diamond (real or fake) in the handle. The tip of the blade was curved a little and had a wicked, serrated edge to it.

That woke me up and got my attention. I grabbed three sodas (no ale) from the mini fridge and sat back down at the table. I could see Chase was trying to decide how to deal with the problem. Merlin was the CEO of Adventure Land, but he'd also stolen one of Alastair's daggers. Maybe Marielle was right and they *were* evil and magical.

"What's so special about this dagger?" Chase asked finally.

Merlin swept his gaze over the blade as though it were

something precious to behold. "This dagger belonged to Harry Houdini, the greatest magician that ever lived. He used it in some of his magic acts. It was stolen right after he died and never found again, until it turned up in Alastair's collection."

"Alastair wasn't old enough to have stolen it," I reminded them. "The website said he was only forty-eight this year."

"That's not the point," Merlin insisted. "This dagger is worth something to any Houdini collector. I'd have been happy to take it off Alastair's hands. Yet he was going broke keeping it."

"As interesting as that is," Chase interrupted, "I'd say the point is that you took the dagger from the collection. Did you steal all of it? Was Alastair alive when you did it?"

Merlin laughed so hard his pointed hat fell off his white hair. "No, of course I didn't steal anything. I actually found it hidden with the rest of the daggers near the castle. It was in one of those old storage units we stopped using."

"What else was in there with it?" Chase wondered.

"A few other things." Merlin shrugged. "Some clothes, female, I'd say. A Barry Manilow CD. I don't know if *that* was in there with the rest of it or not. I found it yesterday. Sorry I couldn't get to you sooner. What do you think?"

Chase yawned. "Did you know Alastair?"

"Briefly. He was a bit too serious for my taste." Merlin chugged down some of the soda I'd given him. "I've heard the stories going through the Village about the daggers being evil and cursed. That's hogwash! But I did see something interesting on the Internet. Apparently, an auction is being lined up for his possessions. The daggers, all twelve of them, are included."

"So someone expects to have all of them," I said.

"Obviously not the same someone who's spreading them out around the Village," Chase agreed.

"We have to find Marielle," I repeated. "She might have stolen the daggers, but she doesn't know what she's gotten herself into."

"Don't forget Onslow had one, too." Chase got to his feet. "Show me where you found them, Merlin. I'd like to get some sleep sometime tonight."

I insisted on going, even though I felt like the walking dead. We walked across the darkened, quiet Village to the old storage lockers near Merlin's Apothecary. The entrance to the castle was nearby, so it would be a convenient place for someone staying at the castle to hide stolen property. Unfortunately, the other daggers, and everything else Merlin had said he found, were gone.

"The rest of the stuff was right here." Merlin looked again through the empty locker.

"I guess someone noticed you had this dagger and didn't want to take any chances," Chase surmised. "I'll have to take it, you know."

Merlin cringed and held the dagger to his chest. "No! Can't we pretend it wasn't here? No telling where the rest are."

Chase held out his hand. "It's stolen, even if you didn't do it. I have to turn it in to the police. That's what you pay me to do. You can bid on it when it comes up for auction."

Merlin finally gave in, but I could tell it pained him to do so. "It will cost ten times what it's worth to bid on it."

"I'm sorry." Chase put the dagger in the pouch at his side. "I wouldn't be much of a bailiff if I let people keep stolen goods."

"That's true," Merlin admitted with a rueful curve to his lip. "You're a good man, Chase. I don't like you much right now, but that's all right. I trust you'll keep my name out of this?"

"If I can," Chase agreed.

"Excellent! Good night then."

Merlin wandered back toward his apothecary, and Chase and I started back to the dungeon. *Again.* I was beginning to feel we should just lie down on the Village Green and go to sleep.

"That was weird," I commented with a yawn.

"Yeah." Chase put his arm around me as we walked. "What isn't weird around here?"

"But you'd rather be here than working for your parents' mega-corp back in Scottsdale?"

"Any day." He kissed the side of my head. "Let's go home and get some sleep, huh?"

I got up a few hours later, cranky and half asleep. Chase had left a while earlier to help with a break-in at Totally Toad Footstools. It probably wasn't a real break-in—someone probably lost their keys and couldn't get into the shop.

I walked down to the bakery, but it was closed. No sign of the monks or even all the flour from last night. I know it was *really* early this morning when the flour fight happened. I just couldn't stand to think of it that way.

With no coffee on that side of the Village, I had to cut across Squires' Lane, through the Village Green and across the King's Highway to Sir Latte's. There was a long line of Village folk waiting for their caffeine. Bart was there, sans tree suit. He asked me what had happened at the castle last night. Lady Lindsey, who trains songbirds at the Hawk Stage, showed us a copy of the Village newspaper.

"So they arrested that guy," Bart said. "I guess that must mean Daisy is off the hook."

"I hope so," I confided. "There hasn't been much sword-smithing going on since I got here. It's only been a few days, so I'm trying to be patient."

"Do you think he really killed Alastair?" Lady Lindsey asked.

"I don't know. He confessed to poisoning him after he hit Chase in the head trying to escape from the castle and head-butted me in the stomach. Not the actions of an innocent man." We all took one small step forward in the long line.

"About Daisy," Bart began again.

"How's Chase holding up?" Lady Lindsey asked. "I hope he wasn't hurt too badly."

"No, he's fine," I assured her.

"Is Daisy out of jail now?" Bart asked.

"I don't know. I haven't been over to the shop yet." I saw Ethan in line ahead of us (of course) and thought about what Onslow had said.

It wouldn't surprise me if Ethan was the one who had shoved the sword into Alastair, not realizing Alastair was already dying. Proving it, as Chase often said, was another matter. I didn't have a clue how to go forward. No doubt Chase would tell Detective Almond and he'd question Ethan. Now *that* was something to look forward to!

We moved one more step in line closer to the whistling, gurgling cappuccino machine and the harried-looking barista behind it. I grabbed one of the last muffins as we passed the food cart. Everyone was going to feel the effects of the Monastery Bakery being closed today. I hoped the monks would get through their bake-off this evening and everything would get back to what passed for normal here.

It didn't take as long to get through the line as I'd thought it would. I was surprised to see how far it stretched behind me. There were no tables available to sit at inside, so I took my double-shot mocha and muffin outside. Bart was already at one of the café tables. He hailed me vigorously from the spot close to Ye Olde ATM.

"I wanted to ask you a favor, lady," he started before I even sat down.

"Okay. But I've only had a few hours' sleep, so I can't promise anything. Merlin was up with Chase after we got back from the castle. He had all these ideas about the rest of the missing daggers."

He nodded as if he understood, then blurted out, "I think I'm in love with Daisy."

"What?"

He glanced around uneasily. "You heard me. I tried to tell you before when you introduced me to Portia. I would like you to help me get Daisy to notice me. Not as a tree, but as a man."

I leaned my head closer to his and whispered, "That's great! You know she recently went through that thing with Alastair, right? She's a little raw right now, but someone with a good sword arm and a soft heart could win her over."

"I don't know. You might have to reverse that. I have a soft sword arm and a good heart. Can you help me, lady?"

"Of course! You've come to the right apprentice. I can give you sword-fighting lessons. Then you can impress Daisy."

Daisy deserved Bart's kind spirit more than Portia did, that was for sure. Would she break his big heart, as Chase and Ethan had said? There was no way to know. Maybe she was ready to settle down and spend her time with one giant.

"I don't know if I can repay you, but I could write you a check for ten dollars an hour while we practice."

Matchmaking and moneymaking at the same time! *Huzzah!* It didn't get any better than this!

We made plans to meet that evening after the bake-off. I thought a few lessons, like the ones they give occasionally to new Village residents, would be exactly the thing. It wouldn't take a lot for Bart to impress Daisy. He was already a giant among men. Women who wear breastplates, in my experience, tend to feel that size really does matter.

With a nice little caffeine and sugar rush going on, I left Sir Latte's and waved to Roger Trent at the Glass Gryphon as I passed. The Three Chocolatiers (three men dressed as musketeers who sell chocolate) were practicing their sword fighting outside their shop. They were too flashy and busy with one-liners to be taken seriously. Their costumes were good, though. I loved the big hats and feathers. The boots were an achievement in footwear also. They paused long enough to hail me. One of them (I can't tell them apart) swept me a low, royal bow, even removing his hat.

I crossed the King's Highway again past Kellie's Kites and Frenchy's Fudge. The knights were practicing their jousting on the Field of Honor. I watched the squires run around after them, remembering the time I was acting as a squire and stepped right in a hot, wet horse dropping. I had many such fond memories of being a squire.

I hurried past Mother Goose, who called out to let me know Phineas was his usual, cheerful self. I waved but didn't stop. I found Daisy in the back of Swords and Such, working her sword arm. When she paused, I ran up and hugged her. I was so glad to see her.

"What, ho?" She guffawed. "What ails thee, apprentice?"

"I'm very glad to see you back home. I was afraid I'd have to go make bagels or something."

"Bagels? What lot is that for a swordsmithing apprentice?" She tossed me a short sword and told me to ready myself for practice.

Whatever part of me the coffee didn't wake up was completely awake after a few rounds with Daisy. It was a good thing the swords had safety tips on them. I still had a few red spots that would probably be black and blue later.

"Nothing like a morning workout!" Daisy wiped her face on a towel and slid her sword back into the scabbard. "Have you seen Ethan yet this morning?"

"At Sir Latte's." Not having a towel, I wiped my face on my sleeve. "About that, Daisy. Onslow said Ethan might have had something to do with Alastair's death. He said the sword Alastair was killed with was made by Ethan."

"Really? You think he's telling the truth? The man is going to jail, after all."

"He'd already confessed to poisoning Alastair. I don't see what he'd have to gain."

Ethan came in as we were talking. For once his beautiful hair wasn't quite as lovely and his clothes were rumpled. "Did you set me up to take your place as a suspect?" he asked Daisy with a wild look in his eye.

"What are you talking about? And what's this I hear about you making swords on the side?"

"I spent the last three hours at the police station being questioned about killing Alastair. They let *you* go, Daisy. What am I supposed to think?"

That was a surprise, sort of, anyway. I knew Chase had been planning to say something about Ethan to the police, but that was before they arrested Onslow. I guess he wasn't completely convinced of Onslow's guilt. Good.

"They let you go, too, obviously," she responded. "What am *I* supposed to think? Did you make a sword for Alastair?"

He looked down at the floor, then tossed his head back. "Yes! You've held me back here long enough! I want to start my own career."

"Nice start," I muttered.

"You tried to sell a sword to Alastair?" Daisy shook her

head. "You didn't have the know-how. He ripped you apart, didn't he?"

"You could say that. He said the sword was a piece of junk and he wouldn't pay for it."

"But he kept it anyway to teach you a lesson," Daisy continued.

"You knew?" Ethan demanded.

"I knew Alastair! You're an idiot, Ethan. You couldn't hope to match wits with him. Did you think he'd be fair?"

That seemed a little harsh, but I didn't say so. Daisy and Ethan stood looking at each other until Daisy finally put her big arms around him and hugged him to her breastplate.

"No matter, lad. You were bound to learn the hard way. I saw photos of that sword at the police station. It was a masterpiece! I am so proud of you! Let's talk about being partners, shall we?"

Ethan hugged her back, crying. "The police let me go, but they still act like they think I put the sword in him."

Daisy laughed and slapped his back. "They said the same to me! We won't worry about it. The chances are Alastair's lackey poisoned *and* stabbed him to prove he wasn't immortal. I told the big blowhard that line was going to get him into trouble." A visitor came through the door, reminding us all that the Village was open for business. "What ho, my partner and my apprentice! Let us ready ourselves for another day!"

By noon, the big crowd (no doubt in response to the TV news about Alastair's death) had wandered away from the shops to the Field of Honor for one of the regular jousts. "Take the shop, Ethan," Daisy said. "Jessie and I are going to the forge."

The forge! The magic words I'd wanted to hear. That was where every sword began its life. I'd done enough research to know that swordsmithing was one of the most difficult and demanding of Renaissance crafts. It required not only great physical and mental discipline, but also an artistic eye and technical prowess. Hand skills like forging, carving, filing, engraving, and finishing were all part of the process.

I was almost too excited to walk next door to the black-smith shop. I'd been in here plenty of times but never as a swordsmith's apprentice. Daisy talked while Hans grunted as he continued working on a piece of metal.

"If you've never worked at the forge," Daisy explained loudly while Hans continued to hit the metal, "you can't work on a sword. Forging takes a lot of practice, making items over and over until you make them perfect. You have to master this to move on to the next level. Hans will take care of you today while you work here. Tomorrow, I want to see everything you've done."

With a brisk pat on the back, Daisy left me in what felt like the bowels of hell. I'd only thought it was hot anywhere else. Because everything had to be as authentic to the Renaissance as possible, Hans heated his metal in a forge that featured real coals and occasional fire. He took out the items he wanted to shape with his incredibly large hammer and put them against an anvil. Sparks flew up every time the hammer hit the hot metal.

"So you want to make swords, eh?" Hans asked in his heavily accented voice.

"Yes. I want to make swords." I remembered Debby (one of my former students) mentioning that Hans was from an Eastern European country. His really big arms were covered in tattoos of fairies, unicorns, and other magical creatures. The tattoos seemed incongruous on this tough-looking man.

"I guess you should start here then." He handed me a heavy apron and told me to put it on. "You see those sparks? Any one of them can set this whole place on fire. We'd never get out in time, and both of us would die."

His words were said in such a monotone that I could hardly believe he was describing his own demise. "Thanks for the heads-up. I'll try to watch the sparks." I managed to get the apron on and still remain standing upright, no mean feat. He handed me some large, dirty welding gloves, and I put those on, too.

"No one ever made a sword by themselves," he told me. "Only in the movies does that happen. Daisy and I work together to create swords that even the gods might envy if they looked down from on high. This is a team effort. Do you understand?"

I nodded with what I hoped was enough solemnity. Hans seemed as hard as his hammer. Still, he'd kept Debby entertained. There had to be something to him besides a big hammer and his kind of cute accent.

"What should I do first?" I asked.

"You watch." He hit the piece of metal he was working for good measure, making me jump. I saw the sly smile that creased his face when I reacted.

So I watched. At first, it was fine. But it was hot and I was exhausted from everything that had happened the night before. I felt myself losing concentration first—my eyes slowly started drifting closed.

An extra loud pounding sound woke me up. I looked at him to see if he'd noticed. He was wearing that same little smile, so I knew he had. "Sorry. I was up at the castle all night helping the bailiff catch what might be Alastair's killer."

He pounded hard again. "Am I supposed to be impressed by that? Do you want to make swords or not? If I tell Daisy you slept through this, she won't let you go on."

"Give me a break!" My temper got the better of me, and

it took over my mouth. "I was trying to explain why I'm not at my best today."

"Do you think you can do this without my tuition?"

"No! Of course not—"

"Fine! I'm going to watch you do it for a while." He put down the hammer on the anvil and handed me a piece of metal that sort of resembled a sword without a hilt. "Show me what you've learned so far."

I wasn't sleepy anymore. I was good and mad instead. I took the erstwhile sword from him while he used an old-fashioned bellows to fan the already red coals. Little flames jumped up everywhere. I could feel sweat pouring off of me. My erstwhile apprentice clothes (an old tunic and short pants I'd borrowed from Chase) would have to be exchanged tonight for sure.

I picked up the thick tongs I'd seen him use to put the metal into the forge. They were heavier than I'd expected. I had to use both arms to lift them even before I'd clamped the sword with them. But I managed to get the metal to the coals. I smiled smugly at Hans, who stood against the wall with his arms folded against his broad chest.

"Look, Mommy," a small child said as a whole group of visitors moved into the shop, "it's a girl blacksmith. They never show those on TV."

"She's an apprentice," Hans told them in his dour tone. "She does what she's told by her master. That was the way things worked during the Renaissance. It was a good system. Everyone had their place. You didn't see serfs trying to be lords. I miss those days."

The adults in the family (wearing cute Village costumes) exchanged glances, then smiled at the education their child was receiving.

"Are you going to leave that sword blank in there all day?" Hans demanded. "It will melt away to nothing."

I took the hint and in a feat of self-restraint, didn't sass him back. Apprentices didn't do that in the 1500s. I picked up the heavy tongs again and managed to get the glowing white metal to the anvil. I realized at that point that I was going to have to lift the big hammer with one hand. The other hand had to use the tongs to keep the metal piece in place.

But no matter how hard I tried, I couldn't do both things. Both tools were too heavy for me to work with at the same time. I dropped the hammer first, then the tongs. I was reaching up to hold the metal with my gloved hand when Hans stepped in to stop me.

"You don't know as much as you think, do you?"

"I didn't say I knew it all!" I glanced at the interested crowd, who stood safely behind a fence that separated them from the forge. "Master."

"That's what I thought. You have much learning to achieve this day, apprentice." He used his ungloved hand to feel my upper arm. "And I think you need to lift some weights before you can do this at all."

I was banished from the forge to watch Hans at work for a few hours. After that, I spent a couple of hours cleaning up the smithy. It was kind of like mucking out the stables, since horses were shod here on a regular basis. No wonder it smelled so bad.

Still, it was almost preferable to watching Hans show off for the visitors who eagerly crowded in to see the blacksmith work. There was one positive result from spending time away from the forge. While looking around the smithy, I found a smaller, lighter hammer I could use to beat my next sword. I hid it where, hopefully, Hans wouldn't see it, for the next time he let me work at the forge.

There was no answer for the heavy tongs. I was going to have to cope with them. I hoped it would make a difference having a lighter hammer, but I wasn't sure I could hold the tongs steady long enough to get the job done. I wasn't ready to give in yet, not by a long shot. Hans might've thought it was funny to embarrass me in front of the visitors, but I was determined to make at least one sword.

The day waned into early evening. I was hot, tired, and smelled like a combination of manure, straw, and smoke. I hadn't seen Daisy again. I guess she was waiting to hear back from Hans on my progress. If that was the case, I might never see her again. Hans didn't let me near the forge the rest of the day. I was going to have to come up with a plan to get through this second initiation.

I stood up straight from finishing one last cleanup job and saw Chase waiting behind me. "How long have you been there?" I stretched the kink out of my back.

"A few minutes. I love seeing women clean up horse poop." He laughed (at his own risk) and said, "I thought you were making a sword."

"I am, can't you tell? Don't make me relate the whole history of sword making to you. Where were you at lunchtime?"

"I had to go to the police station. They definitely arrested Onslow and charged him with Alastair's murder. Apparently, there *was* rat poison in Alastair's body. Onslow swears he didn't stick the sword into him, too, but no one really believes him at this point. Detective Almond said the rat poison would've killed Alastair in another few minutes anyway, but the sword is still the real cause of death. Case closed."

I put down my pitchfork. "Yeah, well, I guess someone had to do it. They talked to Ethan, too."

"But he seemed to have an alibi for when Alastair was killed. Have you seen Marielle today?"

"No. I've been making swords all day."

"I alerted security to keep an eye out for her. She might've wandered away from the Village."

"That would be the best thing for her." I climbed through one of the fences separating me and Chase. "Maybe she'll start thinking clearly if she gets away from here."

"I still think she took the daggers," he reminded me. "You're a mess! We'd better run back to the dungeon so you can take a shower and change clothes before the bake-off."

"I really don't want to be there. Couldn't we bow out or something?"

"If I have to be there as the judge, you have to be there, too."

"Chase!" Hans greeted him with the manly forearm grab and a big smile. "You aren't arresting my apprentice, are you?"

"Not yet. You aren't working my girlfriend too hard, are you, Hans?"

Hans was obviously surprised by this revelation. I was surprised by his surprise. I thought everyone in the Village knew Chase and I were a couple. "No. She's coming along fine. I'm sure tomorrow or the next day we'll have her out of the forge and back at Daisy's place."

Chase grinned (and they did the forearm clutch thing again) before he said, "Thanks."

Hans grinned, too. He reached over and ruffled my hair with his hand. "She's a good worker. A hard worker. A very good apprentice."

They finally completed their man stuff, and Hans took the pitchfork to finish whatever straw moving still needed to be done. Chase and I left the smithy and started toward the dungeon.

I gathered up my change of clothes and headed into the shower, leaving Chase watching CNN while he waited for me. It was a relief to get off all that sweat and dirt. My mind was still working on a way to finish my sword. I planned to look for something smaller to use as tongs tomorrow. No way was that forge defeating me!

I washed my hair a couple of times to be sure all of the straw and smell were out. In this case, my short hair was a blessing! Wearing my pretty skirt and a cute little off-the-shoulder peasant blouse, I made my entrance into the bedroom expecting to find my man waiting for me with open arms.

Instead, he was staring intently at something in his hand. I could tell from the lines in his forehead that whatever it was wasn't good. "Chase? Did you get an eviction notice?"

I thought he might laugh, but instead he held up my pouch in one hand and the check Morgan had written me in the other. I guess he liked to snoop, too. "Sorry. It fell out." His dark eyes stared right through me. "Is there some reason Morgan wrote you a check for enough money to buy a new house?"

Thirteen

I could totally tell he was getting the wrong idea from the check. I went across the room, smiling, and took it from him. "It was something stupid."

"Okay. Something stupid like what?" He gave me the pouch to go with the check, then folded his arms across his chest. "Before you tell me, I should warn you that Morgan bought off the last two women who were serious in my life."

Now he tells me! "Chase, this isn't that much money. I mean, it *is* a lot of money, but I'm not going to take it. I made that very clear to him when he gave it to me."

"Why do you still have it if you don't plan to take it, Jessie?"

I could tell his feelings were hurt. I should've remembered to throw the stupid check into a trash can before this. "I don't know. I forgot about it. There's been a lot going on. But that doesn't mean I meant to take it. I wouldn't still be here if I was going to let him buy me off." It suddenly occurred to me what he'd said. "What do you mean the last two women who were *serious* in your life? Was that something recent?"

"Let's stay focused on my brother offering you money to leave me. Then we can argue about past relationships, although that has to include *your* past relationships, too. And considering I only have three relationships I can discuss, that means you're going to be doing most of the talking."

I thought about it and knew he was right. I wouldn't consider any of my previous romances with men in the Village as serious, but that's why I'd always avoided discussions of past loves. "If it would make you feel better, I'll rip up the check right now and that'll be it."

"Okay. I have a trash can right here." He held it up.

I looked at the number written on the check. It was *so* much money. I could think of so many things to do with that kind of money. Not that it really mattered. I wouldn't leave Chase for a big check, even twice this amount.

"Well?"

"I'm looking at it." I smiled at him. "I might never see a check this big again unless I get shot at the university and they have to buy me off because I've told them their security is lax. It's a lot of money. I know it probably doesn't seem like that much to you. But where I come from, it's a *whole* lot of money."

"I know. And I wouldn't ask you not to take it."

I suddenly had a thought. "How about if I take it and stay with you anyway? We can really stick it to the man, in this case your brother. I could buy my house, and we could thumb our noses at your family while I enjoy their money."

"I don't think so. Nice try, though. I'm afraid it's either me or the money. Your choice."

I sighed and almost rubbed my cheek affectionately against the check, but realized that might be too much.

With a resolve I didn't know I had, I ripped the check to shreds and tossed it into the trash can. "How's that? I never considered keeping it, really. Especially not if it meant I had to give you up."

He put down the trash can and closed me in his arms. "I knew you wouldn't take it."

"But two other girls did?"

"That happened when I was in college." He kissed the side of my head.

"College? You could've mentioned that."

"You don't want Morgan's money."

"You're right." I snuggled up close to him. "I want yours. You could buy me a house. I have no shame about these things. Years of begging for school supplies and asking people to participate in boring programs prepared me for this moment. We won't go back any further than that."

"You could live here full-time with me. We don't need a house."

We'd had this conversation before. I supposed it was the same one Chase's parents had with him all the time. Chase loved the Village and wanted to live here. I didn't want to give up my job in Columbia. It was an impasse.

"Just kidding." I backed off from the subject. "This is fine. We have it all."

He studied my face as he brushed the damp hair back from my forehead. "We don't have to live here if you're really unhappy with it."

I could see he was dreading my response, and I loved him for taking the chance that I would demand that neither of us should live here all the time. Maybe someday things would be different, but for now, I knew this was where he wanted to be.

"Who could be unhappy living in Renaissance Village where history comes to life?" I kissed him hard on the lips and refused to let the future ruin the present. Someday was a long way from here. We were happy now. How many people can ever say that?

I think the kissing might've led us away from our trip to the bakery, but a brisk knock on the door brought us back to the reality of the situation. It was one of the monks, of course, looking for Chase to come and judge the bake-off.

"Later," Chase whispered as we followed the monk down the stairs.

I smiled and took his hand. Later would be okay with me as long as we came back together.

The bake-off wasn't as exciting as the monks made it out to be. All that sifting, stirring, rising, and perfecting was really kind of boring. Like watching a cooking show on TV where no one was worried about the ratings. The perfect loaf of bread was supposed to win. I sat next to Chase at one of the tables and almost fell asleep.

A tap on the shoulder startled me. It was Marielle, no doubt with otherworldly dagger news. The only thing I wanted to do less than watch the bake-off was hunt for another dagger, but I was glad to see her anyway.

She looked awful, like someone who hadn't eaten or slept in days. She'd managed to trade her cloak for a simple, brown peasant dress. Her face was beyond pale beneath the dirty smudges, and her hair was still matted.

"Come with me," she whispered.

"I can't. I have to watch the bake-off." I didn't really have to watch. All the monks cared about was that Chase was there.

"Come with me, please, Jessie! I have to show you something. It may help catch whoever killed Alastair."

I felt bad for her. She was out of the loop and didn't

realize the police had Alastair's killer in the form of Onslow. The least I could do was bring her up-to-date and tell her she didn't have to run herself ragged over the situation. I nudged Chase and told him I'd be back.

Marielle and I moved out of the group of monks who were raptly transfixed on the sight of Brothers Carl and John working on their bread. Outside, away from the ovens, the evening air felt pleasantly cool. We sat on the stairs at one of the manor houses across the street at Squires' Lane.

"I found another dagger." She brought it out of a pouch on her side. This dagger appeared to be made of sharpened stone. It was covered in crosses, and there was a reddish stain on the tip. "It's the dagger that killed the mighty Aslan on the great stone table."

I pretended to find something interesting on the ground at my feet. I messed around with my sandals, anything to keep from telling her that all of these things were myths and, in this case, literature. How could she believe these things were true? I know people in love are slightly crazy, but this was *really* crazy.

"It's quite a knife," I remarked when I could without laughing. "Where did you find it?"

"You see, that's the curious thing. I found it buried outside one of the Village residences. I saw someone bury it out there and waited until he left to dig it up."

"You saw who bury it, Marielle?"

"The tall one who works at the sword shop." She smiled prettily. "He's very handsome. Probably has the best hair of any man I've ever seen."

Ethan! "I knew it! I wasn't looking in the right place." I got to my feet. "Show me where you found it."

Marielle was happy to take me there. On the way, we encountered Fred the Red Dragon, still in costume. He turned back from dinner at Peter's Pub (chicken-wing night) and accompanied us. Obviously we weren't going for stealth! "Where are you two headed?"

"Out for a stroll." I didn't want him telling everyone what we were doing. "Do you know Marielle?" When he shook his head, I introduced them. "Where was the knife buried?" I asked her after the pleasantries were over.

"Over there." She pointed to a group of ramshackle cottages between the Dutchman's Stage and the Jolly Pipemaker's Shop.

Usually groups of residents lived together in a dormlike setting with a small kitchen area and a bathroom. This particular residence was first-year stuff, where you started out. Residents who became named characters had better quarters. Shopkeepers almost always lived upstairs from their shops.

"Who lives here?" Fred asked. "You want me to kick in the door?"

"No!" I said right away. "We don't want our suspect to become suspicious. I guess we'll have to stake out the place and wait for him to look for the dagger."

I pretended I didn't know who we were looking for. I did this for two reasons. The first one had to do with not wanting to be wrong about who Marielle was talking about. The second was to try and keep everybody calm. We couldn't go drag Ethan out of one of the pubs and accuse him of killing Alastair. We had to catch him doing something that pointed to his guilt. Like trying to dig up the knife.

"I'm hungry," Fred said after we'd gotten positioned on the ground behind the fence that hid the trash cans. "I'll go get some food and bring it back."

"No!" I hushed him as I made it clear that he couldn't leave. "If he sees you, it's all over. You have to stay here now."

"I can go and get something," Marielle offered. "I'm

good at sneaking around. I'm not hungry, but I can get something for the two of you."

"No one is going anywhere until we see who comes home. If we're lucky, he'll come right for the knife to check on it."

Fred shrugged his red scales. "I wouldn't look for it yet. Not until this whole thing is over."

"I agree with Fred," Marielle said. "Maybe we could set up a camera to take his picture."

"How would we do that?" I was a little frustrated with their attitudes. I had to remind myself that I was the one with experience dealing in murder investigations. Or at least watching them on TV. "We don't have the equipment to take someone's picture when we're not here."

"I think we should take it all to the police," Fred suggested. "Or maybe even tell Chase what's going on."

"Shh!" Marielle shushed us. "I think he's coming."

Someone *was* coming toward the cottage. It was hard to tell in the gathering darkness if it was Ethan. I hoped he wouldn't notice the large red dragon standing near the fence around his trash can. No matter how quiet we were, there was no way to disguise that.

"Where did you say the dagger was buried?" I asked Marielle in a tiny whisper.

"Back here, by the trash cans," she whispered back.

Exactly where we were waiting. There was no doubt that Marielle didn't have experience sneaking around looking for killers. But there was no time to do anything else. The footsteps continued toward us until we heard a sharp rap at the door followed by a moment of silence as the door opened.

"Alex!" It was Ethan's voice. He'd been inside the cottage the whole time. "What brings you out of Sherwood Forest?"

"Robin sends his regrets on your party tomorrow night. He had a blast when you were visiting us in the forest, but Marion wants to get out for the evening. You know how it is when a woman's involved."

They both laughed. Ethan said, "You don't have to tell me. I work with one! Tell Robin another time. I had a great time Sunday night. See you around, Alex."

The door closed, and Alex's footsteps receded again. The three of us behind the trash can wall sat (and stood) quietly for several more minutes until we were sure it was clear to get out of there.

I was trying to use sign language to let Marielle and Fred know that it was probably safe to move. In fact, I thought it was a good idea to get away before Ethan had to take out some trash. Now that we knew that the knife had been buried right outside his door, that (along with everything else) firmed up my resolve to prove he was more connected to this than he was telling anyone.

Before we could move (try using sign language on a dragon), a loud voice hailed us. "Hey, you guys!" Chase had found us. "What are you doing back here?"

I slapped my hand across his mouth and moved away from the trash cans with him. That seemed to give Fred and Marielle a hint. They followed us away from Ethan's cottage.

"I'll let you go if you promise to be quiet," I told Chase. "We're scoping out a spot where Marielle found another dagger." I pulled the stone dagger from my pouch.

"Sorry. I didn't know we were in spy mode." He looked up at Fred. "Next time it might be better to ditch the dragon if you're trying to hide. Where did you find the dagger, Marielle?"

She pointed and explained that the dagger had been

buried near the trash cans. "I think Jessie may be right. Ethan might be Alastair's killer."

I explained all the reasons (again) that made Ethan a good suspect. "Now we know he was in Sherwood Forest before the Merry Men found the third dagger and after Phineas went missing. That gave him a chance to plant the dagger he'd stolen after he killed Alastair with his sword. I'd say he has a few questions to answer."

"Which is my job, I think," Chase reminded me. "If you find these things out, you're supposed to tell me. I tell Detective Almond. We have a chain of command that works if you let it."

"Okay. You have the information. What are you going to do about it?" Marielle asked him.

"Nothing, actually. This is all circumstantial. Onslow is being indicted for Alastair's murder. It would take more than this to reopen the case."

"How can you say that with what we know now about Ethan?" I said. "You have to admit that's a lot of circumstantial evidence."

"She's got a point." Fred backed me up. "I may only be a dragon, but it seems to me that Detective Almond may not be able to see the tree for the forest."

Marielle giggled. "That's really funny. You're wasted being a dragon, Fred. You belong on stage! You're funnier than the Tornado Twins."

"You really think so?" He gazed down (a long way down) into her eyes. "No one has ever thought I was funny before."

"I've always thought you were funny," I reminded him. "Maybe I didn't say so, but you have great timing."

"While we're all here," Chase began in his bailiff voice, "there's the little matter of Alastair's stolen daggers to deal with. Marielle, were you involved in that?"

"I've been searching for my lord's daggers, Sir Bailiff," she responded. "I didn't steal them. I merely wanted to be sure they were kept somewhere safe where they would do no harm."

"Like the old storage locker?" I added.

She hung her poor, matted head. "I admit I put them there when I first found them. I didn't want to take them back."

"Where did you find them?" Chase wanted to know.

"In the castle," she said. "But some of them were missing."

"The rest are missing now." I explained to her about the locker being empty. "Someone else has them, except for the ones we've found that Chase gave to the police."

"They *are* magical," she countered. "They attract evil the way flowers attract bees."

"The police are going to want to hear this story from you, Marielle," Chase told her.

"I understand." She looked at me. "If I could have a few minutes to clean up a bit. Jessie, maybe you have some clothes I could borrow?"

"Sure. We'll go back to the dungeon and meet you at the main gate," I said to Chase. "Would that be okay?"

"Yeah. Go ahead. I'll call Detective Almond."

"I'll see you around, Marielle," Fred said as we left.

We started back down the cobblestones. Three actors were rehearsing an old nursery rhyme: *The little dog laughed to see such sport and the dish ran away with the spoon.* Farther away, I could hear someone singing to a lute. A fairy, wearing only a little more than blue gauze, ran by with Jack the Pumpkin Eater. I wondered how Jack's wife was going to feel about that.

"This place is like a moment out of time," Marielle said. "It is quite my favorite out of all the places I have been with my lord."

"Why do you call him that?" I asked finally. "Why did you let him treat you that way?"

"Because it was important for me to be with him," she answered. "I learned much. Such as this magic trick. Would you like to see it?"

After listening to impossible stories about fabled daggers, I thought it might be the best of my options. "Sure. Why not?"

She put one hand out. "See? Nothing in it."

"Okay."

I watched as she pulled out the other hand, but this time it wasn't empty. It was filled with a white powder that she blew up into my face. I started coughing and choking, my eyes watering. "What," I gasped, "what are you doing?"

"Eluding you, my friend. I'm sorry. I can't stop until my job is finished. Tell the bailiff that I will turn myself in when it is time. In the meantime, he should seek answers in Sherwood Forest. Farewell."

Whatever it was, the powder she'd blown into my face was like fire in my poor eyes. What was I thinking not letting Chase take her in to the police? I knew I didn't know her well enough to trust her. A little matted hair and dirt made me feel sorry for her. It wouldn't happen again.

I couldn't see anything. My throat felt like it was closing up. I dropped to my knees, wondering if I'd been poisoned like Alastair, and started making hand gestures to attract help. It wasn't too long before someone called Chase.

When he arrived, I gasped out what had happened. He gathered me up in his arms. "It smells like garlic. I know it hurts, but it isn't serious. Let's go to the first-aid station. Wanda should be able to help."

I howled and complained, but it didn't do any good. Chase thought I was complaining about what Marielle had done to me, but really I was begging him to go anywhere other than to see Wanda. The thought of those cold, blue fish eyes was enough to make me try to run away. She had a knack for making whatever was wrong with me far worse. This incident involved my eyes. I could lose my sight completely by the time she was done with me.

I could tell a group of residents went with us across the Village. I could hear them asking what had happened and if they could do anything. Then I heard a door squeak and a voice with a thick (and real) British accent say, "Well, ducks, what have you done to yourself this time?"

Fourteen

Chase explained what had happened. I calmed down as he put me on the chair in the first aid station. I tried to look at Wanda, my eyes burning. "Don't touch me," I managed to rasp out. "Someone call an ambulance."

"Don't be silly." She moved in close so I could see her. "Jessie and I have always been such good friends. Perhaps you should wait outside, Bailiff. I'll call when she's finished."

"No!" I grabbed Chase and clung to him like an octopus. "Please don't leave me."

"It's only a little water to irrigate the eyes and throat," Wanda said matter-of-factly. "She's such a baby, isn't she?"

"I think you'll be fine, Jessie," Chase said. "I have to call Detective Almond and let him know about this. I think Marielle has crossed the line from being weird to being dangerous."

"After she's done." I sounded like I had a bad cold. "Don't leave me alone with her!"

"Jessie, calm down." Chase got to his feet. "You're going to be fine. I'll be right back."

Why doesn't anyone believe me about Wanda? Why does everyone trust her? Am I the only one she's tried to seriously injure? Last time I was here, she wrapped a bandage around my ankle so tightly it cut off the circulation to my foot. The woman is a menace.

"I can splash water in my own eyes." I got up and stumbled right into something that went crashing to the floor.

When I bent to pick it up, Wanda pushed me down and sat on me. "Now then, let's get this over with, shall we? You're interfering with my watching *Torchwood*, dear. That Captain Jack Harkness really grinds my gears!"

I fought her, but she was strong. My grandmother used to say the devil always is. She pinned me to the floor, and I felt water trickle down into my eyes. I coughed, and she irrigated my throat, too. Don't ask me how she did it. I think she has multiple hands that come out when she needs them.

"Get off of me!" I tossed her to one side. I scrambled to my feet, surprised to find that the water had helped my eyes and throat. She hadn't used acid. I was amazed, but not lulled into a false sense of security. This was still Wanda LeFay, witch practitioner of Renaissance Faire Village.

Wanda swept my leg with hers, and I fell back down to the floor. She was on me in a second, glaring down into my face. "There, now. You can see me, can't you? That's a good thing. Seems to me you're a bit hysterical. Have something right here that will quiet you down."

"I'm fine," I argued. "I don't need a—"

Too late. I felt the needle prick my arm, and she sat back a little farther on me, saying, "Now, I think there's time for a trim on this hair. Lucky for you I used to work in a hair salon!"

Her voice was slurred, and I knew I couldn't stop her from doing whatever she was going to do. My eyes closed, and I didn't hear her say anything else.

I woke up in Chase's bed. The numbers on the alarm clock read two fifteen A.M. I could taste the garlic now, but my throat felt normal. My eyes seemed to be working, too. I had managed to evade Wanda doing anything terrible to me.

Then I remembered my hair. I sat up and ran my hand through it. It felt okay. Maybe Wanda had been messing with me. I felt a little woozy still, so I lay back down and closed my eyes.

Chase's hand tickled my side, then brushed over my hair. I turned in his direction and got ready to cuddle a little. It was nice to finally be in bed together.

I pressed my lips to his, but something felt strange. At first I thought it was because my brain wasn't working like it should, but I realized when he kissed me back that it was far more than that.

I felt a thin, cold hand touch me, and I leapt out of bed with a loud scream. Halfway to the door, I looked back and heard laughter. "Who are you?" I grabbed the sword that Chase had used when he was the Black Knight. It had been hanging on the wall since his retirement.

"Don't be so dramatic!" Brooke pulled the blanket off her tousled hair. "I'm sure Chase won't mind if you stay."

I knew this game, having played it, or something like it, once or twice myself. I could see the whole plan now. Morgan wrote me that check, not because he thought I'd take it, but because he thought I'd tell Chase and that would break us up.

Now Brooke was doing the same thing. I could play that

game, too. "Oh, no!" I feigned total jealousy and frustration at seeing her in Chase's bed. "I can't believe Chase would do this to me."

Brooke almost purred with satisfaction. "Cheer up, honey. It's not the first time. Chase has his little flings, but he always comes back to me. We'll get married someday when he gets over this whole medieval thing."

"I don't know why Chase doesn't want me anymore," I whined as I sat down on the bed with the sword still in my hand. "You know, in Renaissance times, there was a way to handle these situations."

"Oh, really? What was that?"

I placed the tip of the sword at her throat as I slowly got to my feet. The look on her face was pure terror. Every ounce of color (real and artificial) faded. Her bedroom-eyes look changed totally as she no doubt questioned my sanity. "In those days, men dueled when they both wanted the same woman. Women didn't have much say in the matter. But that was back then. This is now. Today, in Renaissance Village, a woman can challenge another woman to a duel. The loser steps aside for the winner to take Chase. Are you game?"

"Are you nuts?" Brooke looked from my face to the sword blade several dozen times but didn't try to move. "I mean, this isn't really two hundred years ago or anything. Real people don't duel."

I considered her answer at great length so I could watch her squirm. I gave her a lot of credit for even daring to ask if I was crazy. If I had been, I probably would've run her through. "To begin with, a brief history lesson. The Renaissance was more like five hundred years ago. It was well before the founding of this country. And secondly, in case you haven't noticed, things around here are different than in other places. We still duel here."

"Well, I'm not dueling anybody," she declared. "It's a stupid idea. Chase wouldn't expect me to do it."

"That means you forfeit. Either way, I win, and you leave Renaissance Village."

"You can't make me do that!"

"No, you're right. But Chase can. He's the bailiff, which makes him judge, jury, and sometimes executioner if you consider that he can order vegetable justice."

"Chase won't find against me. He loves me," she spit out. "You don't know what you're messing around with."

"Let's find out." I sent a hastily scrounged pen and an old map of Renaissance Village flying in her general direction. "You sign that you declined the offer to duel over Chase. That means you lose. Then we'll see what Chase has to say about it."

I could feel Brooke sizing me up with her eyes. She was almost as tall as me, which meant our reach with swords would be almost the same. Her little flabby arms would never have the stamina to fight me on the Field of Honor. As far as jousting was concerned, it would be a massacre. I felt pretty safe glaring at her.

"Okay. Fine. If it will satisfy your savage little traditions, I'll fight you for Chase. I was three times tennis champion at my country club, and I played lacrosse when I was in college. You can challenge me all you want. This way, Chase will see how much I really care about him. So lead on, sister!"

Hmm. I wasn't expecting that move. Really, I thought the best I could expect was that she would sign the paper and Chase would put her in the stocks so I could throw tomatoes at her. This was so much more interesting.

"My second will call on yours and arrange the date and time," I quoted her from the dueling handbook. "Because I challenged you, you have the choice of weapons." I lifted the sword from her throat and saluted her with it. "Now, get your clothes on and get out of *our* bed."

I left the room and went downstairs to hang out by the tree swing for a while. Chase returned about twenty minutes later. Brooke was still upstairs. I had no compunction about telling him everything that had happened. Well, almost everything. I didn't know how he'd feel about me holding his sword to her neck, so I left that part out.

"I'm sorry, Jessie." He leaned his head against mine. "Are you okay? I'll go up and get her out of there. I told you she and Morgan would be a pain in the ass."

"If it's all the same to you, I'd rather wait until she comes down on her own. She might try and use her nakedness against you. It's not that I don't trust you, but I don't like the picture I'm getting in my mind."

He laughed and suggested we go across the cobblestones to the Pleasant Pheasant for a while. "Wanda said no ale until tomorrow, but you can have some soda. Then you can come back and see if she's gone. She probably wouldn't try to use her *nakedness* against you."

I didn't enlighten him about our initial encounter. It was enough that he didn't rush upstairs to see her. It would probably be better for me, too, since I was having second thoughts about the two of us dueling.

While it had seemed like a good idea in the heat of the moment, now I wasn't so sure what Chase would think. I wasn't worried about kicking her butt in whatever kind of duel she chose (my gut told me she'd leave first anyway), but now I wanted to keep it quiet. No reason for Chase or anyone else to know about it.

We stayed at the pub for a while. I whined at Chase for leaving me with Wanda, but couldn't argue that she hadn't done the right thing for me. I don't know. Maybe I'd been hysterical while she was treating me. Marielle had attacked me with her magical garlic powder. I hadn't seen that coming.

We talked about Marielle for a few minutes. Chase said he had told Detective Almond everything and had given her picture to the security team in the Village. "I think we can assume she won't leave until she does whatever it is she wants to do with those daggers."

"She told me you should seek the answer in Sherwood Forest, whatever that means. I'm thinking maybe she and Ethan killed Alastair together."

Chase laughed. "We can't accuse people of crimes because we don't like them."

"I can. I'm not a bailiff." I sipped my soda, pretending that it was ale.

The Tornado Twins were working on a new show that they were trying out on the group assembled there. Diego was pretending to be a dog after Lorenzo hypnotized him. Lucky for me there were a couple of fairies for them to call on from the audience. Diego humped their legs and slobbered all over their feet. Better them than me!

"Oh, you have such beautiful fur," Lorenzo said, stroking Diego's hair. "It would make a beautiful coat for some lucky woman." He took out a large pair of scissors.

Diego shook himself and ran yelping into the lap of one of the Lovely Laundry Ladies. The next few minutes were made up of Lorenzo chasing Diego in and under the table and the lady's skirt.

The skit ended with Diego finding a way to pretend-pee on Lorenzo's leg before the "trance" was ended. Everyone in the small group applauded and pronounced the show a hit. Diego bought ale all around, then things settled down.

At least they did until Diego came up and perched on the table when Chase went to the bar to pick up more chili-cheese fries. "What's wrong, Jessie? Didn't you think it was funny?"

"Hilarious. Get off the table." I swallowed some soda and tried to ignore him. The best way to deal with the twins is to ignore them. They thrive on any kind of attention.

"You'd like it better if it was me doing Lorenzo's part, wouldn't you? I could tell by the way you were looking at me." He grinned, showing perfect white teeth against his olive skin. "Or is it that you were jealous of the attention I was paying to that fairy? I swear, she means nothing to me. You'll always be my only love."

"Great. Get off the table." I didn't say it's always *easy* to ignore them.

He jumped on the floor and started that leg-humping thing with me. I waited as long as I could (at least thirty seconds) to see if he'd stop. When he didn't, I tried to push him off with my free foot. In turn, he started sniffing and licking my ankle. I thought I might have to hit him with my empty soda tankard.

"Get off her, Diego," Chase said in a very nonchalant manner. "Don't make me take you to the stocks."

"Oh, Chase," Diego whined, "please take me to the stocks. I want to go to the stocks with you. It's always been you. I've only been using Jessie to make you jealous."

"Chili-cheese fries don't look good on the human face," Chase said.

Lorenzo yelled, "Heel!" and Diego sat back on his haunches until his brother came to get him with a leash. "Sorry about that, Bailiff. I'll put him in his cage now. If you'd like, I can take those fries off your hands to punish him with later."

Chase kind of grunted, and the Tornado Twins whirled out of the pub. I realized as they left that I couldn't wait any longer. If Brooke was still in Chase's bed, she would be sleeping with me. I was too tired to hold my head up.

"I'm going to check on Brooke. If I don't come back down, I'm either asleep or dead. If I'm dead, you'll know who the suspect is."

"Are you sure you don't want me to come with you?"

"Yeah. If she's still up there, I'll handle it. Give me twenty minutes." I kissed his forehead (avoiding his chili-cheese mouth) and left the pub.

It was quiet outside and blessedly cool. I wished I could've enjoyed it more, but I was just too exhausted. I might not be able to kill Brooke with Chase's fake sword, but I could sure use it to herd her out of there.

I heard whispering coming from the shadows close to the dungeon. I couldn't see anyone at first, but as I got closer, I could make out Brooke's and Morgan's voices. She must've called him for help after I threatened her. And I hadn't even mentioned it to Chase! Some women can't handle their own problems.

"She tried to kill me," I heard Brooke complaining. "I don't know if this is going to work, Morgan."

"It will work if you give it some time," Morgan assured her. "Believe me, by the time we get done harassing Chase, he'll be glad to sign over his part of the business to me. He's never wanted to be in the family anyway. We can do this, angel. Just think how much money we'll have when we finally get married."

Whoa! Wait a minute! Morgan didn't want to break up me and Chase? Neither did Brooke? And from the sounds of their lovemaking against the side of the dungeon (*yuck!*), they wanted to be together? I might not ever tell Chase about threatening Brooke, but I sure planned to tell him this. I was sure I could manage to stay awake long enough to regale him with this twisted tale.

I went upstairs quietly so as not to disturb the couple

outside. I changed the sheets (who knew Chase had more than one set?) and crawled into bed. I tried my best to wait for him, but I fell asleep before he got up there.

It was morning when I opened my eyes. My first thought was that I hadn't stayed awake long enough to tell him about his ex and his brother.

My second thought was, who cares? The story was as good now as it had been last night. Chase was gone, of course, but he'd left me a package of clean clothes for the day. It was a nice tunic and short breeches, too. I didn't want to know how he got them from Portia.

I jumped up and raced into the shower, and that's when I noticed what Wanda had done. She'd snipped the ends of my already short hair, making it stick out all over my head even worse than usual. I growled at it in the mirror, promising vengeance for the trespass. Wanda might find herself without BBC America at all when I got done with her!

I met Chase as I was going down the stairs. He was carrying a piece of paper and sort of scowling, but I didn't let that stop me. "Look what Wanda did to my hair!"

He looked up at me. "What?"

Argh! "Never mind! You aren't going to believe what happened last night!"

"No?" He turned the paper he was holding around so I could see it. It was one of the thousands of notices posted around the Village every day. "Does it have anything to do with challenging Brooke to a duel for my hand?"

The flyer detailed in elaborate terms what Brooke and I were willing to do for the hand of Bailiff Chase Manhattan. Apparently, Brooke's choice of weapon was bow and arrow. *Bad choice.* I had apprenticed with Master Archer Simmons two years ago. I was his star pupil. No matter what kind of archery skills she'd managed to get in college,

I'd be able to shoot rings around her. Even Robin Hood himself had been impressed with me that summer.

I shrugged. "Not a problem. I'm really good with a bow and arrow. You don't have to worry. Is there coffee?"

"Did you challenge Brooke to a duel?" Chase didn't sound as happy about the situation as I did.

"You had to be there to appreciate how it happened." I started to explain, but he cut me off.

"Jessie, this whole thing is stupid! I'm not exactly the fair damsel type we usually get in here for this kind of thing. What were you thinking?"

His reluctance to look at the bright side was starting to put me out a little. I mean, maybe it was that I hadn't had breakfast or coffee yet. Or maybe it was that I went to bed last night without him and woke up this morning the same way.

"I was thinking that your ex-girlfriend was naked in our bed last night! It seemed like the best thing to do. I wanted to make a point."

"And that was?" He raised his left brow at me. It was the same expression I'd often seen him use on evildoers in the Village.

"Never mind." I pushed past him on the stairs. "I'll talk to Brooke and call the whole thing off. I wouldn't want you to feel *stupid* because your other girlfriend wanted to make trouble with your present girlfriend. At least I *was* your present girlfriend. I'll see you around."

I stalked out of the dungeon, slamming the heavy outside door behind me. Even without caffeine, my mind was buzzing along too fast. *Chase and I are over. That's it. If that's all he can think about, he can kiss my butt.*

But my eyes kept darting back, hoping he was right behind me. I was already waiting for the makeup part of the disagreement. Yes, I was angry. No, I didn't want to break up. That would be accomplishing what Brooke and Morgan wanted.

I stopped dead in my tracks and realized I'd forgotten to tell Chase what I'd heard last night. Breaking up with him wouldn't accomplish what Brooke and Morgan wanted, I reminded myself. But maybe this flyer making him feel stupid might do it.

I ran back to the dungeon, but he was already gone. I swore as I accidentally kicked the door and hurt my toe. If I had a damn two-way radio, I could call him and we could talk. I didn't have one, so I was going to have to look for him. Not an easy thing to do in a crowd of people.

"I want those boots back by this afternoon!" Portia called out as she passed me on the cobblestones. "And where's my boyfriend? You won't even have a green T-shirt to wear tomorrow!"

I ignored her. Right now, I had to zero in on what was important: Chase. I tracked him down past the camels and elephants on the other side of the Village. Someone said they'd seen him at Sir Latte's, but when I got there, he was gone. Bawdy Betty at the bagel shop said she'd seen him go by with Merlin a few minutes before I arrived. I gritted my teeth and continued down the cobblestones past the Swan Swing and Lady Cathy's Crochet.

"Jessie!" I heard someone call my voice and realized it was Alex from Sherwood Forest. He was sitting at an outside table with Rafe, the ex-pirate king from the *Queen's Revenge*.

It took me by surprise to see two of my ex's at the same table drinking coffee together, especially since they were from two different areas of the Village. As far as I know, Rafe has never been a Merry Man and Alex has never been a pirate. It was too weird. I had to stop.

Rafe held up the flyer that I'd seen at every shop and plastered on the high fence that surrounded the Village. "So you're finally committing to one guy, huh? I knew you'd settle down in time."

Alex laughed. "Yeah, though methinks we got the best of the old girl. How much could there be left for the bailiff?"

That brought forth peals of laughter from both of them. I noticed something unusual on Alex's side. The men of Sherwood Forest carry daggers but not such elaborate models. "Where did you get that?" I asked him.

"This?" He glanced down uncomfortably at the knife that hung from his side. "You know, they hand them out. It's only a prop."

I knew better. After all the summers (I didn't want to think how many) I'd spent here, I knew a fake from a real dagger. "That's part of Alastair's collection, isn't it?"

"I don't know what you're talking about." He nodded to Rafe. "I have to get back. I'll talk to you later."

"Oh, no! You're not going anywhere until I know why you have that dagger."

Alex broke into a fast sprint across the King's Highway and the Village Square. I knew he was heading for Sherwood Forest and the protection the trees and familiar surroundings would bring him. He was involved somehow in all of this. First the dagger already found in the forest, then his hanging out with Ethan, and now another one of the evil, magical daggers in his possession.

I ran after him, but we were equally measured. We passed Leather and Lace and the Treasure Trove before he veered right toward the fountain and the climbing wall. I took the shortcut through the passageway between the houses on Squires' Lane, hoping to cut him off.

The monks were in the street chanting and having a celebration for their new/old leader, Brother Carl. I ran through them, almost getting my foot caught up in their loose robes.

Tavin Hartley, wearing yet another gray suit, was clicking away through the main gate in the general direction of the castle. I barely had enough breath to yell at her, pointing to the dagger at Alex's side. Surely she'd help if she realized what was going on.

To my surprise, she pivoted on her high heels, grabbed one of the fortune-teller's loose rugs from the side of her shop, and threw it at Alex's feet. Less than a hundred yards from the entrance to Sherwood Forest, he fell and skidded to a halt.

"Nice work," I commended when I could breathe. Fortunately, Alex wasn't in any better shape. He lay like a beached whale on the rough grass right off the cobblestones.

Tavin pushed her glasses back on her face and made an expression like a smile. "I understood what you were pointing at. This person has one of Alastair's daggers. Someone should call the police."

"Wait!" Alex managed to choke out. "Wait a minute! I found this dagger. I didn't steal it. I didn't kill anyone. Finders keepers, right?"

Tavin stripped the dagger from the sheath on his side and stood over him like an avenging goddess. "We'll see about that. You'd better have a good explanation for this."

"I do. I really, I do." He struggled to catch his breath.

"We'll wait right here until we hear what it is, right?" I looked at Tavin and she smiled back.

"Right! Huzzah!"

Fifteen

"We found the daggers in the forest." Alex glanced up at Tavin and added, "Well, I found the daggers and the goose. I kept this dagger and put one in the toaster oven before I gave it to Robin. I gave one to Ethan. I figured it didn't matter. After all, Alastair is dead. He can't use them now."

"And did you kill him to take the daggers?" Tavin demanded.

"No! I told you I found them. They were out there near a tree. Phineas was squawking or I wouldn't have noticed. I might borrow the occasional toaster oven, but I've never stolen anything." Alex's eyes pleaded with mine. "Ask Jessie. She knows me."

"That's true," I admitted. "But if I find out you were making a deal with Rafe to sell him a dagger, you're going down."

"But I'm not a thief, right?"

I sighed. "Not as far as I know."

"I still think I should call the police," Tavin said. "This whole investigation has been lax. Daggers all over the Village. I need that collection returned to me."

"Before the auction, right?"

"Yes. Of course! They will help pay off some of the huge debt Alastair left behind. The daggers might not be real, but they have meaning to his followers."

The evil, magical daggers, I added silently. I believed it now.

"Can I go now?" Alex asked.

"No!" We both shouted at him.

"What did you plan to do with this dagger?" Tavin asked him.

He shrugged. "Keep it? I don't know. It's a great piece!"

"Did you know Alastair?" I thought about Marielle and her obsession with the daggers.

"No. But Toby, I mean, Robin did. He went to see him the first night he was here. He wasn't too happy when he came back to the forest either."

"Maybe we should go see Robin Hood then," Tavin surmised. "I can't believe I said that!"

"Not a chance." I turned to Alex. "You have him meet us right after closing tonight at the main gate. Got it?"

"Aye, milady." He nodded. "I'll have him there."

Tavin sat down on a nearby bench as Alex scampered back into the woods. The bench was shaped like an alligator and featured an ad for exotic animal rides at the other end of the Village.

"This whole thing has been hard," she admitted. "Alastair was a good friend. He didn't deserve to die that way. I know they're blaming Onslow for Alastair's death, but no one seems to care that the daggers are gone. They'll probably bring in the biggest amount of money for the estate. Alastair had children, you know. I'm trying to do the best I can by them."

I didn't know the Great Alastair had any children. Being a father didn't seem in keeping with his image. But I suppose when you spend all your time with young, attractive women who worship you, it can happen.

"Some of those daggers are actually valuable," I told her. "I think Marielle might have stolen them. She keeps saying she finds them, but I think she might be using the daggers to draw attention to the people she thinks killed Alastair."

"Doesn't she know about Onslow?" She tried hard to smile but couldn't quite make it.

I explained how Onslow had stolen a dagger from the collection and had hidden it in the monk's flour. "These things really get around."

We came up with the idea of marking places the daggers had been found in the Village. Seven of the twelve daggers were in custody. That meant there were five to go. So far, no one had been hurt with any of them. The question seemed to be, where would Marielle leave the next dagger?

"After she attacked you, your boyfriend must think she's dangerous," Tavin said. "Why hasn't he had her arrested?"

"He would if we could find her. No one has seen her since she blew that garlic in my face."

"Well, you said Onslow left one in the bakery." Tavin wrote on a copy of the Village map. "There were two in Sherwood Forest."

"There was one buried under a trash can," I said, trying to help.

I didn't tell her about the dagger we'd taken from Merlin. I was sure Chase wouldn't broadcast it around and thought I shouldn't either.

"All right. So here we have it. If your calculations are

correct and Marielle is leaving them to attract attention to people she thinks had a hand in Alastair's death, where will she go next?"

I had no idea. "Didn't anyone like Alastair? I've heard a lot said about him but not much of it good."

"You're right, Jessie. No one liked Alastair. Many people were envious or worshipped him, but he had no close friends. He and I were close because of work, but there was a side of him that he would never let anyone see. He was a very private person."

I could see in her eyes that she had wanted to be closer to him. Was she another spurned suitor like Daisy? What did these women see in him? Reputation could only get someone so far!

Thinking about Daisy made me realize I had to get to Armorer's Alley before I lost my apprenticeship. I'd have to find Chase and make up later. It was time to get back to making swords. "I have to go," I said to Tavin. "Are you leaving the Village soon?"

"I don't know yet. I guess I'll give it a day or two to see if the other daggers turn up. I hate to leave without them. Alastair wanted his collection to go to a museum. Several museums have bid on the daggers. Since that's all I can do for him now, it's important to me."

She stood up, squared her thin shoulders, and stuck out her hand in my general direction. "Thank you for your help, Jessie. I'm glad I met you."

We said good-bye, and I followed the cobblestones to the sword shop. Karl, one of the knights who served the Village, and Daisy, were sparring in the backyard with a nice-sized crowd of visitors watching. I didn't bother going there, since I knew Hans wasn't finished with me.

I patted my side pouch with the smaller hammer in it and walked in the direction of the forge, thinking about

Chase instead of my work. I didn't understand why he was so angry about my dueling with Brooke. If she wasn't up to it, she shouldn't have accepted. I wasn't worried about the tournament. I was too good with a bow to even consider it.

Maybe he was embarrassed, though I've never known anything to embarrass Chase. I finally had to give up trying to guess—I'd just have to wait until I could talk to him. I wished I hadn't been so mad when I'd walked out of the dungeon. It had already been a long day knowing things weren't right between us.

"There you are!" Hans greeted me with something like a glad-to-see-you expression on his face. "I think we're going to get some good things done today, Jessie. The forge awaits!"

Hans led the way, and I looked at the big, heavy tongs again. Somehow I had to manage to hold them without dropping the sword blade or I was lost. The smaller hammer had to be my salvation.

"A blacksmith must have a thorough understanding of metallurgy and heat treating," he said, beginning yet another lecture. "It took me years to come to this knowledge. Obviously you won't get so deeply into it, but I think we can get a blade made for you anyway that will be what you need."

He looked at the tongs and his hammer sitting on the side of the forge. The coals glowed red hot from the middle of the pit. It was time to put up or shut up. He handed me my slightly blackened blade, and I advanced to the forge.

I needed time to look around for something more accommodating than those tongs. There had to be some similar tool that someone besides Hercules could lift. That meant I had to distract him, otherwise we'd be standing here all day looking at the forge.

My chance came when a group of visitors wandered

into the smithy. I stepped aside from the forge submissively so the master could take charge. Hans launched into his speech about how metal is forged and how things were made during the Renaissance.

I scrambled toward the workbench, which looked as though it was hardly ever used. Tools were scattered all over it, covered with a fine dusting of black ash. I didn't know what most of these things were, but I recognized a pair of tongs when I saw one. They were as large as the ones Hans used but thinner and lighter. They probably would heat up much faster, but if I could hold them at all, I could live with it. I was fast, just not strong.

Hans was hitting a sword blade (not mine) for the crowd when a squire brought in a horse that needed to be shod. I knew Hans wouldn't do a job this big for visitors, so I led the horse into a stall and gave him some water. I was still there when Hans came to tell me the visitors were gone.

Armed with superior tools, I approached the forge with more confidence. I used my lighter tongs to pick up my sword blade and put it into the coals. I hooked the hammer I would use to begin work on it into my side pouch where my tankard (free drinks) usually lived.

"Well done!" he said, slapping me on the back. "Ingenious!"

There were a few other adjectives, but I couldn't understand them in his foreign tongue. When the sword blade glowed bright red, I secured it with the tongs again, pulled it from the coals, laid it on the anvil, and held it firm as I hit it with the hammer. Maybe the job would take me longer with this hammer, but it would get done. Hans didn't seem to mind.

We spent the next few hours getting the blade into shape so that it was ready for the handle. Mine would be very plain, but effective. I swished it around in the air a few times after it had cooled, wishing Brooke had chosen swords instead of arrows. Of course she'd seen me fight with a sword, so she was probably afraid to confront me that way. Pity, because I could've brought out my new sword.

"You'll have to practice with this and get a feeling for the weight in your hand," Hans said. "Daisy will work with you on the grip. It will probably be wood, since that's easiest and cheapest."

I had burned my hands and shirt in a few places, but the finished blade was smooth and ready to be partnered with a grip. It needed some serious polishing, since it was still dirty from the fire and the pounding. "Thanks for your help. I think it will be a fine sword."

"And I think you're starting to build some muscle." He grinned and pushed at my arm. "I hear you won't be fighting for Chase with a sword. Why a bow?"

"It wasn't my choice," I assured him. "I challenged her. She got to pick the weapon."

"I can't wait!" He rubbed his hands together. "If you're as courageous with a bow as you were with a sword facing Alastair, it should be quite a show!"

I took my sword back to Daisy with great pride. She was too preoccupied to notice it or think about the next step. "I can't find Ethan. He's not at his place, and no one has seen him this morning."

"I haven't seen him." I held up my sword blade, but she turned away without looking.

"I have this gut feeling that something bad has happened to him." Daisy kept sorting through huge amounts of receipts and other paperwork. "Don't ask me why. But I feel it."

"What could've happened to him?" I admit to being a little annoyed. So Ethan was missing. Big deal. I had a viable sword blade ready for a handle. That seemed more important to me.

"Ethan is *never* missing. He's always here. Something has to be wrong."

I could see I wasn't going to get anywhere this way. "You could call Chase and ask him to look for Ethan."

Her face brightened. "That's a great idea, Jessie. Too bad I don't have one of those radios everyone carries around. Do you have one?"

"No." I hated to admit it. "But I know a few people who do. I could ask one of them to call him."

"Do that. Thanks a bunch. I shall attend the shop until the bailiff's arrival. Make sure you tell him how important this is. Ethan could be hurt somewhere."

I agreed and struck out on the cobblestones toward Mrs. Potts's shop. I knew she had a radio. I was hoping to run into Chase and not need to call him, but the Village was crowded and I wasn't sure I'd see him unless he walked right by me.

I did manage to run into Tony, who was perambulating in the direction of Harriet's Hat House with a lovely lady dressed in green silk. It was unusual to see him with a woman wearing so many clothes, since he tended to prefer fairies.

"Lovely to see you, sister!" He doffed his small green Merry Man cap and smiled at me. The lady with him stood rigidly upright, with not so much as a nod in my direction. I was totally beneath her station, and she was acknowledging it. "What brings you out on such a fine day?"

"I'm looking for Chase or Ethan, I'll take either one. Have you seen either of them?"

Tony laughed and the lady giggled. "Sister, you sell yourself too readily."

"And why is she dressed in these rags?" The lovely lady

in green wanted to know as she put a dainty white handker-
chief to her nose.

"I'm dressed as a swordsmith's apprentice," I snarled,
not in the mood. "And I'm not selling anything. Ethan is
missing. Daisy can't look at my sword until we find him.
She wants Chase to look for him."

Tony seemed to consider the question, then responded,
"I haven't seen either of them today. But I'll tell them you're
looking for them if I do see them."

I started to continue down the cobblestones but then
thought of something else. "Alex said he found three daggers in the forest with the goose. Do you know anything
about that?"

"If it doesn't involve the computer in Robin's tree house,
I probably haven't seen it. That guy wants me working on
that blog thing 24/7. This is my first time out all day."

"So you didn't even know about the daggers and the
goose?" I found that hard to believe.

"I heard about it. At least I heard about one of them.
Wasn't it an iron dagger stuck in a toaster oven?"

The lady next to him gasped. "Wasn't that the one used
to kill Conan?"

All I could do was shake my head. I thanked them and
moved on, hopefully to people who knew some helpful
information.

A brainstorm hit me when I reached the Honey and Herb
Shoppe. Instead of sending Chase to Swords and Such,
I could have Mrs. Potts ask him to meet me here and walk
with him back to Daisy's place. Maybe then we'd have a
chance to talk.

On the other hand, maybe he'd be right here having tea
with Brooke and Morgan while Mrs. Potts bustled around
in her white mobcap serving them honey cookies.

I started to walk back out of the shop before they saw

me. Brooke and Morgan didn't know that I knew about their scheme. I didn't want to tell Chase in front of them. And I certainly didn't want to sit at their table pretending everything was fine while the three of them drank tea and ate cookies.

Too bad Mrs. Potts's sharp eyes saw me come in. "Bless my soul! It's Jessie! I suppose you're looking for Chase. Sit down and I'll get you a cup for tea. Would you like some cookies or a scone? They're fresh this morning."

"Jessie!" Chase got to his feet and rushed over to me. "I was so busy all morning. I haven't had a chance to look for you."

He folded me in his arms, and I closed my eyes on the rest of the world. "You know me. I was figuring out how to make a sword." I didn't even mention the fact that I obviously *wasn't* in the Honey and Herb Shoppe. It didn't matter. "I'm sorry you were upset about Brooke."

"It's okay. I don't care. If you guys want to fight, have at it. But don't fight over me. You *know* who I belong to."

I thought my heart was going to melt. How did he always (most of the time) know exactly what to say to make me feel better? "Thanks."

"I'd ask if you want to have tea and cookies, but—"

"Yes! Please, join us," Morgan gushed, turning around in his chair to look at us. "No hard feelings. We're almost family."

Mrs. Potts darted her eyes back and forth between us before muttering, "Oh, dear," and going back into the kitchen.

Morgan nudged Brooke, who grudgingly turned around and said, "Yes. Join us, Jessie."

"I'm supposed to be working," I explained to Chase. "But Ethan is missing and Daisy is frantic. Can you help?"

"Sure. What's up?"

"I don't know. She says he's never missing. She won't look at my sword blade until we find him."

"Let's check his place." He told Brooke and Morgan he was leaving.

"See you at the duel, Jessie," Brooke said as we walked out the door.

"Sorry about them," Chase apologized as we walked. "I wish they'd leave. I don't know what's keeping them here."

"I do." I told him about them wanting his part of the family company. "And she's pretending to still want you when she really wants Morgan."

"That doesn't surprise me. And if that's what it will take to get them to leave, I'll be glad to give them my share of the company."

"Wait!" I stopped walking and faced him. "You can't let them win like that!"

"Why? I don't ever plan on going back."

"Really?" It was such good news, I almost lost track of what I was going to say, but then I rallied. "Chase, you could regret that someday. I don't think you should let it go that easily."

"They'll keep coming back."

"They don't bother me. And now that you know the truth, they shouldn't bother you either. Let them stay as long as they like. Don't give up what's yours."

"Yeah?" He smiled and kissed me. "You sure?"

"Absolutely! And if Brooke wants to duel—"

"Did I mention she chose the bow because she was the president of the archery club in college?"

Hmm. That was annoying. Was there anything she *wasn't* president of in college? "I don't care. I'm good with the bow, too. And it's been a long time since college!"

"Okay. Let's find Ethan!"

We marched right over to Ethan's place and pounded

on his door. A few seconds later, a tall woman with carefully mussed hair answered the door. "Where's Ethan?" I
demanded.

"He's not here." She was obviously trying to decide if
she should let me in or not.

I didn't bother asking. I brushed by her and looked in
the two rooms. Ethan wasn't in either one of them.

"Have you seen him today, Denise?" Chase asked her.

"Earlier." She yawned. "He left with some girl. I don't
know who she was, but he followed her out of here like she
put a spell on him or something."

"I'll call security." He took out his two-way radio. "He
probably stopped for another latte or something. Don't
worry. We'll find him." He smiled at Denise, who smiled
back.

"I'm not worried," she said. "Would you like to have an
ale or something?"

Right there in front of me! I couldn't believe it! "No, he
wouldn't. Call security if you see Ethan."

Sixteen

Chase called Detective Almond, who was not interested in missing people unless they'd been gone at least forty-eight hours. He wasn't interested in missing daggers either, now that his case was closed.

We sat around with Daisy outside Swords and Such, Chase taking notes on the dozens of places Ethan could be. "All I know is that Ethan is always here," Daisy said. "Since he's not here, that means trouble. You have to find him."

"This list will help," Chase told her. "It will give security some places to look for him. You know how it is around here. When someone could be anywhere, it's hard to say where they are."

"Like Marielle," I added, then realized it wasn't the most helpful thing to say. It was true, though. Now Marielle and Ethan were both missing. Of course, Marielle seemed to like it that way.

"I appreciate whatever help you can give me, Chase," Daisy said. "That boy is important to me."

"I'll get everyone out on it, Daisy," he promised. "Of course, if he doesn't want to be found, that's a whole other story."

"I know." She blew her nose loudly on a green rag, then wiped her eyes. "But I know that's not the case. We have to find him."

Chase agreed, and then I walked him out the shop door. "I guess I'll stay here with Daisy and help with the visitors, if nothing else." I sighed heavily in frustration for the loss of sword-making time. I guessed I would have to make due until Daisy could focus again.

"He's around here somewhere." Chase kissed my forehead. "I'll see you later."

I went back inside as a few visitors entered the shop. They weren't dressed in Renaissance garb, but their interest in swords and blades of all types was as keen.

I got Daisy to talk with them, thinking it would give her something to think about besides Ethan. It didn't take more than a few minutes before they were fully immersed in a discussion and had decided to go down to the pub to continue their conversation over a few pints of ale.

"Do you think you can handle the shop by yourself?" Daisy asked.

"Sure. Not a problem. I've worked alongside Lady Visa many times. Go and talk swords. Maybe they'll buy something nice."

That's all the convincing it took. I told myself I was doing a good deed. Daisy really cared about Ethan even if he didn't seem to feel the same about her. *Snake.*

A few visitors wandered in and out of the shop, but mostly the hot afternoon wasn't conducive to selling swords. I sat around with my new sword blade, polishing it until it shone. It would get dirty again when the handle was put on, but that was okay. I did a few practice thrusts and parries in the empty shop and was satisfied with what I had created.

Daisy returned right before closing with a big contract to make a few swords. "Those guys have a club where they get together and do role-playing. Selling swords that are already made is one thing, but custom designs are where the serious money is. Any word from Chase?"

"Nothing. Sorry. But he'll find him."

"I know he will. Chase is a good man. You're lucky to have him." She grinned and slapped me on the back. "He's lucky to have you, too, Jessie. And I've been neglecting my responsibilities to you as your master. I think you had a blade to show me."

Overjoyed, I brought my blade out and showed it off to her. "It took some doing, but I figured out how to make the forge work for me."

"If you learned nothing other than how to make something your own, that would be a substantial lesson. But this is a good blade. It still needs a little work before we add a grip. You need to round these edges. Otherwise it will nick and ding too easily. You'll need a file to wear it down, and then you can hand sand the radius to a smooth edge. I have a file and some sandpaper. Let's see what we can do."

She showed me how to use the file on the edge of the blade. "We want it to look sharp, but it has to be strong to endure me hitting it with my sword."

"It seems like this would make it weaker." I hated to see my perfect blade changed.

"Not at all. The more you temper it, the stronger it becomes." She laughed and kept working the metal. "Like a good apprentice. You have to work them to make them stronger."

"Like Ethan?" The words slipped out of my mouth before I realized I'd said them.

She put down the file and wiped her hands on a rag. "Like my Ethan." Daisy looked down at her hands for a long time before she looked back up at me. "I want to tell you something I've never told anyone. I feel like I can trust you, Jessie. It's something I don't want everyone to know."

I felt honored that she trusted me. She was so strong and smart. If she felt the same about me, it was a compliment. "Of course! I'd never tell anyone."

"You swear?"

"Yes. I won't tell a soul."

"Not even Chase?"

"Not even Chase."

Daisy took the end of my blade and cut her hand with it. I watched in horror as her red blood dripped on the metal. "Here. You do the same. We'll swear to our silence over the steel that binds our lives."

This seemed a little extreme to me, not to mention that it was messing up my beautiful blade. But there were many rituals within the various guilds, some involving blood, others involving flour and toaster ovens. I wanted Daisy to trust me, so I closed my eyes and cut my hand. My blood joined hers on the blade between us.

"Ethan is my son. Alastair was his father." If Daisy's pretty blue eyes weren't so intent on mine, I might've laughed out loud.

"Are you sure?" Once again my words came out quickly, no doubt influenced by the painful cut on my hand and the fact that I was still bleeding on the metal.

"Of course I'm sure!" Daisy got up and got us both clean polishing rags to tie on our wounds. "That's why I left him all those years ago. I never wanted Alastair to know. I let someone else raise Ethan for a while. I was afraid I couldn't take care of him. He believes his real mother abandoned him, but I was never far away. He lacked for nothing. I just didn't want him to know I was his mother."

This made me want to cry. How could I not tell Ethan? He had to know she was his mother. No wonder she was so worried about him.

"Say something, Jessie."

"I don't know what to say. I'm surprised. And I think you should tell Ethan."

"No, I can't! And you swore in blood that you wouldn't either. A blood bond is for life. I don't even want to tell you what the consequences are of breaking that bond. But if you think your hand hurts now, imagine that all over your body."

I swallowed hard and reiterated my pledge not to tell. It was going to be difficult, especially when I saw Chase again. "Your secret is safe with me."

She nodded, apparently satisfied. I put the rag around my hand, then cleaned my sword blade. "That will be a much better blade for the blood spilled on it," she promised. "Go to your man now. We've done enough for one day. I'll see you in the morning."

I felt shocked and stunned as I walked out of the shop and into the street. Visitors were scurrying about looking for last-minute bargains. The flower girls were trying to sell the last of their wares for the day. I could hear the musicians starting to play at the main gate, one last serenade as the Village got ready to close.

I wished there was someone I could convince to cut their hands and swear they wouldn't tell anyone so I could tell them about Ethan and Daisy. It was so sad that Ethan would never know she was his mother. Of course, knowing about Daisy would mean knowing his father was a cheap monster who'd disparaged the wonderful sword he'd made so he wouldn't have to pay him. But knowing about Daisy seemed like it would make it worthwhile.

"There you are!" Tavin joined me on the cobblestones. "I've been looking for you everywhere. We're supposed to meet Robin Hood when the Village closes. You didn't forget, did you?"

Between my hand bleeding through the rag and the knowledge Daisy had shared burning in my brain, I stared at her without comprehension. It occurred to me that she'd gone native, like so many others before her. The gray suit was gone, along with the tightly pulled back hair. Tavin was wearing a costume, a sheepherder's pants and shirt, but a costume nonetheless. I thought the day couldn't get any stranger.

"You changed." I cleared my throat and managed to get the words out.

"I know!" She twirled around. "What do you think?"

"I like it." I didn't tell her how many people before her have been affected by the Village, leaving behind their everyday garb, and sometimes their normal lives, to join the residents here.

There are police officers, doctors, accountants, and various other professions and services represented by Village folk. They become pirates, shopkeepers, Robin Hood, and all the other characters. Sure, there are plenty of transients, high school and college drama students. But the real heart of the Village is its permanent residents.

"I don't know why this never happened to me before," Tavin gushed. "I've been to hundreds of Ren festivals with Alastair. I've never been moved to become part of them."

It was always funny hearing someone become a convert. I'd fallen in love with Renaissance Village the first time I visited here. I probably sounded the same way. Of course, my love of the Village might have been influenced by the fact that it was where I first saw Chase. The combination of the Village and its bailiff was too powerful for me to resist.

"So what do we have lined up to make Robin Hood talk?" Tavin asked. "The sooner I discharge all of Alastair's bequests and everything else, the sooner I can be out here on the cobblestones full-time. Did I show you my new boots?"

She held up one foot so I could see the ankle-high boot. It had to be a novelty for her to walk around without six-inch heels. "I don't have anything particular in mind. I guess we'll talk to him and see what he can tell us."

"Too bad. I was hoping the dungeon had some torture devices or something. You know, the Village could probably use a museum for that kind of thing. What do you think? I could become a shopkeeper."

"That would probably work." I saw Robin waiting by the main gate as we approached. Alex had been as good as his word. We must've put the fear of something into him. "There he is. We have to focus. He can be slippery."

"Don't worry about it." She put one arm around me. "We make a great team, Jessie. You should let me help you with that hair once we get all of this settled. You know, there's not a salon here either. I could call it Rapunzel's. What do you think?"

I didn't answer. Clearly, she was in the thrall of the Village. There was no reasoning with people in her state of mind.

A few stragglers were still making their way through the main gate to the parking lot. The bulk of the traffic was gone, so minstrels and singers were packing it in for the night. The girls throwing flower petals were already gone. It was a nice farewell ritual.

"It's about time you got here," Robin, formerly Toby, said. "I have things to do."

"So do we," I countered. "This is Tavin Hartley. She's Alastair's lawyer. We're trying to round up the last of the daggers."

"I gave you the one I found in the toaster oven. I don't know what else I can do."

Tavin walked up to him, grabbed him by the front of his leather jerkin, and pushed him against the wall. "I think there's plenty you can do, Green Boy. You met with Alastair before he died. Why?"

Robin glanced at me in surprise. I shrugged and let the new shepherdess wield her power. "I met with him. He told me he needed money. I told him I didn't have any. End of story." He struggled away from Tavin and straightened his clothes. "Don't think the bailiff won't hear about this assault. You'll both spend some time in the stocks."

"I don't think so," Tavin taunted him. "She's his girl-friend. It's more likely you'll spend time in the stocks unless you tell us *exactly* what happened."

"Alastair wanted to sell me a sword. It was a nice piece, but I couldn't afford what he was asking for it." Robin collected himself. "A long time ago, he did me a favor and helped me out of a legal jam. He threatened to tell everyone about it if I didn't give him the money."

"He didn't realize that would only accentuate your status as Robin Hood, I take it?" I mean, honestly, who wouldn't expect Robin Hood to have had a run in with the sheriff?

He laughed (his big, head-back guffaw) and nodded to me. "You are a girl after my own heart, Jessie. Why did I ever let you get away? If you get tired of being with the good guys, let me know. I'm always ready for the next Maid Marion."

Tavin looked at me oddly, but she seemed satisfied with Robin's answer. "I'm looking for the rest of those daggers. I need them to close out Alastair's estate. If you hear any-thing about them, tell Jessie."

She stalked away, leaving Robin and me alone by the gate. "Sorry about shepherd commando," I offered. "She's new."

"Watch out for her, Jessie. I don't think you should trust her."

"You know how newbies are. She'll be fine. Just make sure she doesn't find any other daggers in Sherwood Forest."

"I will. My best to Chase."

He went back into the forest, which was starting to look shadowy and dark despite the fact that night wouldn't come for a few more hours. Some large clouds had lodged overhead, threatening rain, as they filled with moist air from the Atlantic.

I hurried after Tavin, catching her going past Fractured Fairy Tales near the Village Green. "Wait up! What's the hurry?"

"I'm mad, I guess," she admitted. "I was hoping he'd have all the answers. Instead, it was the same old thing. I'm beginning to wonder if I'm ever going to round up those daggers. I'll be stuck wearing a business suit forever."

"I don't think that will happen." A big thunder boom and some lightning punctuated my words. "But I think we're going to get wet if we hang around out here much longer. Polo's is right over there. Let's head that way and see how the food is."

I felt bad for her. That's why I was willing to share some time with her. I figured if I ate a little pasta, I could always still eat a little something else with Chase later. With his job, who knew how much later that would be anyway?

Polo's wasn't one of the friendlier Village eateries. They never seemed to have leftovers they wanted to share with residents when the day was over. I wasn't sure whether that was on purpose or they were just better judges of how much food they needed.

Whatever the reason, Tavin and I sat across from each other in the plush, Venetian-themed eatery with a glass of wine and several breadsticks between us. The Polo's folks didn't kick us out, but they didn't encourage us to stay either.

"I don't know how you go back and forth," Tavin told me. "Now that I've discovered my inner Rennie, I don't ever want to go back to that other world again."

I shrugged. "I'm working on my PhD. I guess I've been going back and forth for so long, I don't even notice anymore." Which wasn't true, but I didn't know her well enough to share my life story with her. She seemed like Chase to me: someone brought up with money and the best of everything. I didn't think she could relate to my insecurities about living in the Village.

She nodded and munched a breadstick. "My law firm has offices in twelve states. I commute regularly between them. But right now, I never want to see any of them again."

"It happens." The hard rain on the roof was underscored by thunder and the occasional arrival of another resident looking for a dry spot to get out of the storm.

"What about Chase? Is this what he wants to do for the rest of his life?"

I had a brief intermission before I had to answer. Lady Godiva and two of the King's Tarts from the pie shop made a loud entrance, demanding something besides wine and breadsticks. When they had settled down, I smiled and said, "Who knows? This is all he wants right now. We'll have to wait and see."

Fred the Red Dragon shot through the door and looked around the dining area until he saw me. "Jessie! Exactly the person I wanted to find."

I introduced him to Tavin, and he apologized for not sitting down at the table. "I'm on my way to get my tail sewn." He showed us the offending rip in his behind. "Can you believe it? Some idiot stepped on it while I was walking. It wasn't a kid either. Some days, I think I should bring a Taser to work."

"You were looking for me?" I reminded him.

"Yeah. Merlin told me to tell you that he saw Marielle today. He said she took some stuff from Wanda at the first-aid station."

"What kind of stuff?" I was envisioning everything from cardiac resuscitators to scalpels.

"Some gauze and stuff you use on cuts. Something like that. Anyway, that was earlier today. She probably isn't there anymore." Fred was rubbing his dragon head. He had a habit of doing that.

"I'm assuming he called Chase after he saw her?" They both had radios. That put me out of the loop. It was almost seven P.M. No telling when Merlin saw Marielle.

"I guess so. I haven't seen him since he told me." He glanced out the window beside us. "I better go. You know how Portia is. Nice meeting you, Tavin."

When he was gone, Tavin asked me what the conversation meant. "Why are you looking for Marielle?"

I told her about Marielle's obviously fragile state of mind. "I tried to help her. She's not eating or sleeping. I'm afraid she might hurt herself or someone else." I explained that I'd gotten garlic powder in the face for my efforts, but I was still willing to help her.

"Poor thing," Tavin said sympathetically. "She always seemed like a nut job to me. Maybe we should go over there and see if we can pick up on her trail before she hurts someone else."

"It's been a while. She could be anywhere by now. If I could get in touch with Chase, we could find out what happened."

She smiled. "Jessie, sometimes I think you're afraid to do anything without Chase. Sure, he might know something, but we'd all know by now if someone had found Marielle and the daggers, right? It would be all over the Village grapevine."

I had to admit she was right about the grapevine. Robin would've told us if he'd heard about the daggers when we were questioning him. It would've been an easy out. The remark about not doing anything without Chase kind of rankled. I never thought of myself that way. "I guess it wouldn't hurt to check it out. We can always follow up with Chase later."

Tavin got to her feet. "That's my girl! Maybe the two of us will outsleuth the bailiff. That would be sweet, wouldn't it?"

She was singing my song, and my feet couldn't help but go along for the dance. "On to the apothecary, my good shepherdess! The game awaits!"

Seventeen

Merlin's Apothecary is one of the most frequently visited places in Renaissance Village. People love seeing the stuffed birds and jars of bugs and worms. Bottles and vials filled with every color powder and liquid sit on shelves that seem to be suspended in midair. A fine layer of dust and cobwebs cover everything because no one ever touches what's on those shelves.

The items in the counter display cases—magic trick sets, wands, cards, and other paraphernalia you'd expect to find in a wizard's store—are new and competitively priced. And, of course, there's Merlin sashaying around in his purple starred robe and hat, and Horace, a motley old moose head, observing it all from the wall. Visitors like having their pictures taken with both of them.

Going inside is kind of like entering a maze. There's no order to the shop, no clear way to walk through it. You have to do the best you can. I explained this to Tavin, who'd never been in the apothecary. She kind of shrugged it off, until we got inside.

"This place is creepy," she declared less than three steps inside the door. "How do we find the old wizard?"

"You don't." Merlin appeared in a puff of purple smoke. "The old wizard finds you. What do you want?"

"We're here to talk with you about the Marielle sighting. Jessie and I are looking for her."

He peered at us through squinted eyes, his one hand holding a walking stick taller than any of us. "What do you want with her?"

Tavin glanced at me, and I shrugged. Sometimes Merlin was easy to talk to. Sometimes he wasn't. "You know what we want," Tavin said. "We think she stole Alastair's daggers, and we want to get them back."

He put back his head and laughed so hard I was afraid his hat would fall off his white hair. "Of course she stole the daggers! Everyone knows that!"

"Merlin, Tavin needs the daggers back so she can settle the estate," I said, butting in. "Marielle can't keep hiding them all over the Village. They don't belong to her, and they're making her crazy."

"Why didn't you say so? I saw her. She was stealing some stuff from Wanda. Looked like bandages to me."

"Why didn't you call someone?" Tavin demanded. "Isn't stealing illegal here? During the Renaissance, didn't they chop your hand off for stealing?"

Merlin glanced at me. "She's intense, isn't she?"

"Do you have any idea where she was going?" I asked him.

"I might. But I think if you want that information, we should play a little wizard's game."

It was Tavin's turn to look at me. "Is he serious? Should we call the police instead of wasting our time here?"

"Please, dear lady, call the police. I'm sure they'll come right out if you tell them someone stole bandages out here. You can use my phone. I can't reach it, but it's in the inside pocket of my robe."

Tavin actually started to reach for it. I couldn't think of any other way to stop her, so I slapped her hand. Not hard, just enough to let her know reaching into Merlin's pocket was a bad idea.

"What's wrong?" She drew back her hand and glared at me. "This crazy wizard isn't getting us closer to the daggers and outsleuthing Chase."

"Believe me, you don't want to stick your hand in *there*."

"What's this about outsleuthing Chase?" Chase asked as he joined us in the apothecary. "What exactly are you ladies up to?"

"Nothing." Tavin shot a warning look at me.

But I'd known Chase a lot longer than I'd known her, and even if we were new best friends, I didn't think I wanted to keep him out of this loop for the mere satisfaction of solving the case without him. "We heard there was a Marielle sighting around here. It sounds like she might be hurt or something." I explained about her stealing stuff from Wanda.

"Why don't we pay Wanda a visit and make sure that's what happened?" Chase suggested. "Sometimes things are different than they look. No offense, sir."

"None taken, Sir Bailiff. You do your job admirably well for this Village. Please continue." Merlin settled back to listen.

"I never take anything for granted," Chase replied. "What looked like gauze could've been napkins. She might not be hurt, but she might be hungry."

"Bravo!" Merlin applauded. "Let us hie to the healing station!"

"If it's all the same to you guys, I'll wait on the bench outside," I said. "I'm not up to seeing Wanda again so soon. I might not have *any* hair when she gets done with me this time."

Tavin tilted her head to one side and gazed at me. "So that's what happened to your hair. I was wondering, but it seemed rude to ask."

"Your hair looks like it always does." Chase glanced at Merlin for backup.

"Don't ask me," the wizard answered. "I don't take notice of these things."

"Apparently, neither does Chase," Tavin added.

"It doesn't really matter." I put an end to the discussion. "I'm not going in there right now. You can fill me in when you come out." *If you come out alive.*

Since there was no way any of them could talk me into helping interrogate Wanda, Chase, Merlin, and Tavin went in the first aid station without me. I sat on the camel-shaped bench outside on the cobblestones and watched what was going on in the Village.

We were close to the castle, and the royal jugglers were working on their routine using the usually off-limits grass plot outside the castle door to cushion their mistakes. Of course, there were plenty of pirates wandering around, since the *Queen's Revenge* was anchored on this side of Mirror Lake.

I waved to my friend Adora, who runs Cupid's Arrow, a nice little shop that has Renaissance-flavored intimate apparel, candles, and perfumes. I could smell the breeze wafting the scent in my direction. Unfortunately, Chase was uncommonly allergic to patchouli, and everything in Cupid's Arrow seemed to be infused with it.

I saw Master Archer Simmons come out of the Feathered Shaft, his archery shop. He looked to be headed toward dinner at Baron's Beer and Brats. I quickly waylaid him, hoping I'd have this chance to talk to him about borrowing a superior bow and some arrows for the upcoming tournament with Brooke.

"Yes, I saw that," he said with a grin. "She picked the wrong weapon to challenge you with, my girl! Come see me tomorrow and I'll have something ready for you. Of course, we expect you to do the Village proud and knock her on her butt. Winning the fair knight is no small part either, though I daresay Chase wouldn't leave you even if you lost."

I agreed to meet him at his shop tomorrow. The day after would be the tournament, which wouldn't give me a lot of time to practice, but I felt confident I wouldn't need it.

There was always the chance Brooke would call the whole thing off and leave the Village now that Chase knew what she and Morgan were up to. In a way, I hoped she would for Chase's sake. Otherwise, I was looking forward to seriously trouncing her.

Talking with Master Archer Simmons made me feel much better. Enough that I could wave to Wanda when she accompanied Chase, Merlin, and Tavin out of the first aid station. "Come and see me!" she yelled across the cobblestones, then laughed her evil witch's laugh. I shivered at the sound, and she seemed to laugh even harder.

"Well, it looks like Merlin is right," Chase said when they'd reached me. "Marielle took gauze, tape, and antiseptic. It looks like she might've hurt herself."

"I am occasionally correct about such things," Merlin added.

"Now that we have that little tidbit in place," Tavin quipped, "when are we going after my daggers?"

"As soon as you find Marielle," Chase said. "She could be anywhere in the Village. There are thousands of places she could hide."

"She'll have to eat," I said. "We could make flyers with her picture and put them up. Someone's bound to see her."

"We could do that," Chase agreed. "If Ms. Hartley has a photo of her. We don't have one, since she worked for us before we started using digital photos for employee IDs."

"I'll take care of that." Tavin took out her cell phone and turned away from us.

"I'm going to have some dinner, hopefully something someone else pays for," Merlin told us. "If you need any other help, let me know."

Chase thanked him, then, when we were alone, whispered, "You could've told me what you and Tavin found out today."

"I could've if I'd had a two-way radio," I reminded him. "Tavin stayed with me after we'd talked with Toby. Otherwise, I would've been alone."

"Maybe that would be a good thing." Chase moved closer to me. "I don't trust her, Jessie. Watch your step."

"She's already gone native. Notice the clothes? What's not to trust?"

He shrugged. "I don't know. But until all of this is settled and Alastair's pack is out of the castle, I want to be careful."

I wanted to ask him why, but Tavin turned back and put her cell phone away. "I have a power buyer on the hook for those daggers, Bailiff. We need to find Marielle and get them back. The police already said I could have the ones you turned in once the case is over."

"We're doing the best we can," Chase said defensively. "I'd feel better if you and Jessie didn't get involved."

She laughed. "I'm sure you would. But someone has to get the job done, right, Jessie?"

I wasn't in a good position to say anything with Chase frowning at me. I smiled and nodded in a noncommittal kind of way. I wanted to help find the daggers and Marielle as much as the next person, but I didn't want to make Chase angry while I was doing it.

My ambiguous nod seemed to make Tavin happy anyway, and she wandered off down the cobblestones looking for someone else to torment, no doubt.

"What?" I looked at Chase as he started walking in the opposite direction. "What did you want me to say? You know I think you do a great job. But you can use the help, right?"

"I don't think so. Shouldn't you be practicing with your bow for the tournament?"

I walked alongside him as we passed the frog catapult game and Lady Cathy's Crochet. "Are you trying to change the subject?"

"Maybe. Where do you want to eat supper?"

"Look, if you really don't want me to look for Marielle and the daggers, I won't."

"Okay. I really don't want you to look for Marielle or the daggers, especially not with Tavin Hartley. We don't know anything about her, and putting on a Village costume doesn't make her one of us."

"Okay." I thought about that as we continued past Lolly's Lavender Shoppe and Wicked Weaves. "Why don't you want me to look for Marielle? We both agreed she needs help."

"That's exactly why. She already attacked you once. We don't know what she's capable of."

"But she trusts me. I think I could probably draw her out if I hang around down by the apothecary." It seemed like a logical strategy to me.

Thunder rumbled in the distance, and a few raindrops scattered across the Village. It looked as though the storm wasn't finished with us yet.

Chase stopped walking outside Sir Latte's. "You said you wouldn't do it if I asked you not to. I'm asking you not to look for the daggers or the girl. Either you honor your words or not. That's up to you. What about supper? I heard the Lady of the Lake is trying to get rid of leftover cheese-cake and some kind of stew."

The Lady of the Lake was at the other end of the Village, the end we'd recently left. A few more raindrops fell on the cobblestones, and a damp breeze blew past the houses and attractions around us. This was going to be a good night to be tucked up inside.

But we had to come to some understanding first. "I won't look for the daggers," I promised. "And if it means that much to you, I won't look for Marielle either."

"Thanks. That makes me feel better. Supper?"

He turned to walk in the other direction, past all the places we'd come by in the last few minutes. "You know you're crazy, right?"

"Crazy about *you*!" He swooped down and picked me up right there on the cobblestones and started back down toward the Lady of the Lake.

"Okay! That's the way women should be treated!" Three pirates I didn't recognize laughed as they ran past us, prob-ably trying to get back to the *Queen's Revenge* before the storm returned.

"Aye!" Chase returned with a hearty whack on my backside.

"Hey! Cut that out or I won't be responsible for what happens tonight while you're sleeping."

"Coward!" Chase growled. "You can't do any better than that?"

By this time, it was pouring rain and everyone was hustling to get inside. We all knew how personally Portia took it when we returned damp costumes. We were closest to Bawdy Betty's Bagels, so Chase ducked in there and put me back on my feet.

"I think I can take you in a fair fight," I said.

"Yeah? What's a fair fight?"

Betty, the proprietor, came out with her quasi-sleazy manner and asked us if we wanted some bagels. "They're fresh. I can scramble up a few eggs with them, if you like. I know a man like yourself needs his protein."

All of this was said as she rubbed her hip against Chase. If I hadn't been soaked and wondering what was up with him in the first place, I would've suggested we go out in the rain again and make a dash for the Lady of the Lake Tavern.

But I knew everyone would be there if they'd said they needed to get rid of some cheesecake. No one was in the bagel place besides us and Betty. Betty would have to be in the kitchen for a while making bagels and eggs. I was willing to take my chances.

When she was gone and Chase and I were sitting down near the window that overlooked the cobblestones, I took his hand. "You know you can tell me anything, right?"

"What do you mean?"

"This thing with Tavin. Does it have some basis in fact, or is it just that you don't like her?"

"The police call it gut instinct." He smiled and entwined his fingers with mine. "We'll call it that for now. It's not that I've heard anything about her. I'd just feel better if the two of you weren't partnering up to get in trouble. You do a good enough job on your own."

The smile stayed on my face, but my fingers weren't quite so happy to be with his as they had been a moment before. "I think I've saved your butt a few times."

"True. And I've returned the favor. But this is my job, not yours. You're supposed to be making swords for your dissertation. When Marielle threw that powder on you, I realized it could've been something much worse. You were only trying to help, but things can get out of hand."

Part of me was touched by his concern. On the other hand, I was angry that he didn't think I could take care of myself. Did I ask him to stop being bailiff because he might get hurt? No. And I wouldn't. "I understand. But I don't want to make promises I can't keep. If you're not around and I see Marielle run out of her hidey-hole, I'm going to go after her. I don't know how else to be."

He paused and smiled at me. "I guess it's too much to expect that you'd act any differently. Fine. Do what you have to do, but be careful of Tavin and Marielle. The more I find out about Alastair and his crew, the sorrier I am that they came here. We've already had one death. Let's not encourage any more, okay?"

I kissed him, so I didn't notice as Bart (out of his tree suit) lumbered into the eatery. I heard him, though.

"Jessie! I've been looking for you. What about those sword-fighting lessons you promised me? If I'm ever going to impress Daisy, I have to know how to fight."

"Matchmaking again?" Chase asked with a sigh.

"Still." I grinned. "Join us, my large, leafy friend," I said to Bart. "Chase still has his old sword from when he was a knight. I'm sure he'd be a big help teaching you what you need to know."

We all donned padded vests that we got from Phil at the Sword Spotte. He was more than happy to equip us with practice swords and lend his expertise.

Phil gets a little overlooked because the Sword Spotte is the number-two sword shop in the Village. He doesn't make his own swords as Daisy does, but he has a wide

array of swords from every culture. He has a vast knowledge of blades, too. It's hard for some people to get past his
short stature and glasses (he looks more like a librarian)
and ask him for help.

"So is this a workout for you guys?" he asked Chase and
me. "Is the big guy going to fight?"

After the rain had stopped, we assembled on the Village
Green where Alastair had fought Daisy. The wet grass, torn
up in some places, still bore mute testimony to that battle.

"We're showing Bart some moves," I said after intro-
ducing Bart and Phil. I realized my faux pas after Phil
didn't call him by name. I always think everyone knows
each other here. "We're looking at some basic moves like
they teach here every once in a while."

"Yeah," Phil mused, reminding me of Rick Moranis in
Ghostbusters II. "I wonder why they stopped doing that.
They used to give those classes to all the newbies."

"Probably not to him." Chase got the feel of the sword
Phil had loaned him. "He was the Grim Reaper, and now
he's the Green Man. Deathlike figures and walking trees
don't really need sword practice."

The concealed lights came on, even though it wasn't that
late. The storm was gone, but the clouds lingered, making
it darker than it should've been. Chase swished his sword
back and forth. I tried mine a few times. It was lightweight
and easy to handle with a shorter blade than most swords. I
have a long reach so it didn't matter to me. I was sure Phil
was trying to get me something feminine to compensate
for the female anatomy having less-developed muscles—a
frequently mistaken viewpoint. Take Daisy, for example.

Phil's sword was even smaller and daintier than mine.
He swished his sword around and jumped back and forth
with some loud warrior cries. I couldn't help but feel that
he'd be fine against Bart as long as Bart never touched him

with his sword. Otherwise, one blow and Phil would probably be down for the count.

Bart's sword was big and bulky. It was a Scottish claymore, really more for bludgeoning an opponent than sword fighting with any finesse. It looked small in his hands as he moved it with clumsy deliberation. "What do I do first?"

"The first thing you have to remember is that you want this to look realistic," Chase said. "You're never out for blood. This is playacting."

"Chase is right," Phil said. "But you have to make it look good or the crowd won't buy it. We have many experienced swordsmen and swordswomen who know when they see something fake. At least they think they know. That's what you have to do."

"The important thing is to think about your stance and how you move," I added before he was hopelessly bogged down by stupid rhetoric. "It's kind of like dancing. You thrust and you spin around. You parry your opponent's blow, and you spin around."

"You're gonna have him doing the hokey-pokey next," one of the pirates who were watching us called out. Of course a crowd had begun gathering. No one was so busy getting ready for the next day that they couldn't watch a fight.

"Like this?" Bart held his sword out and spun around a few times. Phil jumped out of the way (even though the swords have tips on them, it still hurts when you get hit) and yelled at him to be careful.

"Never mind the dancing stuff." Chase glared at me. "This is serious. I'm your opponent. Come at me with your sword."

The first response from anyone who's never used a blade before is to hold it up in the air and charge forward like in those old Western movies where the cavalry attacks whoever gets in their way. That's exactly what Bart did. Chase sidestepped his charge and smacked him on the backside with the flat of his blade as Bart went by.

"Hey! What's that for?" Bart yelled at him.

"You have to hunch down a little, look at your opponent, and come forward toward his midsection. The only thing raising your sword above your head is going to get you is sore ribs when you get jabbed in the chest." Chase did some fancy hand maneuvers with his sword, then waited for Bart to attack again.

"Okay." Bart did as Chase had suggested and came back at him with his sword aimed at Chase's chest.

"That's good!" Phil encouraged him. "Remember to keep your head up, eyes on your opponent."

The pirates and other Village rabble who had assembled to watch shouted out a mixture of praise and abuse as Bart's thrust came closer to Chase. The two men went at it, the swords clanging in the damp evening air. Thunder still rumbled in the distance.

Bart was about a head taller than Chase and probably a lot stronger. I could see when their blades actually hit that it was hard on both of them. But Chase was in better shape than Bart. He worked out with a sword a few times a week, so he could take the punishment and give some back.

As I watched their blades connect, I realized I could've handled the first hit or two from Bart's sword. Then I would've needed to take a break while I tried to stop my teeth from chattering and find some way to hold my arm up again. No wonder they'd invented guns. They were a much easier way to kill people during wars.

Bart was really getting the hang of it. He and Chase were well matched. I watched as Bart charged toward Chase across the grass, glad this wasn't the real thing. Chase was ready for him, but a voice rang out across the Green. "Hey, Manhattan!"

Chase looked aside for an instant, his attention wavering from Bart's charge. In that instant, Bart's sword hit Chase directly in the chest, knocking him down to the ground, his sword arm outflung.

Thunder boomed directly overhead, but everything else, including Chase, was still.

Eighteen

There was a flash of lightning in the sudden stillness. Rain started pouring down on us as everyone rushed to Chase's side. I felt like I was running in slow motion because I couldn't get to him. Pirates ran past me, and Phil threw down his sword to reach him.

Bart lifted Chase and held him in his arms like a child. He let out a keening wail that sent shivers up my spine as the rain pushed my hair into my face and made the wet ground even more slippery.

From out of the crowd, someone else called out, "No!" It was Brooke. She was on her feet and closer to Chase and Bart than I was. She reached them and started yelling at Bart, hitting him ineffectually (she might've been the rain for all she could do) while she called for Chase to wake up. "You have to be all right. You know it was always supposed to be me and you. You can't die, Chase! I know I've hurt you. I swear I was only pretending to love Morgan. I would never have married him."

I couldn't see Brooke's face, but I could see the look on Morgan's as he got to his feet to follow her. Even the rain streaking across his features couldn't hide the anger and frustration there. Intuition told me that Chase had always beaten out his younger brother for everything. This was one more nail in the coffin of their relationship.

Of course, I knew Chase wasn't dead. There was a wide plastic tip on the end of the claymore. He'd probably had the wind knocked out of him, and he'd have a nice bruise that would be sore for a few days. But he wasn't dead. Even so, I moved a little faster to reach him.

"He's fine," Phil yelled to a chorus of "Huzzah!" from the group around us.

I was glad he'd said something because I couldn't wade through the bodies pressed close together around Chase and Bart. *Of course he's fine. Didn't I say so?* No one gets killed practicing with swords in the Village.

Bart finally stopped his terrible wailing. The pirates moved off when they saw Chase was okay. I saw Bart put Chase back down on the wet ground, and Brooke buried her face in his shirt. I should've been there, but I wasn't. I could only watch as Chase moved around a little and finally sat up. "What happened?" he asked.

"That man over there got your attention, and I almost killed you," Bart explained. "I'm never picking up another sword again." He handed the claymore to Phil with ominous sincerity.

"It's okay," Chase said in a breathless voice. "Really, I'm okay. Jessie?"

That made me feel better. Even though Brooke was there first, Chase was looking for me. How sweet was that? "I'm here," I called out. "I knew you were okay. I've seen you take hits much worse than that while you were jousting. I can't believe you let someone distract you."

"Thanks." He laughed a little, but that probably hurt. He looked at Brooke, who'd finally raised her pretty, tear-streaked face from his shirt. "I'm not dead, honey. Why didn't you tell me about you and Morgan?"

"Didn't you hear me, you big dumb whatever they call you here? I said I love you, and I don't want to be with Morgan. You have to believe me."

Didn't she know Morgan was right there? He was standing behind her, listening to every word. From the look on his face, this wasn't part of the act.

"I believe you, Brooke." Chase managed to get to his feet with Bart's help. His hand was on his chest where the claymore had struck. "But you don't know what love is, so it doesn't matter. I'm in love with Jessie. You and I are never going to be together again."

If Brooke really loved Chase, she had to be in a lot more pain than he was. She demonstrated this by jumping to her feet and giving out a loud growl as she located me in the thinning crowd and ran directly at me. Her hands were outstretched, nails ready for the kill, like the talons of some avenging harpy.

I instinctively put up my sword to defend myself and crouched into a fighting stance as Chase had instructed Bart. I don't know if I would've used the sword or if I would've punched her lights out, but I didn't get the chance to find out.

Morgan reached out and put an arm around her waist, drawing her back. "Save it for the tournament," he grated. "If you really want to hurt her, Brooke, do it while all of her friends are watching."

This advice seemed to calm her down. She glared at me but walked away with him. I took a deep breath and looked up as Tony put his hand on my shoulder. He'd been directly behind me all the time. Maybe he was going to defend me from the murdering harpy. I'd never know that either.

But I did know Chase was on his feet and I was on my way to him. Bart was carrying Chase's sword as if it were the Holy Grail. "Are you sure you're okay?" I asked as I reached his side.

Chase put his arm around me, wincing as he did so. "I'm good now that you're here." He smiled and kissed me.

"If you're finished fooling around out here in the rain, Manhattan," Detective Almond said, "I've got some serious issues you need to take care of."

"*You!*" Bart gave me Chase's sword, which I then handed to Phil. "You're the one who distracted him. You yelled his name."

Before anyone could even guess at what he'd do, Bart picked up Detective Almond and placed him squarely in the Good Luck Fountain. Bart stood over him with his hands on his hips while the rain-enhanced fountain completely soaked Detective Almond.

Everyone stood silently, waiting to see what Detective Almond would do next. Chase finally stepped forward and offered his hand to him, pulling him out of the fountain. Detective Almond shook off, kind of like a wet dog, and looked up at him. "I think I'm gonna need some coffee."

And that was it. Either Detective Almond had a well-hidden sense of humor or he'd always secretly wanted to climb in that fountain. We went to the dungeon, where Chase made coffee and I found towels for us. I sat down on the edge of the bed while they sat at our little table. There wasn't enough room for all three of us.

"The DA isn't willing to prosecute your friend Onslow Chivers. He doesn't like the case."

"Why?" Chase asked, without adding that Alastair's right-hand man wasn't our friend. "Onslow confessed to giving Alastair rat poison. What more does the DA want?"

"He wants him to confess to sticking the sword into Alastair. Without that, the DA won't budge and the guy walks." Detective Almond slurped his coffee and stared at Chase. "Any ideas?"

"Beyond the obvious, no. Maybe Onslow *didn't* stab Alastair with the sword. Maybe someone else did it." Chase sipped his coffee, frowned, and put it back down. Apparently, he was spoiled by Sir Latte's coffee.

"And pigs fly," Detective Almond said. "Maybe they do in here, but in the *real* world, two people don't murder the same person so close together that it's hard to tell if the poison or the sword killed him first. This boy killed your master swordsman. It's up to us to prove that he did it."

"How do we do that?" Chase wondered.

Detective Almond outlined an elaborate plan for proving Onslow killed Alastair. He was bringing in another forensic team first thing in the morning. The castle would be closed except for the people who lived there. In the meantime, he expected Chase to investigate everyone in the castle until they got enough evidence to convict Onslow.

"The DA is only giving me forty-eight hours to prove this one way or another," Detective Almond said. "I need your help, Manhattan. You've got a good eye and some decent instincts. If you ever want to get a haircut and put on a uniform, I'd be happy to give you a job."

"I'll do the best I can without a haircut and a uniform." Chase smiled and winked at me.

"That's all any of us can do." Detective Almond got up (still dripping) and went to the door. "You people are complete whack jobs out here, you know that?"

That was it. He nodded at Chase and left the dungeon.

I realized I'd been half holding my breath the whole time he'd been there. I finally inhaled deeply, like someone who'd recently finished swimming twenty laps. "I can't believe he isn't going to arrest Bart for throwing him in the fountain."

Chase rinsed out the three coffee cups and shrugged. "Maybe he's a whack job like the rest of us. I don't know. I'm not looking forward to tomorrow. Hot shower?"

"I thought you'd never ask!"

Because I had nothing to wear besides my street clothes, I was up early with Chase. We parted ways with a kiss on the cobblestones. Someone had called at six A.M. about a camel running loose in the Village. Chase found some rope and was going to round it up and return it to the animal shelter near the Field of Honor and the petting zoo.

It was misty and foggy after the rain last night. The storm had finally passed over after midnight, leaving behind cooler temperatures and higher humidity. A few residents were up and about: a knight exercising his horse and a few serfs running errands. Most people in the Village weren't even eating their Pop-Tarts yet. The Village didn't open until ten. Why get up before nine forty-five?

I had my wet, dirty clothes with me as I marched down to the costume shop. I didn't know what kind of mood Portia would be in this morning. I didn't care. I needed clean clothes. That was part of my contract working here. Even if I couldn't find her a mate she was interested in, she still had to provide me with clothes.

I put my wet, dirty costumes into the dirty costume bin and faced Portia with what I hoped was the perfect mix of defiance and gratitude. Before I could say anything, she reached out of the costume window and hugged me. I was a little frightened at first, since I didn't know what she was doing.

"Oh Jessie! How can I ever thank you? You were completely right about Ethan."

"I was?"

"Of course you were. And if you hadn't pointed out that we were wrong for each other, I don't know if I would've even noticed Fred when he made his play."

"Fred? The Red Dragon?"

"Yes! We ran into each other yesterday and had tea. It's like a match made in heaven. Neither one of us can imagine why we didn't notice the other one before now. We're so happy, and I want you to be happy, too."

I wasn't sure how this new and improved Portia would affect my clothing allotment, but I waited, withholding judgment, until I saw what she put on the counter.

"I dug up these outfits, which should be perfect for your apprentice duties with Daisy." She put brown shirts and short pants on the counter with matching vests. "I sewed your name tag inside them so you'd have enough to wear while the others are being cleaned, but you should get all three of them back each day."

I was too stunned to do more than croak, "Thank you."

She looked around a little, then said, "And I have something *really* special for your tournament tomorrow."

She put a Robin Hood-esque costume on the counter. It was scarlet instead of green. There were matching long gloves, a cape, boots, and even a cute little hat. "I talked to Master Archer Simmons. He's expecting you this morning. He found you a matching quiver for your arrows. You're going to look terrific out there tomorrow."

This was above and beyond normal. I almost couldn't find the words to say thanks. I looked at the scarlet costume wrapped in plastic and smiled at her. "I don't know what to say."

"I know. I'm the best." Her usually tired face was almost

glowing. "Thank you for pointing me in the right direction. You go out there tomorrow and kick that outsider's butt. Don't let her take your man!"

"You don't have to worry, Portia. Chase isn't going any-where."

"Great. Now get out of the way. I see Fred coming. How does my hair look?"

I told her that her hair looked wonderful. It wasn't a lie exactly, since it looked the way it always looked: tired, like the rest of her. But who am I to argue with love or four cos-tumes? I felt like I'd won the lottery.

I hurried across the King's Highway, past Our Lady's Gemstones. The *Queen's Revenge* floated serenely at anchor. There was no visible sign of activity at either place. The pirates usually didn't stir until noon.

This end of the Village was even quieter than the area around the dungeon. The castle rose high above Mirror Lake, mist and fog swirling around its artificial parapets. The lake was like a sheet of glass, smooth and calm, the castle and the *Queen's Revenge* reflecting on its surface. It was an awesome sight that made me glad to be here, especially holding four costumes and going to get custom arrows for the tournament. I felt loved.

My pleasant thoughts were interrupted, however, when a figure concealed in a black cloak suddenly cut across the King's Highway a few hundred yards in front of me. The figure was clearly headed for the castle and wasting no time getting there. I couldn't tell who was in that dark, hooded cloak, but I was willing to bet it was Marielle. True, the fig-ure looked bulkier than Marielle's thin form, but that could be part of the disguise. She'd last been seen at this end of the Village, so it made sense to believe it was her.

I carefully hid my costumes in an old wooden crate as I passed Eve's Garden. The crate was clean and dry, and

I'd never seen anyone use it. Marielle was moving past the Hanging Tree and the Lady of the Lake Tavern. She'd be lost in the fog if I didn't hurry, but I had to protect my costumes.

I could already smell the barbecue at the Three Pigs and hear a few of the musicians practicing at the Merry Mynstrel Stage next to Merlin's Apothecary. I darted in and out of the fog banks, trying to stay close to Marielle without her seeing me. The way she was moving, she was probably too eager to reach her destination to notice me anyway.

I was a little worried I might not be able to find her once she disappeared into the labyrinth of the castle. I could save Chase a lot of time and trouble if I went ahead and hauled her in for questioning.

The cloaked figure reappeared as we reached the grassy area outside the castle entrance. I didn't stop to question whether what I was doing was right or wrong. I ran up behind her and tackled her on the grass. I knew as soon as I landed on top of her and heard the guttural swearing coming from inside the cloak that it was *not* Marielle.

I pushed the hood away from the face beneath it. "Daisy?"

"Who were you expecting?" She started pushing at me. "Get off of me, Jessie. What the hell are you doing out here anyway?"

"I thought you were Marielle. What are *you* doing out here this early?"

She got to her feet and brushed off her cloak. "Why? Aren't people allowed to walk around before eight in the morning? Is that some kind of new rule?"

I didn't know why she was so angry. Sure, I'd tackled her, but only because she looked suspicious. "No. But you usually aren't up so early."

Daisy kind of shook herself off and mustered a facial

expression between a smile and a grimace. "I guess it was only a case of mistaken identity. No harm done. I'll see you later at the shop."

"Okay. Have you heard anything from Ethan?"

"No. But the boy can take care of himself. I've got to go now." She scuttled away, going back toward the opposite end of the Village. Whatever had brought her out this early, she must've decided against doing it.

I shrugged it off and went back for my clothes. As I turned around, I saw Daisy do an abrupt about-face and head toward the castle again. This time I didn't stop her, and she disappeared into the mist that surrounded the structure.

I didn't know what was up with her. Whatever she was doing, she didn't want me to know. I also thought it was odd that she wasn't worried about Ethan anymore. But there was no point in hyperventilating about it. If she wanted me to know, she'd tell me.

Master Archer Simmons was waiting for me at the Feather Shaft. He had the scarlet quiver ready with twelve red-feathered arrows in it. "These are the best in the shop. They'll fly straight and true to your target, Jessie. I can't wait for the tournament. I'm taking all my pupils to see you shoot the pants off that outsider."

I thanked him for the arrows and quiver. "I appreciate your faith in me. I know with these arrows, I won't miss."

I put the quiver of arrows and the red bow he gave me across my back, bundled my costumes together, and set out to find breakfast and coffee. The Monastery Bakery still wasn't open, so I decided to drop everything off at the dungeon before trekking across the King's Highway to Sir Latte's.

The inside door to the apartment was unlocked. My heart leapt up when I thought Chase must be back. I took the stairs two at a time and opened the door only to find Morgan snooping through the apartment. I should've realized he and Brooke had a key, since she'd managed to get inside previously. Chase needed to have the lock changed.

"Looking for something in particular?" I got great satisfaction out of seeing Morgan jump when I spoke.

"What do you want now?" he snarled at me. "Haven't you done enough damage already?"

"Apparently not. You and Brooke are still here."

He laughed in a vicious way, making me aware that it was only the two of us in the apartment. "You think you're hot stuff, don't you? You're not the first girl Chase thought he was in love with. You probably won't be the last. But when it comes right down to it and Chase gets tired of living like this, who do you think he'll turn to? He'll forget all about you. You should've taken the money, Jessie."

He walked past me, knocking into my shoulder a little before he disappeared down the stairs. I closed and locked the door, then sat down on the bed. Morgan knew how to push my buttons. Somehow he was able to hone in on my fears about Chase. I didn't like it, but my brain seemed to resonate with his words. *He'll forget all about you.*

I looked around the little apartment. Nothing seemed out of place. I realized calling the large room an apartment was a stretch. Chase was used to so much more. How long would it be before he got tired of this and went back home?

There was only a tiny mirror in the bathroom above the sink. I looked in it and tried to envision what I'd look like in ten years. Would I have gray hair by then? I was already getting wrinkles by my eyes. Of course, I could always Botox those, but would the rest of my body hold out? Would Chase still want me?

I changed clothes, replacing my street clothes again with one of the nice brown costumes Portia had given me.

I needed some coffee and maybe an extra muffin to get out of this funk. I tried to take consolation from the fact that Brooke would get old, too. That didn't work as well as I wanted, so I hit the cobblestones to join the other Village folk waiting for breakfast.

As I walked past the privies and Da Vinci's Drawings, a large figure dressed a little like one of the musketeers (the queen's, not Mickey Mouse's) jumped in front of me and swished his large sword. He was wearing a mask, but it would've taken whole body camouflage for me not to recognize Bart.

"Take care, young woman! I am in search of my lady fair, and I will stop at nothing to find her."

Nineteen

I sniffed, feeling a little melancholy about the whole love thing. "I saw Daisy at the castle this morning. She might be back at the shop by now."

"What's wrong?" Bart lifted his mask so I could see his concerned face.

"I think I need caffeine." I pushed a tear from my eye. "Ignore me. I'm indulging in some drama this morning, good sir."

"Okay." He fell in step with me as we crossed the King's Highway. "What do you think of my costume? Do you think Daisy will like it?"

"Sure."

"Did you and Chase have a fight?" He hugged me close to him.

"The course of true love never did run smooth." Shakespeare joined us on our quest to find breakfast. "But let us not to the marriage of true minds admit impediments."

"What does that mean?" Bart asked.

"It means Jessie and Chase make a great couple and they shouldn't break up," Shakespeare clarified. "What's the problem? Whatever it is, I'm sure my fine green friend and I can help you solve it."

Bart held up his sword. "No longer am I a walking tree. Today, I am a gentleman, fighting for my lady love."

I didn't question what made him change his mind about picking up another sword after last night. A few other residents joined us (mostly from the Knave, Varlet, and Madman Guild). As they all discussed Bart's infatuation with Daisy, I was forgotten. That was okay, too. I was only feeling sorry for myself. I was giving Morgan what he wanted. I vowed, as I swerved to go to Fabulous Funnels instead of Sir Latte's, not to be so predictable that he could get under my skin.

I know I vowed something like this before, but I meant it this time. I stepped right up to the counter in the funnel cake shop and ordered one with strawberries and whipped cream. That's right. I was throwing caution to the wind.

"I thought you wanted caffeine." Bart followed me and let the rest of the group go to Sir Latte's.

"I did." I ordered an extra-large Coke with my funnel cake. "Sometimes, it's all about changing things up. You have to do what feels right, right now. Who knows if any of us will live to see forty? This may be all the time we have."

Bart ordered the same thing. "You're right, lady. We have to go for what we want, when we want it."

We got our funnel cakes and ate in silence for a few minutes (except for the occasional slurp of the straw) while our deep, consciousness-expanding decisions weighed down on us.

"You know, it will cost me a year's salary to pay for these clothes," Bart told me. "I bought them special."

"Yeah. I won't be able to eat anything else the rest of the

day if I want to wear my scarlet archer's costume tomorrow either. You have to take the consequences."

"Will you introduce me to Daisy this morning, if she's at the shop?" Bart looked nervous in his really nice musketeer costume.

"Yes. I think you're ready. What you lack in skill, you'll have to make up in finesse."

After polishing off our funnel cakes, we marched out the door and headed toward Armorer's Alley. There was still very little resident traffic, since the main gate was still closed. The sun had begun to burn through the mist and fog. Several serfs drenched themselves in the fountain near Kellie's Kites, trying to stay cool.

Whether by luck or not, Daisy was behind the shop, practicing some of her moves. She was dressed in her standard short pants and breastplate over a black T-shirt. She had a black metal head band holding her springy curly hair out of her face.

Bart and I watched her over the fence for a few minutes. I finally nudged him and nodded toward her. "It won't get any easier than this. Go and woo your lady fair."

"But what should I say?"

"Don't say anything. Let your sword do the talking."

He smiled in a jaunty way I wouldn't have expected from him, put his hands on the fence, and vaulted over the top of it. His cape spread out behind him as he sailed through the air. His plumed hat hit the ground at the same time as his boots. He picked it up, dusted it off, then set it back on his head at a rakish angle.

"Bart?" Daisy whirled and frowned at him. "What the hell do you want?"

He drew his sword without hesitation and saluted her with it. "I have come to woo you, fair lady."

"Great! That's exactly what I need right now." She

turned away from him. "Go home. I don't have time for this today."

But he didn't take no for an answer. He ran up and did a smashing, spinning leap that landed him between her and the door to the shop. "I shall not leave without your heart in my hands."

Well, maybe that was a little over the top (the graphic image was almost too much), but Daisy seemed to like it. She drew her sword from its scabbard and laughed. "All right. If you're determined to do this, let's get it over with."

Not exactly enthusiasm, but better than nothing. Bart guffawed, and they went at it, their swords ringing in the quiet of the Village morning.

"What's going on?" Chase asked as he came up. "Don't tell me Bart and Daisy had a falling out."

"No. They're in love." I winced as Daisy's sword sliced through part of the feather on Bart's hat. "At least Bart's in love. I'm not sure about Daisy. But at least she's letting him give it his best shot."

"Is this a love-by-the-sword kind of thing?" he asked.

"You know it." I glanced away from the love match to look at Chase. "Where have you been all morning?"

"Don't ask. It's hard to imagine so much can go on in this little place. I don't want to think about the things that go on in big cities. We almost need a task force here to counter nightly activities."

We watched Bart and Daisy thrust and parry in the ancient fashion. I was totally amazed at how good Bart was. He must've had some training before yesterday. Or Daisy was seriously cutting him some slack.

"Who knew he had it in him?" A winsome wench dressed in green brocade with a matching parasol sighed as she watched the match. "He's a big hunk of man. Exactly what I'm looking for."

It never fails. If someone else wants you, everyone wants you. There must be some parable for that.

Daisy's sword caught the edge of Bart's cloak. He detached it at a critical moment, and she lost her footing, almost falling as she got tangled in the material. Bart scooped her up in one arm and spun her around to confront him again.

"Wow! Is that the tree guy?" one of the Village madmen asked as he watched. "He's good. Probably make a good knight."

"Only if he rode a buffalo," Sir Reginald, the queen's champion, retorted. "He'd squash a normal horse."

"I don't know," Chase said. "If you had a two-hundred-pound man wearing a full suit of armor, he'd weigh in about the same as Bart. A Percheron could handle it."

Sir Reginald made a snickering face. "Let's hope we never have to see it."

Chase smiled. "You mean let's hope you never have to face him in a joust, right?"

A few of the dozen or so residents watching the battle laughed a little at the idea of prissy Sir Reginald facing the giant musketeer on the Field of Honor. Sir Reginald took his leave.

"Thought he'd never get out of here," Hans the black-smith remarked, sniffing. "Methinks there is a foul stench in his place."

This didn't surprise me, as there is no love lost between the Craft Guild and the nobility. Like most of the groups in the Village, they only tolerated each other.

"He's got some stamina," a pretty pink fairy cried out at a surprise riposte from Bart.

"What are you doing after this?" Chase asked as the sound of swords clanging together continued.

"Maybe making the hilt for my sword. Why?"

"I was thinking about taking you up to the castle with me to take notes."

"Is that a different pay scale from apprenticing?" I smiled at him. Naturally, I'd rather be anywhere with him, even on the same pay scale.

"No. But there's lunch at the castle in it. Maybe dinner, too, if it takes that long. I've got a few extra security guards out here keeping up with things. And Diego and Lorenzo are taking care of vegetable justice for me."

I groaned at the thought. "Then yes, I definitely want to be at the castle as long as the Tornado Twins are yanking people off the cobblestones to throw tomatoes at them."

Bart dropped down on one knee to fend off a flurry of movements from Daisy. The crowd grew quiet enough that we could all hear both of the combatants' heavy breathing. The match was taking its toll on both of them. We all knew this could be the make-or-break moment.

"You're mine now!" Daisy crowed as she lifted her sword arm for the blow that would take Bart's blade from him.

But as her sword came down, he reached up and took it from her. The stunned look on her face was immediate. He followed that move with another, wrapping his big arms around her from behind. She was defenseless and unable to move.

"Do you yield?" he asked in a breathless voice.

"No!" she yelled. "You won't take me that easily, sir."

Bart stood there, not moving, not letting her go. We all watched them, wondering what would happen next.

"Do you yield?" he asked again with a little more authority to his voice. "I shall not release you unless you agree to have tea with me at the Honey and Herb Shoppe."

Daisy held herself rigidly in his grasp a moment longer, then sagged against him. "Make it a cold ale, sir, and you have won my heart."

He shrugged and released her, bending down to pick up her sword. "That sounds good to me. You're a very good fighter, you know. I like your costume, too."

She laughed. "And I like yours, too. You make a better swordsman than a tree. I'll take that ale now, and we'll see what happens after."

I heard people sighing as they left the fence. It was a good match. Whether or not it would lead to a relationship between the pair was anyone's guess. No matter what, Bart would never be a tree or the Grim Reaper again. He'd won respect from the residents. It wouldn't surprise me if the queen knighted him.

"Let's go tell Daisy about you helping me." Chase grabbed my hand. "She looks like she might be kind of busy for a while."

I thought about my meeting her (okay, tackling her) at the castle earlier. I started to mention it to Chase, but it seemed unimportant. We caught up with the happy couple right before they got to Peter's Pub, and Chase asked Daisy about me working with him.

"That's fine," she said. "Maybe Bart can give me a hand at the shop if I need someone."

Bart acknowledged her with a deep head bow. "My pleasure."

"Have you heard from Ethan?" Chase asked her.

Daisy's pretty blue eyes kind of fluttered a little, and she waved her hand at him. "It doesn't matter. He'll get back to me when he's ready."

I was surprised again by her attitude. Ethan was her son. Of course she was still worried about him. Obviously she hadn't heard from him. Acting as if his disappearance was nothing seemed out of character after her concern yesterday. What game was she playing?

Chase seemed surprised, too. "I'm sure he's fine. Probably

sleeping it off somewhere. Alone, I'm sure." He turned to go toward the castle. Bart was walking in the pub door.

For a split second, Daisy and I were alone on the cobble-stones. "Are you okay?" I asked her.

"I'm fine, except for being bruised where my apprentice knocked me on my butt this morning."

"Is Ethan still missing?"

"Yes." She bit her lip. "But I don't want Chase to look for him anymore. You either."

"Why? He might be in trouble. I know you're worried about him."

"Drop it, Jessie. I'll handle it." When she looked at me, her pretty blue eyes weren't so pretty. They were laserlike, with a tinge of frost. "You understand?"

"Sure. Whatever." I walked away, my feelings hurt at first. It didn't make any sense why she'd be so hostile about Ethan. I wished I could tell Chase that Ethan was Daisy's son, but she had way too many swords for that. She probably knew how to kill a person with one heavy blow.

I caught up with Chase, and he slid his arm around my shoulder. "Girl talk?" he asked. "Or sword talk?"

"I'm not sure. Something is up with Daisy. She's acting really strange."

He laughed. "I can't even imagine what strange would be for her. No, wait. Don't tell me. Let me die in my inno-cence. Do you have some paper to take notes as we ques-tion everyone in the castle?"

O f course I didn't have any paper, but it was conve-niently given to me as soon as we walked into the royal living quarters. Lord Dunstable was also there, pre-sumably to keep us from looking in the queen's drawers.

I was also given a real quill pen (the kind made from a feather) by the assistant scribe, Marcus Fleck. His job, it seemed, was to hold the royal inkwell as we walked around the castle chaperoned by Lord Dunstable. I asked Marcus how he was doing. The last time I'd seen him he was the Village crier.

He shrugged and looked up at me (way up, since he's barely three feet tall and I'm usually a giant among women). "It's okay up here. The castle gig isn't too bad. I'd like to be a pirate, but the pirate queen rejected me. I'll try again in a few weeks."

Lord Dunstable insisted we should begin our investigation with the king and queen, since they had things to do once the main gate opened. "We shall not inconvenience the royal personages more than necessary, Bailiff. They await you in their private quarters. I'm not sure if your serf should accompany you." He looked at me with distaste.

"She's not my serf, she's my assistant." Chase defended me. "And if she doesn't go, I don't go. That would leave Livy and Harry to the tender mercies of the real police. I don't think they want that, do you?"

"No. They would not. Please follow me."

"Like we don't know the way there," I said sarcastically. He ignored me.

"This whole Alastair thing has been strange, huh?" Marcus made conversation as we walked down the hall. "I like the evil daggers best. Have you actually seen one?"

"More than one. They don't look like all that much," I said. "And as for their mythology—"

He let out a long whistle. "I know. When I heard Alastair had the stone dagger that killed Aslan, I was seriously impressed. Wonder how someone gets something like that? I heard it was worth more than a million dollars."

I could only roll my eyes at his gullibility. I didn't bother explaining to him about Aslan being a character in a book. It wouldn't do any good.

King Harold and Queen Olivia received us in one of their sitting rooms. It was magnificent. There was a gorgeous mural depicting the travels of Odysseus shown off by a crystal chandelier that created prisms across the room. The furniture was a very good (and probably very expensive) reproduction of Louis XVI style. The Persian carpet on the floor was real enough. Harry and Livy might not be a real king and queen, but they certainly lived the lifestyle.

"Your majesties." Lord Dunstable swept them a low bow, almost touching his forehead to the floor. He stood up again without any problem. Who knew he was in such good shape? "May I present the bailiff and his assistant?"

"Of course, Dunstable." Harry got to his feet and shook Chase's hand. He was always the more normal of the two of them. "Thank you for coming, Sir Bailiff. The queen and I are grateful for your intervention."

Chase shook his hand, then bowed low to the queen. "It's my pleasure, Your Majesty."

A castle servant (I recognized him as one of the squires from last year) moved two chairs closer to the king and queen. He moved a satin-covered footstool over for Marcus.

Lord Dunstable took his leave, asking Chase to send for him before we went anywhere else in the castle. The heavy doors closed behind him, and the room became dead silent.

"Where to begin in such a problem." King Harry shook his head (always careful of his crown). He was a large man, over six feet, with a barrel chest, but the rest of him was quite thin. His legs looked especially small in his pale blue tights.

"It's best to begin where things started happening,"

Chase told him. "Where were you the night Alastair was killed?"

"Here, of course. With my queen."

Livy made a gasping sound and put her hands on the arms of her chair. Her bright red hair was piled high above her crown. Her pale blue satin gown matched the king's clothing and as usual, threatened to spill her bosom out of her bodice. What can you say? It's Renaissance style.

"Do you have something you want to add, Your Majesty?" Chase asked her.

"No, of course not. Proceed, Bailiff." Her retort was short and snappy. The look she threw at Harry was questionable.

"All right. Where were *you* that night, Queen Olivia?" Chase questioned despite what seemed to be the obvious answer.

Livy threw her head back so hard I thought her crown would fly off. Obviously, it was well attached for this performance. Her whole round body shook as though she were having a seizure, and she put one arm across her face. "Oh, God, no!"

Have I mentioned that Livy is the queen of melodrama? Even in a place where melodrama is not only celebrated but expected, she excels at it better than anyone else I know. It might be more for that than her skills as a saleswoman that Adventure Land tapped her for this gig.

"My dear!" The king went to her side and held her hand. "You were with me. Bailiff, I have already told you we were together. What part of that don't you understand?"

Chase's eyes narrowed on Livy's face. "I'm sorry, Your Majesty. But I have to ask these questions."

"You can see this is upsetting the queen," Harry protested. "If there were a real dungeon in this castle, I would surely throw you into it for your impertinence."

"I'll be glad to call in the forensic team," Chase responded. "They're right down the hall going through everything in the room where Alastair was killed."

"No!" Livy shot to her feet. "You are my only hope. As you were once my champion, I implore you to defend me again."

Chase nodded. "I'll do what I can. But you have to tell me the truth."

"I was with that vile creature the night before he died," Livy confessed. She opened a silver brocade purse that dangled from her side and withdrew a small dagger. "Someone knows my secret. I found this dagger on my bed this morning."

Twenty

Livy cried for a few minutes. Chase tried to comfort her and got her a glass of brandy, even though it was barely nine thirty in the morning. Drinking ale this early seemed different somehow. Harry immediately distanced himself from her and the situation, standing aloofly to the side with his arms crossed against his chest.

The pair had a joint history of infidelity, and they'd broken up a few times in the years since I'd been coming to the Village. It was even part of one of the Tornado Twins' comedy routines.

But last year, there was a big, well-publicized reunion, even a marriage redux that was carried in the *Myrtle Beach Sun* newspaper. Apparently, the whole thing had come crashing down when Livy saw Alastair. What was it with women and that man? He hadn't appealed to me at all. I felt like I had when I was watching *The Witches of Eastwick*. I wanted to shout, "He's only attractive because he's the devil!" except that in this scenario, Alastair, rather than Jack Nicholson, was the evil one.

"We'd known each other for years," Livy confessed, still sniffing. "I swear I had no intention of sleeping with him. I didn't even want to *see* him. He bewitched me."

"There's a lot of that going around," I muttered over my notes.

"It's true!" Livy obviously heard me and defended herself. "You didn't know him."

"Come on, Liv," Harry said, disgust raising his voice. "We promised each other we wouldn't do that anymore."

"I couldn't help it." She blew her nose and glared at him. "I tried. Don't you think I tried?"

"Whatever." He completely turned his back on her.

"What time did you leave him?" Chase questioned, a little coldly, I thought.

"About two A.M.," she replied. "What about the dagger? Am I going to die?"

Harry said something about finding a chastity belt and left the room, slamming the door behind him.

Chase stared at the door for a few seconds, then turned back to Queen Olivia. "What about Harry? Where was he when you got back?"

Livy fanned her blotchy face with her hands. "You aren't thinking he was involved with all this, are you?"

"I'm thinking he looks kind of angry. Maybe he knew where you'd been when you got back after being with Alastair. Maybe he went and drove the sword into him before the poison had a chance to work."

"No!" Livy got to her feet. "Harry was there sleeping when I got back. I stared at the ceiling for a long time before I fell asleep. He never even moved. He didn't know about Alastair until this morning."

I was impressed at Livy's defense of Harry. I would've

thought she'd be too worried about dying because she'd found the dagger to focus on him. Maybe there was something to their reconciliation after all. Or at least there *had* been something to it. This probably threw some water on the forge, as Hans was fond of saying.

"You're not going to die because you found this dagger," Chase said. "I'd like to have the police forensic team go over your bedroom and see if they can figure out how the dagger got there."

"Of course, my good Bailiff." Queen Olivia was starting to get over her trauma. She had acquired her customary haughty tone again. "Whatever we need to do to get this evil influence out of our Village. Now if you will excuse me, I must speak to my husband."

When she was gone, Chase looked around the room in a cursory sort of manner. Probably wondering where the metaphoric skeletons were hidden. "So you think Harry killed Alastair?" I asked. "I mean, after or before Onslow killed Alastair?"

"I don't know. What do you think?"

"I don't think Livy or Harry is capable of coming up with that kind of interest in another person." I smiled at him. "But maybe that's just me."

"I feel the same way, my faithful assistant."

"Maybe," a voice joined ours. That was when I realized Marcus hadn't left with Livy or Harry. He was still sitting on the footstool. "But there's been a bunch of whacky stuff going on here since Alastair died. Some of the kitchen wenches say he's haunting the castle. There's been food missing from the kitchen and clothes gone from the laundry. Not to mention lights in the hallways after everyone is in their chambers. Spooky stuff. Makes me wish it was Halloween again."

"I may be wrong," Chase said, "but I don't think ghosts need clothes or food."

"Or lights," I added. "Wait a minute! Were there bed sheets missing?"

"Very funny," Marcus replied. "We haven't found any bed sheets with eye holes cut out either. But something's up here. I don't know if a forensics team is going to figure it out."

"You might be right," Chase agreed. "Let's pay a visit to the laundry and the kitchen."

Marcus raced to the door in front of us and bellowed for Lord Dunstable. He might as well not have bothered, since the nobleman was standing right outside the door. He apparently wasn't taking any chances on us wandering around by ourselves.

Chase told him we wanted to go to the kitchen, and we walked in procession toward that end. I could see uniformed crime-scene people moving stuff out of the suite of rooms where they'd found Alastair.

I wondered whether the room looked more like in *CSI* where the investigators neatly looked through everything, or more like in *COPS* where they rampaged through the room. I was destined not to find out, since the kitchen was in the other direction.

Halfway there, we met Tavin Hartley. She was wearing another Renaissance costume (I was right, she'd gone native). This time she was dressed as a woodsman, from what I could tell. Many Village costumes are difficult to pin down.

"There you are!" She started walking with us. "I've looked all over for you, Jessie. Are you two investigating something here again?"

"None of your business," Lord Dunstable told her. "Away with you, rabble."

"I wish I could away," she retorted. "But I'm stuck here until this is over. I might as well make the best of it."

Marcus growled at her, but Chase asked, "Have you heard any ghostly happenings around the castle?"

"No. Is there a *ghost*?" She looked at all of us like we'd been keeping the secret from her.

"You know about it," Marcus said. "You're always wandering around, sticking your nose in places it doesn't belong."

"My nose has nothing to do with you, little man. Until I find my daggers, I'm supposed to be looking for them."

"Another one turned up in the queen's bedroom." Chase held up the dagger Livy had given us. "How many does that make still missing?"

"Well, your delightful police detective won't give me access to the daggers that have been found so far," Tavin replied with an edge to her voice. "I'm guessing there might be four still out. But don't hold me to that."

"Don't worry, I won't," Chase assured her. "Have you noticed anything unusual going on at the castle the last two days?"

She laughed. "You're kidding me, right? This is a *castle*. It's filled with unusual. There's nothing normal that goes on in this whole place."

"Witch!" Marcus hissed at her.

"It might be better if we do this without you," Chase said.

"All right." Tavin turned to me. "I don't know if I told you this, Jessie, but I took archery in school. I'd be glad to work with you later. Maybe we could meet up after dinner."

"I appreciate it, Tavin, but I'll be fine." I smiled at her, but Chase and the others kept moving down the hall. "I'll see you later."

I caught up with the group, and Chase glanced at me. "Why am I not surprised that she has experience with weapons of some sort?"

"You know, it's not like we're going to shoot arrows at

each other," I reminded him, thinking he was still worried about Brooke. "I'm going to practice with targets. There's no reason Tavin can't be there."

"I suppose not," he agreed.

We finally reached the kitchen, where smells left over from breakfast were colliding with smells from lunch preparation. The castle had about twenty kitchen staff there each day. On special occasions, like the King's Feast, it could go up to forty, with extra serfs and wenches on standby.

Rita Martinez had been head of the kitchen staff since I'd worked there my first year at the Village. She was a large woman who wore an oversized white and brown cotton gown. She stood around a lot barking out orders in her hoarse voice (she sneaked out for a smoke every hour or so), but she was a fair, calm person. She needed to be to keep the kitchen running.

She was glad to tell us about the missing food, which had escalated in the last few days. "It's been noticeable but not bank breaking or I would've reported it. I thought probably some of the castle guests were having late-night snacks. Those people are big eaters to be so skinny."

"But you think something else now?" Chase asked.

"There was a whole leg of mutton missing this morning," she said. "I had castle security keep an eye out last night. No one saw anything or anyone move in or out of the kitchen. Explain *that*!"

"Ghosts," Marcus added. "Or at least, one ghost. Alastair had a big appetite for everything."

"He *did* order a leg of mutton straight away when he got here," Rita said. "There have been some odd movements. Salt and pepper shakers missing. Mustard bottle missing."

"Which could go with the mutton," Chase said.

"I guess." Rita shrugged. "Somebody's getting the food."

"Thanks for your help." Chase left without looking

around the rest of the kitchen. "Let's go to the laundry and see what's missing there."

The laundry was in the basement, still accessible by the elevator that had been used in the old Air Force tower. It squeaked and groaned, barely moving, but eventually it reached its destination.

There was a damp, moldy smell to the basement despite the constant influx of bleach and detergent added to the laundry each day. It was cooler down here under the weight of three stories of mortar and stone. Five large washers and dryers sloshed and slapped in the small space.

Storage surrounded the laundry area. Chairs, tables, saddles, ropes, and cannonballs were all thrown together with no particular order in mind. Everything and anything that had ever been used in the Village could be found here. There was even part of the original *Queen's Revenge*, destroyed by fire right after it was built.

"This place is a hazard." Chase looked around at the debris. "It should be cleaned up. A fire down here would take the whole castle out."

"I shall inform their majesties of your concern," Lord Dunstable said.

Esmeralda, a tiny birdlike woman I remembered from my time in the castle, was still in charge of the laundry. I couldn't imagine it. She had to have plenty of opportunities to get out of the basement. Maybe she preferred to be the proverbial big fish in a really small pond. Here, she was queen of her laundry world. Not a pleasant thought.

She and her two serfs wore stone gray clothing, except for the white mobcaps on their heads. "What can we do for you today, young Bailiff?" she asked.

Chase ignored the *young* part and went right for the information. "I was wondering what you can tell me about the missing laundry items."

She nodded, her gray hair not quite covered by the mob-cap. "There have been some things missing, especially the last few days. But there are *always* things missing. I don't know that it really means there's a ghost in the castle."

"If you could tell us what kind of things," Chase reiterated. "We're trying to understand what's happening."

"Good luck with that," she said with a wry smile. "Well, there have been some women's garments missing. A few men's garments have gone missing, too. Some tea towels. The king's socks—"

"Anything *unusual*, madame." Lord Dunstable tried to hurry the process before she got to anything more embarrassing than socks.

"No. Not really. A bit more than normal but nothing strange enough to be remarkable," Esmeralda summed up. "Sorry not to be more helpful. But people lose things all the time. Sometimes I think there's a void that opens up on the laundry chute and swallows them. Only last month, the queen—"

"Thank you for your time, madame." Lord Dunstable did not acknowledge her with even the barest nod of his regal head. She was so far beneath his station that he couldn't even see her.

"I was only going to tell the story about the queen's knickers."

"I'd like to hear that story," Marcus said, nudging me. "How about you, Jessie?"

"I hardly think that would be appropriate at this time," Lord Dunstable added.

"I'd like to hear it anyway," I agreed with Marcus.

"Me, too," Chase said. "But Dunstable's right. Thanks for your time, Esmeralda." His slight bow was courteous, if not deferential.

"Oh, come back anytime," Esmeralda invited. "I have

a million stories about Livy's knickers turning up in odd places."

We started to leave (not a minute too soon, since I could feel the weird smell starting to affect my nose), but one of the serfs said, "Pity he didn't ask about all the bloody towels. Now *there's* a tale."

We all turned back as one to look at the real laundry ladies of the Village. "Do you mean that as in *human* blood?" Chase asked.

The serf nodded. "Yes, sir. I believe so, sir. There were dozens of them yesterday. It looked like someone got cut real bad. No one knew anything about it. People said it was Alastair trying to stop the blood from pumping out of his body."

"But you would've seen those towels if they were from a few nights ago, right?" Chase asked Esmeralda.

"Oh, these were fresh bloody towels," she explained. "Probably happened within an hour or so. The police took all the linens from the suite where Alastair was killed."

"Why didn't you mention this before?" Chase wondered.

"You didn't ask about bloody towels, Bailiff," she pointed out. "You asked about missing items. These towels were accounted for."

"I understand. Thanks. Any chance one of them wasn't bleached?" Chase looked at her hopefully.

"Not a chance," she answered. "We bleached every one of them. They're all white again now."

We left at that point. Lord Dunstable promised reparations for Esmeralda's insolence, as he termed it. "Don't worry about it," Chase said. "That's what happens when you ask the wrong question."

"Where do you think those bloody towels came from if not from Alastair's ghost?" Marcus asked.

"Probably from someone who also needed gauze from

the first aid station," I replied. "Someone who was injured but didn't want anyone to know."

Lord Dunstable glanced at me. "If there is someone hiding in the castle, I should alert security."

Chase shook his head slightly, and I dropped the subject. He obviously had developed a plan to find Marielle, since the information we'd just heard pointed to her being the one hiding in the castle. And probably scaring Livy by putting the dagger in her room. No doubt another way of trying to point the way to possible suspects in Alastair's death. Why didn't she believe Onslow was responsible?

We walked through the rest of the castle, but the laundry had the only interesting information. We finally left about an hour later, Chase promising Dunstable to let him know if Detective Almond had any further plans to question the king and queen. Marcus seemed unhappy to see us go as I handed him the quill pen. I considered putting in a good word for him with Crystal, the queen of the pirates. Too bad she wasn't all that crazy about me. It might do him more harm than good.

Brilliant sunlight, and Gus, greeted us at the door. "Anything of interest?" the master at arms asked Chase.

"Not much. Have you seen anything of Alastair's ghost flitting around?"

Gus laughed. "If I had, I would've run him through again. He doesn't deserve to be a spook any more than he deserved to be alive."

"What did *you* have against him?" I was sorry afterwards that I'd drawn his attention. What was I thinking?

He smiled at me in that male predatory fashion. "I'd be happy to discuss that with you tonight, Jessie. Come over to my place after the Village closes."

"Not right in front of me, Gus, huh?" Chase put his arm

around me, and we walked away from the castle. "Now I know how you feel about fairies."

I laughed and almost walked into a visitor (the main gate was now open) who seemed to be dressed like Attila the Hun. He had the biggest sword I'd ever seen, and that's saying a lot. It dragged on the ground behind him, making it difficult for anyone else to walk close to him. But it was peace tied, as Village rules decreed, so there wasn't anything Chase could say about it.

"What do you make of the whole thing?" he asked when we were clear of Attila and headed down the cobblestones toward Swords and Such.

"I don't know. I don't think it's Alastair's ghost messing up towels and eating mutton. I think it's gotta be Marielle. I hate to think she could be seriously hurt somewhere in the castle and we can't find her."

"I can have the entire security team sweep through the unused parts of the castle," Chase said. "Someone had to see her when she went to the kitchen and the laundry room. This is why I've tried to get Adventure Land to put cameras in that labyrinth. They don't want to spend the money."

Merlin was coming toward us, a large group of visitors trailing in his wake. "Maybe now would be a good time to ask again," I told Chase. "I'm going to see about finishing my sword. I'll see you later."

We kissed quickly and he was gone, also following Merlin. Maybe he'd be able to convince the wizard CEO to spend some money on cameras.

I hated that it had to be this way. Ghosts, I could handle. Even evil, magical daggers. But murder was something else. I didn't like the real world intruding here.

I grabbed a pretzel from a pretzel-and-pickle vendor's cart. It was late already, but I figured I could skip lunch and make up for the time I'd missed. Chase probably wouldn't stop to eat anyway with so much going on.

I'd hoped Bart would be gone by now, but he was still lingering over coffee, and what smelled like brandy, with Daisy. The two seemed happy together. I hoped for Bart's sake that it would last longer than Daisy's legendary infatuations. I didn't want to think about his big heart breaking. I knew I might have to put a word or two in for him with Daisy.

"Hello, lady." He got to his feet without his usual lumbering. There was a big smile on his face that I didn't think had anything to do with the brandy. Love suited him.

"Hi. I didn't expect to see you here. Are you totally giving up working as the Green Man?" I thought a little lightweight conversation might be in order.

"I'm going to the castle to see King Harold and Queen Olivia," he explained. "The queen wants me to become one of her men."

I stifled a laugh, but Daisy took it seriously. "Verily?" She stood up close to him, laying her heavily ringed hand on his chest. "Be sure to tell Her Majesty that I'll give her a haircut with my sword if she touches you."

"You're jealous?" Bart smiled and caressed her face with a loving hand. "That makes me happy."

"I'll see you later, dear heart," she whispered, then kissed him.

I tried not to watch, but it was hard, especially considering I'd brought them together. Matchmaking was so worthwhile. Chase didn't know what he was missing.

"I suppose you'll want to make that handle for your sword now," Daisy said in a slightly hoarse voice when Bart was gone.

"No. Actually I have another plan. We're going to find Ethan."

Twenty-one

Daisy put her sword in its scabbard on her back. "We're not talking about that again, Jessie. Drop it."

She started walking through the shop, straightening swords and other knifelike paraphernalia as she went. But I couldn't let that answer go unchallenged. "I don't understand. You were upset, even crying about not being able to find him yesterday. What changed?"

"Nothing changed." She looked back at me. Her normally sparkling blue eyes were dead in her face. "Leave it alone."

"So we're completely forgetting that your son is missing. Even though there are so many other things going on, like crazy Marielle, dead Alastair, and evil daggers."

"I said drop it!" she ordered in a commanding voice she usually used only for sword drills. "He's gone for now. That's it. I don't want to talk about it."

I thought of something else. "Have you heard from him? Is that it?" I couldn't believe her attitude and that she didn't want my help. Something had to be wrong.

Daisy took a deep breath and closed her eyes. "Jessie, do you want to finish your sword or not? I don't have time to waste arguing with you. I'm very busy."

I looked around the empty shop and wondered what she was so busy with. Something in, or near, the castle was my guess. Was she somehow involved with Marielle's disappearance? I couldn't imagine how.

But I could tell from the look on her face that she wasn't going to tell me what was going on. And I really wanted to complete my sword. So I gave in. "I guess I'm ready when you are. I thought you might be worried about Ethan and want to do something besides waiting for Chase to find him."

She put her hand on my shoulder. "I'm sorry, Jessie. You're a good friend, and I know you mean well. But this is not the time for us to look for Ethan. I know in my heart he'll return when he's able."

That brought a hundred other questions to mind. Did Daisy and Ethan have a fight? Did she tell him she was his mother and now he needed some space? That last part wouldn't surprise me after all the things he'd said about her. I wished I could've been there when he found out she was his mother. I'll bet even his hair didn't look so good at that moment.

But Daisy's word was law, at least as far as swords and talking about Ethan went. She took me to the Sword Spotte across the King's Highway and conveniently located beside the privies. Phil was a master at carving sword handles (furniture, as they're known in the trade), and he was happy to see me again.

"This looks like a fine blade." He complimented my sword. "You'll need the right furniture for it, not only to show it off but to help you use it. It must be perfectly balanced with the blade for optimum usage. Let me show you."

Daisy thanked him and told me to head back to Swords

and Such when I was ready. "Take your time. Phil's right. This part is as important as forging your blade."

Phil swished a few swords back and forth to give me the idea. I knew basically what he was talking about. I wasn't exactly a novice. But I knew I was fortunate to learn at the feet of these two masters.

I went around the shop and checked out the furniture that might be right for my blade. Many of the handles were too ornate for use with a flat sword. They would be better for dueling swords, which were lighter. I liked the simple, wood handles without fairies (*please!*) or gargoyles. The lighter the sword in my hand, the faster and more effectively I could wield it. I didn't have Chase's or Bart's (or even Daisy's) arm strength.

Phil's shop got busy at that point, and I got tired of looking around. He already had two assistants helping him, so he didn't need me to do anything. I had several choices for my furniture picked out, but I couldn't move forward until he was ready.

My stomach grumbled, reminding me that I'd left my pretzel at Daisy's shop. This seemed like a good time to go back for it—and grab a pint of ale to wash it down. I told Phil I was taking a break and headed out the front door.

King Arthur had amassed a large audience to watch him pull Excalibur from the stone in the middle of the street. The Glass Gryphon across the way was doing a glass-blowing demonstration, and the King's Tarts were trying to lure visitors into their shop for pie. It was a fine afternoon in the Village!

I wandered into Brewster's for my ale (free, since I had my own cup) and then headed across the King's Highway through the Village Square. It was kind of a long route to take back to Armorer's Alley, but I figured I wasn't in any hurry.

A group of visitors was looking at some posters announcing the tournament tomorrow between me and Brooke. My picture was incredibly bad, but Brooke's was really good. I didn't have to ask who created those posters. Renaissance Village wouldn't care, since they didn't have to pay for them. I waited until the visitors were gone, then took the posters down and stuffed them in Ye Olde Trash Can.

I knew if I was smart I would call the whole tournament off. I mean, what was there left to prove? Even if I lost, Chase didn't want to be with Brooke. She and Morgan would probably go home and that would be that.

But some ancient (probably masculine) urge kept me from forgetting about it. I wanted to master her and show her there was nothing for her here. I wanted to beat her so badly that she'd never come back again pretending to be in love with Chase. I had no doubt that if something happened between her and Morgan, she'd come back here, wanting to cry on Chase's shoulder.

That wasn't happening. At least not in *my* Village. So I had to kick her butt. I had no choice. I hoped Chase sort of understood.

I wandered back toward Swords and Such. As I was approaching the shop, I saw Daisy leaving. She locked the door behind her and put out the Closed sign.

I wasn't as surprised about her closing as I was to see her in street clothes. She was wearing jeans and a red tank top. In her large sunglasses and floppy straw hat, she looked more like someone going to visit the county fair rather than an artisan on a stroll through the Village.

I don't really know why, but I ducked behind the fountain in the middle of the cobblestones. I turned my back to her and waited until she went past. It crossed my mind that she might be angry if she knew I was following her, but I told myself it was for her own good. Something was very wrong, and I needed to find out what it was.

A thick crowd of visitors were being entertained by everything from a sweet young woman with a goat cart to some wisecracking jesters who had run afoul of the Tornado Twins at the stocks. The crowd pressed in to see vegetable justice delivered. I kept my eye on Daisy's red tank top.

It was weird that she would disguise herself in ordinary clothes to walk through Renaissance Village. Usually the residents here wanted to stand out—it was good for business. The red tank top made her easier to track even when a team of knights with horses separated us. She was headed for the main gate, and probably no one else realized it but me.

I thought she was going to leave, which would've made following her a lot harder. Then she stopped at the ATM right beside the first-aid station and pulled out her bank card. I saw her push the buttons and take out what looked like a huge amount of cash. I couldn't be sure exactly how much, but it was more than dinner and some ale. Maybe now she was going to leave.

A part of me felt kind of stupid standing there watching her. After all, she might be going shopping for groceries or something. Maybe I was getting too caught up in what was going on. After all, even Ren folk have needs beyond swords and shields. For a minute I was ready to concede that I was wasting my time spying on her.

Then she tucked the money into her wallet and started toward the castle. Now all I had to do was stay with her until she got to wherever she was sneaking off to.

I hadn't figured in the daily rituals of the Village. One of these involved the Sheriff of Nottingham catching and displaying one of the Merry Men from Sherwood Forest

each day. Today appeared to be my brother Tony's turn.
He was trussed up like a pig on a stick and being led out
of the forest by the current sheriff, who was riding a large
black horse. He was accompanied by a large group of varlets and knaves who booed and hissed at the group of the
sheriff's men.

The group pushed between me and Daisy. I couldn't
get around them, and I lost sight of her red shirt. Visitors
flocked to the scene to watch as the tableau unfolded, only
making matters worse for me. I was stranded on the cobblestones with no way to get past the loud group of actors
hamming it up for the visiting Rennies.

"Came to watch me suffer, didn't you?" Tony called out
from his precarious position on the back of the big horse.

"I told you not to play with them," I said, still trying to
find Daisy's red top in the crowd.

"I remember you used to say things like that to me when
we were growing up."

"And I was always right."

He laughed. "I'm not sure about the other times, but I
think you might be right about this time. I'm not getting
paid enough to do this."

"There are always other options." Out of the corner of
my eye, I saw Daisy crest the hill leading to the castle and
pause to look around. *Ha! Gotcha!* But how would I get out
of the crowd around me in time to reach her?

The sheriff's booted knee came into view (right by
my face), and I had an idea. I didn't stop to think about it
because I knew I wouldn't do it if I did. I grabbed his stir-
rup and lifted myself up behind him on the horse. I used to
do it all the time when I worked as a squire. That had been
a while ago, and it was harder than I recalled. But a large,
gloved hand reached over and helped me get situated so
I wouldn't fall.

The sheriff's expression was comical disbelief. "Hallo! Do I know you?"

He was quite good looking, very blond and good teeth. He had a rugged, athletic build that enhanced his sheriff's costume, which was trimmed in rich cream-colored ruffles and gold lace. I hadn't seen the sheriff for a while, but I remembered him being older and definitely not in this kind of shape.

"I don't think so." I held out my hand. "Jessie Morton, apprentice."

"Nottingham, evil sheriff, at your service, ma'am." He kissed the back of my hand and grinned. "Will you be staying?"

"No, I'm afraid not, but I appreciate your help. I'm trying to get to the other side, like the proverbial chicken."

"Not at all. A pleasure to meet you." He assisted me down from the horse's broad back on the other side of the crowd. "I hope we meet again soon."

I shrugged. "It's a very small Village. See you!"

I knew any minute now the Merry Men, led by Robin Hood, would storm the area and retrieve Tony from the sheriff. They'd disappear into Sherwood Forest, leaving the handsome sheriff cursing and yelling after them. The crowd would applaud, then move on to the next event. That's the way it worked each day.

Daisy was long gone, of course. I searched the high area at the entrance to the castle as far as I could before butting heads with the police. I was sure visitors kept trying to wander into the crime scene.

I sat down on a horse-shaped bench and tried to determine where she could be going. Obviously not into the castle, as I'd originally thought. The police wouldn't have let her in. But, if not the castle, where?

The Feather Shaft was right next door to the castle,

along with the Hanging Tree and the Lady of the Lake Tavern. There were a few vendors with movable carts selling flowers and other trinkets. Across the cobblestones was the first-aid station. Merlin's Apothecary was beside the Merry Mynstrel Stage, and Cupid's Arrow was next to the privies.

The good ship *Queen's Revenge* was docking, the pirates getting ready to attack the tavern as they did a few times a day. I knew they came up from the basement through a natural cave in the side of the hill that had been enhanced for the act. That's why you couldn't see them until they were already on the tavern. It was a nice effect for visitors.

Today something seemed to be different. The pirates were scuttling up the side of the hill beside the tavern and attacking from the front. I saw my friend, Tom Grigg, who was once a respected member of the Myrtle Beach Police Department before he went native like Tavin. He was in the thick of things, cutlass in his mouth, a red scarf tied around his head.

"Avast, me hearty!" I greeted him. "Why are you attacking from up here?"

"Arr! The cave be closed, good lady. Some scallywags are doing work on it. What's a decent pirate to do?"

"Drink rum and steal things!"

He rattled his saber at me and grinned. "Exactly!"

I watched him and the other pirates in the group rush into the tavern and heard the screams from inside as they did their worst for the crowd. I'd never seen the cave closed, but on the other hand, repairs had to be made from time to time. It struck me that the cave would make an easy and convenient hiding place in this area—the very same area where Marielle kept popping up. Maybe she knew something the rest of us didn't know.

I decided it would take only a few minutes to find out

if that's where she was hiding. I'd lost Daisy's trail and would have to pick it up later anyway, but maybe I could find Marielle.

Someone poked something into my back and whispered, "Ahoy, matey. Don't look now, but I have the drop on you."

It was Tavin pushing her finger into my back. "I had you, didn't I? Are there any female pirates? I think it might be fun being a pirate."

I was amazed at how much she'd changed in the last few days. Her face was a little smudged, and her blond hair was wild. "I think there's only one female pirate, and she's the queen," I explained. "I think she likes having the men around her."

"Just an idea. Only one of hundreds. What are you doing out here, Jessie? Has Chase found all of the daggers yet?"

"Not yet. As for me, I'm still looking for Marielle. She's out here somewhere. I'm wondering if she's hiding in the pirates' cave. Want to help me explore?"

"Sure! Sounds like fun. Do pirates really have gold or is it fake?"

"As fake as Alastair's evil, magical daggers," I replied, starting down the side of the hill toward the edge of Mirror Lake.

"Yeah. Well, they may be fake, but they're worth some money to his followers."

"And his children, right?" I pushed aside some brush that had been piled up by the maintenance crew trimming bushes in the area. It was always a challenge keeping things hidden from visitors.

"Oh, yeah. Them, too." She followed me.

The pirates' cave was securely situated so that it would be difficult for a wandering visitor to find. Even many of the residents didn't know where it was.

For one thing, you had to approach from the lake, like

the pirates did. There was a small footpath that ran from the *Queen's Revenge*'s dock to the cave. It was nothing more than some sand between plants, stones, and pieces of tree bark.

"Are you sure you're going the right way?" Tavin asked a few times as we went down to the edge of the lake, then started back up again.

"Besides being with the pirates one summer, I've had a few run-ins with them. I know where the cave is."

"And why do you think Marielle is hiding here?"

"Because she keeps showing up in this area. I didn't think about the cave until I heard it was closed to the pirates. It would give her easy access to the castle and the first-aid station."

"First aid? Did she cut herself on one of the daggers or something?"

"I don't know." I explained about the bloody towels and the gauze. "Maybe we'll find out."

"Maybe Marielle and the queen got into it over Alastair. Maybe that's why she hid the dagger in the queen's bedroom."

At the mouth of the cave there was more loose brush that the pirates used to camouflage the entrance when it wasn't in use. A small sign, the kind Adventure Land normally used to close something for renovation, was tacked to the side of the cave. But I could tell the brush had been moved recently. Half of it was still on one side of the cave. Sloppy work. I'd have to speak to Merlin about it.

"It looks like someone might be here," Tavin said. "I hope it's Marielle with the rest of the daggers. I'd like to get that over with so I can really have a good time and forget about everything else."

I couldn't say why, but something about the tone of her voice bothered me. It sounded fake, unlike Grigg, who'd also gone native. Tavin seemed stressed, more so than she normally did. I wished I'd come down here by myself, but it was too late. The door to the cave opened in front of us, and Daisy stepped out.

"You had to keep looking, didn't you?" She pulled out her sword and held it on me and Tavin. "Come on in, but you won't be going back out for a while."

"What's going on?" I walked into the cave with Tavin, Daisy and her sword flanking us until the door was closed again.

"Nothing much," Daisy explained. "I'm trying to help Marielle and Ethan get out of the Village. We've got everything together now. We only have to wait until it gets dark."

There was a dim light in the cave. I could see Ethan and Marielle standing close together. Obviously, Marielle's undying allegiance to Alastair had changed. I knew there was more to this than I had realized. It certainly happened very quickly.

Daisy motioned to me and Tavin with her sword, and we sat down on some crates. "We're all going to sit here and wait until dark. Then Marielle and Ethan are leaving. I'll let you two go as soon as they're gone."

"I'm sorry, Jessie," Marielle said. "I didn't mean for you to get involved this way."

I noticed the bandage on Ethan's hand. That's where the bloody towels in the castle had come from and where the medical supplies were being used. "Why are you doing this? The police aren't looking for Marielle, except for her own good. It's not like she's a suspect or anything."

"You don't understand," Ethan explained. "Marielle took the daggers to show the police who could be guilty of Alastair's death. When the police figure out she took them, they'll arrest her."

I laughed. "They already know she took them. Chase and I figured that out a while back. I can't believe you've been holed up here because of that."

"It's not only that," Marielle cut in. "Ethan and I fell in love with each other when I asked him about the daggers. It was love at first sight. He was hurt trying to save me from an attacker. Someone tried to kill me, Jessie. Whoever it is wants the daggers. I think it might be the same person who killed Alastair."

Obviously the evil, magical daggers were at work again. Ethan had been with several different women in the last few days before he fell in love with Marielle. It was just as likely they'd be with other people next week, as soon as this adventure was over. Sometimes life in the Village is like a soap opera.

"I've been trying to keep them both safe," Daisy added. "This seemed like a good place to hide where no one would notice what was going on."

I heard Tavin chuckle beside me. "Good thinking. I couldn't have set it up any better myself. Thanks, Daisy." She drew a small gun from her pocket and pointed it at her. "Now, put down that stupid sword and let's have a little chat."

Twenty-two

"What are you doing, Tavin?" I asked.

"Collecting what belongs to me." She nudged me with the gun. "Join your friends, Jessie."

"I knew it wasn't Onslow." Marielle took the opportunity (however bad her timing might be) to declare her triumph. "He might be willing to poison Alastair, but he'd never shove a sword into him."

The distinction was lost on me. "Are you saying Onslow was too scared of Alastair to kill him with a sword?"

"Exactly! We were all in awe of him. No one would be brave enough to do something like that to him." Marielle grinned at me.

"Will you all shut up?" Tavin snapped. It was a command, not a question. "I can't think with all of you babbling."

"Poor Tavin," Marielle taunted. "Alastair wouldn't even look at your skinny ass! You wanted him like a fish wants water, but he *never* wanted you."

I realized that Marielle might have saved us a lot of

trouble if she'd said that a few days ago. I'd had the impression that Tavin might be one of Alastair's conquests, but she'd seemed too rational. How could someone that rational put a sword into a man?

"Don't make me kill you, Marielle," Tavin threatened. "I never wanted to hurt anyone, especially Alastair. He abused me, you know? He took money from me and swore he loved me, but he slept with you and all those other girls. You people are all insane, you know that? With your stupid Renaissance clothes and stupid ideas about having fun. I never understood what Alastair loved about this."

"I don't think anyone else has to die." Daisy got up and approached Tavin with her hands held out. "Take the rest of the daggers and leave us alone."

Tavin played with her hair, her eyes frantic. "I'm afraid it's not that easy. Now that all of you know, you'll go to the police. The daggers aren't worth enough money to keep me in the lifestyle I'm accustomed to unless I go live in a third-world country. I don't see any way to leave the four of you alive."

It was a tough spot, more for us than for Tavin. Daisy remained standing, looking at Tavin. I was wondering what she had in mind.

"For right now, you can get me the rest of the daggers," Tavin yelled at Marielle. "Trust me, you're the only one I'd really like to shoot. He loved you, you know. He wanted to give up everything and go away with you somewhere. After he used me all those years to build up his reputation, I wasn't going to let that happen. I won't ever get that money back, but everyone wants those stupid, worthless daggers. I'll be able to retire on what I can get for them at auction."

Marielle got to her feet. "I don't have any of them left. I put them all in the Village, except the one Onslow took. I think the police have the rest of them."

"I don't think so." Tavin waved the gun at her with a shaky hand. "The police only have eight of them. I know. I checked. Where are the other four?"

"I told you. I hid them around the Village," Marielle replied. "And I'd rather you shoot me than take you to them. You don't deserve our lord's daggers, even though they would no doubt kill you for taking his life. His blood is on your hands."

"It wouldn't do much good to kill her," I told Tavin, maybe hoping to create some kind of rapport with her. "She wouldn't be able to tell you where the daggers are."

"Maybe I should kill her boyfriend then." Tavin held the gun on Ethan. "He got in my way the other night. I meant to hurt *her*."

"Don't hurt Ethan, you witch!" Marielle ran at her, knocking Tavin to the floor of the cave. The two women wrestled, rolling toward the mouth with Tavin's gun pointed toward the ceiling.

Ethan jumped on top of Tavin, heedless of his injured arm and perfect hair. The three of them looked like a clump of wrestlers going at it in a dirty ring. Dust billowed up around them.

"Ethan!" Daisy shouted his name, then added her bulk to the fray. It was difficult to tell one from the other as they all tried to reach the gun. I saw arms and hands flailing out, but the torsos stayed glued together. I didn't know how anyone could tell who they were fighting.

A shot rang out, echoing through the cave. It was inevitable. Everything stopped. I couldn't tell what had happened and didn't dare move close enough to find out. I was frozen in place, waiting and watching. Was someone hurt or did the bullet go into the cave wall? Had someone upstairs in the tavern heard it and help would shortly arrive?

The last was useless as the pirates attacking the tavern

were even now firing their fake pistols and crashing furniture. They were making too much noise to hope it hadn't covered up the gunfire in the cave.

It's what they do every day. Ten and two and six like clockwork. Visitors expect it. Everything else is exactly as it's supposed to be. We're the ones out of sync.

Finally someone in the bunched-up wreck of bodies on the ground groaned. It broke the silence that followed the gunshot and seemed to move everything forward at an accelerated pace. I rushed to the group and tried to sort them out.

Daisy fell back against the ground, her hands clutching her chest. She'd been shot. Blood was gushing through her red tank top, soaking it darker. "The only time I'm not wearing my breastplate," she joked, then closed her eyes, passing out as her life's blood trickled to the dirt beneath her.

"Daisy!" I knelt down and tried to revive her. I pushed her shirt up and looked at the small, ugly hole in her chest. How could so much blood come out of such a small hole?

"I'm not playing games here." Tavin got to her feet behind me. "Jessie, tie lover boy up over there." She waved the gun at me. "You, Marielle, and I are going for a walk through the Village to find those daggers."

"Daisy needs help," I argued. "We can't leave her like this. She'll die."

"I don't give two figs about Daisy dying." She pushed the gun against the side of my head. "Tie him up or you'll die a lot faster than Super Sword Woman. Then I'll start to work on Marielle."

"Do it, Jessie," Ethan urged. "I can't live if something happens to Marielle."

"What about your mother?" I blurted out, not realizing what I'd said until it was too late. Oh well, in for a penny, in for a pound. "Daisy's your mother, okay? Alastair was your father. He's dead. We can't save him, but we can help her."

Tavin pushed the gun a little harder against my head. "Shut up and do as you're told. You're not helping Daisy by making this take longer. If Marielle cooperates, maybe we can find those daggers and come back here in time to call EMS and save her."

"Like that's going to happen." I glared at her, wishing an evil, magical dagger would jump up and stab her in the eye. That seemed like the only thing that might save us.

I didn't know what else to do but comply. The heavy smell of blood, sweat, and gunpowder made me feel sick. I tied Ethan against some barrels with the rope that was lying around the cave. In the tavern, they used it for mock hostages. Those people were released and given a coupon for a free tankard of ale.

I don't know why I was focusing on these irrelevant details in the face of such terrible trauma. None of it seemed real, even with Daisy dying on the cave floor. My mind refused to function. But then, suddenly, miraculously, a small, sane voice echoed in my head: *Get Tavin out in the open. At least you'll have a chance to get away from her or find help. There's nothing you can do in this cave but die.*

As I finished tying Ethan, Marielle stuffed some torn material from her dress against Daisy's wound to staunch the bleeding. Daisy's face was completely white, her eyes shadowed and lips pinched tightly together.

"Are you *sure* she's my mother?" Ethan whispered as I made a show of securing the knots.

I told him how I *knew* she was his mother, and he grimaced. "Did you think she let you get away with so much crap because you have such great hair?"

His face turned as red as Daisy's shirt. "I don't know. I never thought about it. *My mother?*"

I nodded and left him there to stew, his perfect hair not so perfect, a streak of dirt on his cheek. He looked human for once instead of too good to be true. I couldn't tell him that I had left the knots loose so he could get away and find Chase. I had to hope he'd test them as soon as we were gone. It was my backup plan in case my first plan to escape from Tavin and get help didn't work out.

"Okay, that's enough blubbering and whispering," Tavin said. "Let's get on with this."

Marielle turned to walk out of the cave and vomited. I felt like doing the same but managed to hold it in. Ethan urged her to be strong. Tavin threatened to shoot him if he didn't keep his mouth shut.

"Which way first?" Tavin grabbed Marielle's arm. "And don't take too long doing it. I don't want you to get any stupid ideas about wandering around until someone takes notice. You got it?"

Marielle wiped her mouth on her dress and nodded. Tavin positioned herself between me and Marielle, probably trying to make it look as if we were three friends out for a stroll. That was good for me because she was focused on Marielle—giving me a better chance of slipping away when we hit some crowds.

"Don't think I've forgotten about you, Jessie." Tavin gave me a nasty smile, then handed me a friendship bracelet sold commonly around the Village. It was shaped like a figure eight, the idea being that two friends, or lovers, could use it to tie themselves together. "Put it on. We wouldn't want to get separated, would we?"

So much for my plan. The gun might be on Marielle, but how was I going to get away when I was attached to the she-devil?

My brain started on Plan C. That would be Chase seeing the three of us together and realizing it was an unholy alliance. He'd want to know why I was with Marielle and hadn't found a security officer to take her. Tavin probably wouldn't realize that, I hoped. Maybe she was too engaged in finding the daggers before she killed all of us.

Of course, that meant running into Chase, which might or might not happen. The Village was packed as we reached the side of the Lady of the Lake and started to walk down the cobblestones. Marielle seemed unable to speak. She pointed when Tavin asked her which way we should go. Apparently, the dagger we were looking for was on the opposite end of the Village.

Plan D formed in my mind when Merlin waved and said hello as he passed us, his robe flying out around him. If I ignored enough people, someone was bound to ask what was wrong. Maybe I couldn't *tell* that person, but maybe he or she would get the idea.

It wasn't Merlin. He kept walking at a fast clip toward the apothecary. It wasn't my friend Adora standing outside her door at Cupid's Arrow. She waved, then resumed talking with a visitor.

We passed Galileo, who nodded in my direction but was quickly consumed by questions from his students. We were on our way to a good part of the Village for me. Wicked Weaves was right across the cobblestones from the Glass Gryphon, which was next to Bawdy Betty's Bagels and the Peasant's Pub. I knew all of these businesses very well. Their owners were bound to speak to me.

Too bad Marielle pointed off the cobblestones toward the Village Square. Foot traffic was thick through here but unremarkable in Village folk who might get suspicious if I ignored them.

"Enough with this silent crap." Tavin shook Marielle. "Tell me where it is."

Marielle's head rolled on her shoulders like a rag doll's, but the harsh treatment seemed to bring her back to herself. "Over there. I hid it behind the dais where the king and queen scorned my lord Alastair. I wanted to remind them that they were part of his death."

Tavin laughed. "The only thing that was part of Alastair's death was his stupidity. He shouldn't have claimed to be immortal if he didn't want it to be tested."

"Is that why you shoved the sword into him?" I asked.

"He was dead already," she replied. "He just didn't know it. Onslow saw to that."

"Which you didn't know when you skewered him," I reminded her.

"True. I had my own issues with his stupidity."

"Like him ignoring you and giving Marielle his chastity belt to wear while she slept on the floor next to him?" I stared at her, catching her wild-eyed gaze. "What was it exactly that made you want him?"

"He was Alastair," she answered so quietly I could barely hear her over the crowd noise around us. "He was . . . *everything*."

We located the first dagger exactly where Marielle said it would be. I looked around for a friendly face but saw none. I knew so many people in the Village, it seemed impossible that no one noticed us. Where was Chase? Had Ethan figured out yet that he wasn't really tied to the wall?

I didn't hear the wail of a paramedic siren coming our way, so I had to assume he was still sitting there waiting for us. Marielle told Tavin the next dagger was at the Hawk Stage.

"Why there of all places?" Tavin demanded.

"Because my lord was spurned by Lady Lindsey," Marielle explained. "I thought it appropriate to hide a dagger there."

"That's because there's something wrong with you," Tavin said. "Let's get moving."

We walked from the Village Square past the Lovely Laundry Ladies. We walked right by Da Vinci's Drawings,

but Sam must've been out for a break. No one was there.
I tried to keep myself from panicking. We were going to
pass someone who would stop and want to chat. We'd pass
Chase and he'd realize something was wrong. Ethan would
figure out he could escape from the cave and go for help.
Something was going to happen that would save us from
becoming bloody heaps of flesh to be found sometime later.

There were minstrels playing a lovely Renaissance
piece with harp and flute, their copper pot ready for
tips. A beggar wearing only strips of cloth was holding on
to a visitor's leg as he tried to walk away without leaving
any alms. Fashionable ladies strolled by with parasols to
shade them from the hot sun, their pretty gowns dragging
in the sandy dirt behind them. Jugglers tossed apples and
loaves of bread while acrobats did cartwheels down the
cobblestones.

It was another afternoon in Renaissance Village, only
now I couldn't appreciate any of it. All I could think about
was Daisy dying and the rest of us following her while
Tavin got away with the daggers.

Where is everyone? Any other time, thirty people would
have wanted to chat as I went by. Even the elephants and
camels seemed quiet as we approached the Hawk Stage.

Lady Lindsey was performing with her songbirds. She
whistled, and they flew up above her, doing tricks for treats.
She had three little bluebirds, a few robins, and a cardinal.
They swirled colorfully through the hot afternoon, flying
out over the heads of appreciative visitors in the audience
and returning to the stage.

"Where is it?" Tavin demanded.

"In her closet, behind the stage," Marielle answered. "I
thought she'd have found it by now."

"This is as good a time as any." Tavin directed her toward the back of the stage after briefly taking in the situation. "Lead us then."

There had to be something else I could do. Some way to get free. I chanted this mantra over and over in my head as I looked all around me for an answer. Maybe I could grab a rock and hit Tavin in the head with it before she could shoot Marielle. Maybe if I could snatch some popcorn from a nearby vendor, I could throw it in her face.

But nothing feasible came to mind.

How could we be so invisible in a village full of people? Someone had to notice Tavin was carrying a gun. But would it be in time?

As I scanned the area, frantically searching for an answer, one came to me. We were walking in the small green space between the Hawk Stage and the elephant rides when I saw Brooke and Morgan.

Brooke was practicing her archery with a target set up on a bale of hay, probably borrowed from the elephant handler. Her aim was straight and true as she let fly a few arrows. The tips hit the bulls-eye and sank deep into the straw. She obviously knew what she was doing choosing archery to challenge me.

I watched her practicing as Tavin, Marielle, and I waited to enter the rear of the stage. Lord Maximus was coming out with his group of trained hawks. He was the centerpiece act, or was supposed to be, but birds of prey seemed to draw smaller crowds than beautiful Lady Lindsey and her low-cut gown.

Tavin fretted impatiently, pulling Marielle closer to her, trying to shield the gun. I stared at Morgan and Brooke, hoping to attract their attention. But they were focused on their target: beating me in the tournament tomorrow.

There was a small brown hawk in a cage right by my

foot. It was waiting to be retrieved by Lord Maximus, fed and watered, then put up for the night. Knowing Tavin's attention was on the big trainer and her goal to retrieve the dagger, I took the opportunity to nudge the loose cage door with my foot. It came open, but the hawk remained stubbornly in its cage. No help there.

I need you, I mentally implored the creature but got no response. The bird's eyes were half closed. My psychic communication wasn't working with Chase either. Obviously not a good day for it. There was probably something in my horoscope about it.

I kicked the cage a little. The hawk brought up its wings and opened its eyes, but still didn't try to escape. *What would it take?*

I glanced at Tavin, who was busy shoving the gun harder into Marielle's side. She hadn't noticed me trying to free the hawk. I kicked the cage harder, and this time the hawk gave a loud screech and flew out of the cage. Unfurling its large brown wings against the sky, the bird looked back down at all of us but then noticed Lady Lindsey's colorful snacks doing their routine.

"Great!" Lord Maximus put down a cage that held an eagle. "That's Penelope. She's crazy. Lindsey's little birds are history. How did she get free?"

He glared at me and I nodded toward Marielle and Tavin, hoping he'd see our predicament. I didn't know Maximus well, but I hoped for the best.

In the meantime, Penelope began chasing Lindsey's birds. That attracted plenty of attention from the audience as well as passing visitors. People began shouting, even screaming, as they realized the peril the little birds were in. Everyone moved toward the Hawk Stage to see what was going on. Morgan and Brooke joined them.

I had to admit Brooke looked magnificent in her black

archer's costume. Her aim had been good. She stood a better than average chance of beating me tomorrow. She wouldn't, of course, not if I survived today.

I tried to make eye contact with the deadly duo, but all eyes were glued on the smaller birds' flight for survival as the hawk ignored Lord Maximus's orders to return to her cage. Brooke and Morgan weren't close enough for me to kick them and get their attention. And Maximus was too worried about his hawk to realize what was going on right beside him.

"We'll have to come back for this one." Tavin decided to leave as Brooke noticed me standing close by. "Where's the next one?" she hissed at Marielle.

No! I'm so close! Not yet.

"The next one is hidden in the clock shop," Marielle replied.

"I don't even want to know why," Tavin said. "Lead the way."

"I hid it there because my lord lost so much of his time here on earth. It was stolen from him by you and Onslow." Marielle's voice carried a hazy ring of prophecy.

"I don't care," Tavin said. "Get moving."

We were about to leave the area when I felt a tap on my shoulder. It was Brooke and Morgan, smiling smugly at me. For once I was happy to see them.

"Jessie, I thought you'd be practicing," Morgan said. "Instead, here you are spying on us. Are you worried after seeing how good Brooke is with a bow?"

"Good? You call that good? I shot better than that when I was a kid. She doesn't stand a chance."

"Get rid of them," Tavin whispered as she jerked my arm with the friendship bracelet.

"Maybe we should have a side bet to spice up the competition," Brooke suggested.

"That would be fine with me," I goaded her, "except you'd have to put your money on me to keep from losing."

"I said get rid of them," Tavin whispered close to my ear. "Do it now, unless you want Marielle to end up like Daisy."

Twenty-three

"I don't know what Chase sees in you," Brooke taunted.

"Obviously something he never saw in *you*!" I retorted.

"Bitch!" she muttered.

Someone jostled Marielle, and Tavin had to shift position to keep the gun against her. She was off balance, still waiting to get away from the crowd pressing in. There would never be a better time to make my move. I knew it was going to be painful. But painful was better than dead.

I had to up the stakes. I needed more than a shouting match between me and Brooke. I brought my free hand back and slapped her hard in the face. Her eyes widened and her cheek turned red. She threw her bow on the ground and slapped me back, grabbing my hair and pulling me toward her as she howled in rage.

I saw two security guards out of the corner of my eye. They weren't paying attention. They had to come closer and investigate. I needed them to be right here when Tavin finally realized what was going on.

So I kicked Brooke before she could move away from me. She made a little sound in the back of her throat (like a growl) and did exactly what I'd hoped she'd do. She launched herself at me, knocking me to the ground. The friendship bracelet that bound me yanked at Tavin's arm, dragging her down with me.

Marielle ran away and disappeared into the crowd that was suddenly more interested in a catfight than a hawk chasing some songbirds. Maybe I should've been upset that Marielle left me there with Tavin, but I was relieved to see her go. No matter what else happened, she was free. She'd go back to the cave to save Ethan and Daisy. Maybe we wouldn't die after all.

From my unique vantage point on the ground I couldn't see whether the security guards were coming our way. Brooke pummeled me—I protected my face with my free hand. We grunted and rolled around in the grass. Tavin was still connected to me, dragging behind. I couldn't see where the gun had gone. Had she dropped it, or was it pointed in my direction now?

Someone grabbed my shoulders and forced me to my feet. The friendship bracelet finally snapped (I was surprised it had lasted that long), freeing me from Tavin. Another security guard was holding Brooke back as she kept trying to come at me. There was no way to tell her she was only a diversion to save our lives. I didn't try.

"What's going on here?" the security guard who'd picked me up snarled. His tone changed when he recognized me. "Jessie? What are you doing? Chase is on his way. He's not happy about this commotion."

I looked for Tavin and saw her trying to sneak away. "Never mind me. Grab her! She's the one who killed Alastair and shot Daisy!"

No one moved. This wasn't something covered in the

security guard manual. The two security guards looked at each other and shrugged, obviously content to wait for Chase as the final authority.

Tavin was going to get away. I saw Brooke's bow on the ground near my feet. I snatched it up, then grabbed one of the target arrows from the quiver still on her back. She screamed and struggled to get away from the security guard.

I took careful aim at Tavin as she tried to push her way out of the crowd. I'd never shot an arrow at a person before, but I had no choice. I fitted the arrow to the bow and pulled back on the string. As I released it, I kept my eye on my target, not breathing until I heard Tavin yell as she fell to the ground.

"My God!" Brooke cried. "You killed her! Someone arrest her. She's a murderer."

"What the hell is going on out here?" Chase demanded as he finally reached us.

"Jessie shot that woman with an arrow!" Morgan pointed toward the spot where the crowd had moved aside when Tavin fell to the ground. "She's lost it, Chase. She attacked Brooke and shot that other woman."

"It's Tavin," I explained to Chase. "She's the one who killed Alastair. She shot Daisy and left her for dead in the pirate's cave. Ethan's there, too. Marielle got away when Brooke and I started fighting."

Before Chase could speak, his two-way radio crackled and a security guard near the cave reported finding Marielle and Ethan along with Daisy. He'd called an ambulance and reported the situation to the police at the castle. Daisy was on her way to the hospital.

"Jessie still attacked me and that woman," Brooke complained. "I don't care why she did it. I'm going to the police to file charges against her."

Chase didn't say a word. He went through the crowd like a serf through ale to get to Tavin. The tip had only pierced the shoulder of her baggy peasant shirt. It was the impact that had knocked her off her feet.

"What a shot," Morgan said as Chase brought Tavin back toward us. "You only winged her shirt." He looked at Brooke, who shrugged away from the security guard and stalked off through the crowd.

Applause broke out among the gathered residents and visitors. *Huzzahs* rang through the area. I thought the accolades were for me, but they were actually for Lady Lindsey, who had coaxed the hawk out of the sky and down to a perch. She was stroking Penelope's brown feathers with a careful hand as her songbirds flew above her head.

Oh well. I was still alive. I hoped Daisy was, too. Chase handed Tavin over to the two security guards after taking the gun from her. They were escorting her to the police at the castle. The crowd began to break up in search of other entertainment.

"Are you okay? Do you need to go to the first-aid station?" Chase put his arm around me and looked into my face.

I shuddered. "I'm fine. All I need is a shower and a good-natured bailiff to scrub my back. Maybe we could check on Daisy after that."

"I think we can work all of that in." He kissed me. "Really nice shot, by the way. Too bad the hawk was more interesting."

"It's all in a day's work at the Faire."

I got up the next morning and dressed in my scarlet archer's costume. Despite everything that had happened the day before, I felt rested and ready to take on Brooke.

Chase wasn't called out early for once, and we had a nice breakfast together before we headed toward the Village Green for the tournament. "Detective Almond will want to talk to you today," he said. "He was willing to wait until after the tournament."

"I thought you said Tavin confessed to everything after they got her to the station?"

"She did. But he has to interview you, Marielle, Daisy, and Ethan. Speaking of which, I heard a rumor last night while you were at the hospital visiting Daisy. Someone told me he heard that Ethan is her son."

I was *so* on top of this. "She swore me to secrecy about it. I couldn't tell anyone about her and Alastair."

He frowned. "Am I *anyone*? I think you could've told me."

"I think Daisy was more worried about me telling you than anyone else. She didn't want Ethan to know she was his mother and Alastair was his father."

"Get out of town! I didn't hear the part about Alastair being Ethan's father! You were hiding some valuable information. I know you were protecting Daisy, but if she'd actually been the killer, you could've been in danger."

"I knew Daisy didn't kill anyone."

"Like you trusted Tavin?"

"I think it's time to go slay my personal dragon. I'm hoping to get back to the hospital to see Daisy again later."

"I'm glad it was only a flesh wound. Daisy's lucky Tavin wasn't as good with a gun as you are with the bow."

"I hope you don't mind if I kick Brooke's butt today. I know you don't want us to do this—"

"Forget about it. Do what you need to do." He kissed me. "Just be careful."

We walked to the Village Green together, hailed a dozen times by friends (where were they yesterday when I needed them?) who were also on their way to the tournament.

Adventure Land had decided the tournament would be held before the main gate opened to the public. Merlin had said last night that they were worried about getting any more bad publicity. So the tournament would be held this morning in front of residents rather than visitors.

That was okay with me. After yesterday, I'd almost opted out anyway. I didn't need to prove anything, and I was really grateful to be alive and know everyone else was all right, too. Tony had actually talked me into going through with it by invoking a lot of sentimental stuff about not giving up. I'm fairly sure he laid bets on it to make money.

I was surprised to see so many residents at the Village Green already. As I think I've mentioned, no one here likes to get up early. People are usually getting ready for the day if they're out of bed. But we all enjoy a spectacle, so I was determined to give them what they came for.

King Harold and Queen Olivia were up on their dais in royal purple splendor. The crowd let out a loud "Huzzah!" as soon as Chase and I stepped onto the Green. I looked around for the black archer but saw no sign of my opponent.

King Harold got to his feet and held out his hand to calm the crowd. "Good people of Renaissance Faire Village, I bear news for you on this glorious morn. Our champion, Jessie Morton of Swords and Such, is the winner of the tournament by forfeit. The challenger, an outsider and coward, to be sure, has decided not to face our champion."

There were louder boos from the crowd and a lot of spitting as residents spoke of the matter. I was totally okay with not facing Brooke. Chase smiled and hugged me.

King Harold held his hand out again, and the crowd reluctantly grew silent. "Since we have all assembled here this day, the queen and I have deemed it fitting to take this opportunity to thank our champion for her bravery in the face of death. Come forward, Jessie of Swords and Such."

I glanced at Chase, who shrugged, obviously not know-ing what was going on either. I walked toward the platform as the king and queen descended toward me. Not sure what to expect, I knelt before them and took off my red cap, hop-ing whatever it was would mean more money or some other Village perk for the summer. Maybe free ale.

King Harold stood before me and raised his hands for silence again. "We declare on this day that Jessie Morton shall become Lady Jessie with all the rights and privileges appropriate for her station. Huzzah!"

The crowd of residents yelled and stomped their feet. It actually brought tears to my eyes, even though all of those rights and privileges wouldn't mean anything more than a deeper head bow from people who recognized me. Queen Olivia placed a thin tiara on my head and smiled at me. "Rise, Lady Jessie, and take your place among us. We thank you for your bravery."

There were more echoing *huzzah*s and lots of foot stomp-ing. The king and queen waved to the crowd as we stood there, basking in the glory.

King Harold raised his hands once more to ask for silence. When it was finally quiet he said, "Lady Jessie, the queen and I would ask one boon from you. We would surely enjoy seeing some of the archery skills you employed yes-terday when you captured the murderous fiend who stalked our kingdom and scared the challenger into submission."

How could I say no? I spent the next thirty minutes shooting at targets Chase put up around the Green. Master Archer Simmons laughed and applauded, joining me on the grass. It was fun showing off, but by the end of the thirty minutes, my arm and shoulder were killing me. There's always a price to pay.

With only twenty minutes to prepare for the opening of the main gate, the cheers and applause finally died away.

Many of the residents shook my hand, bowed, or patted me on the back as they returned to their places in the Village.

"You were really good!" Bart said. "You should have your own show at one of the stages."

"Don't get rid of my apprentice," Daisy said. "The summer isn't over yet."

I swung around, amazed to see her there with her arm in a sling. "Did you escape from the hospital? You're supposed to be there for at least three days."

"And miss Alastair's funeral tonight? I dare not think so. And if you're done showing off, I have a shop that needs sweeping and swords that need polishing. We need to work on that furniture for your blade, too."

I wondered about Ethan and how he was dealing with the knowledge about his parents. I didn't see him or Marielle in the crowd. I knew Daisy would be lost without him. I could only hope he'd be able to handle it with time.

"I think Lady Jessie needs a mocha before apprenticing, Master Armorer," Chase said, wrapping his arm around me.

"So say we all, Sir Bailiff," Daisy agreed. "Lead us to that divine beverage."

Despite Chase's security fears about holding Alastair's funeral at the Village, Merlin overrode his concerns. The funeral was planned for sunset, after the Village closed for the day. In that manner, Merlin had declared, the crowds would be kept small.

Merlin's definition of *small* clearly differed from mine, though. As I approached Mirror Lake from the side of the main gate, I saw what looked like thousands of people in Renaissance costume holding candles in the fading sunlight. If this wasn't a crowd to Merlin, I hated to think what was.

Chase had also compromised on the whole funeral-pyre

issue by allowing Alastair's already cremated remains to be put on a small wooden boat (far away from the *Queen's Revenge*) and set on fire as it crossed the lake. Two Myrtle Beach fire trucks were on hand in case of emergency. Because of the low risk factor, both bright red engines were covered with camouflage netting that supposedly made them blend in with the setting. Merlin hadn't been happy about the trucks, but Chase wouldn't agree to the event without them.

Alastair's bier was brought out of the castle, carried by Chase and three other members of the security team. King Harold, Queen Olivia, and the Nobility Guild followed it in rich garb and ceremony. In turn, they were followed by the heads of the other eleven guilds. I didn't even want to know what behind-the-scenes fighting had gone on to determine who would go first.

But I had to admit, it was a spectacular funeral. The flowered bier was placed in the wooden boat, and Chase set it on fire with a torch. The boat was pushed out into the middle of Mirror Lake, the flames reflecting in the water and off the castle walls, drawing thousands of camera flashes as people paid homage to the erstwhile master swordsman.

Once the flames had consumed the boat and been swallowed by the water, music began playing across the Village. Every restaurant contributed to the feast that was too big to be contained in the Great Hall, so it was served on the ground wherever people could find a place to sit and eat. Jugglers juggled, acrobats bounced and cartwheeled, and the Tornado Twins were completely obnoxious.

Portia, in the thralls of love for Fred the Red Dragon (and recognizing my part in the relationship), made a beautiful blue gown for me. It was studded with silver stars that matched the blue velvet doublet Chase wore for special events. I wore my tiara and my new nobility lightly as I staked out a spot near the lake for Chase and me to eat dinner. I knew he was coming with the feast, and I waited with the wine.

I didn't realize Marielle and Ethan were beside me at the funeral until I sat down to wait for Chase. Ethan was a little banged up, but his hair was perfect. Marielle had her share of bruises, too, but she looked lovely beside him. I could only hope that his perfect hair rubbed off on hers if they stayed together. Maybe being rich would be some incentive for them, since Ethan appeared to be Alastair's only child (the other children were made up by Tavin as a diversion). It seemed Ethan would inherit the evil, deadly daggers, which I felt sure he'd auction as Tavin had planned to.

"Thanks for your help, Jessie," Marielle said with a smile and a hug. "You saved us."

"You're welcome. But I'm sure Ethan had figured out that he wasn't really tied up when we left the cave."

Ethan's expression could only be called sheepish. "You didn't really tie me up?"

Chase joined us with the food. He put his arms around me as we sat down to eat. A new crescent moon rose in the sky. "All's well that ends well."

Ye Village Crier

Welcome back to Renaissance Faire Village and Market Place! There's so much to do and see at a Renaissance event. Sometimes it can be hard to take it all in. I know at my first event, I was amazed at how many people were needed to make it all happen. As with anything of this size, a Renaissance Faire requires a lot of work behind the scenes to keep the whole thing going.

You'll notice that there are signs of respect interwoven through the fabric of life here. These can include a head nod, a curtsey, a way of speaking, or even a deliberate snub.

The general rule is, the deeper the nod, curtsey, or bow, the more respect shown to the individual. The reverse is also true. If you want to show your contempt for someone, you do a quick curtsey or head bow.

To show absolute disrespect, ignoring a person sends the clearest message. It's like saying that the person is beneath your notice or acknowledgment.

Of course, during the real Renaissance, if you snubbed

someone of a higher station than you, you could face a flogging or worse for not acknowledging them. Very few peasants would have had the nerve to do this to a lord or lady.

There were other signs of respect during the Renaissance. Many of the table manners we use now were born during that time. Elbows off the table, don't use a knife to pick your teeth while you're eating, and my all-time favorite: no double dipping in the salt bowl!

Renaissance Recipe

APPYL TARYT

Renaissance festivals try to emulate history, but most of the foods offered—chili, pretzels, turkey legs, and so on—are those everyone is familiar with today. This is more to accommodate easy outdoor eating than to maintain authenticity.

But some of the dishes we eat today were a part of the Renaissance diet. Apple pie, for example, has been around for centuries. Because apples are usually plentiful and store well, they have been a favorite for as long as there have been cooks.

The modern pie shell we eat today was called a coffin by Renaissance folks. It was never eaten, but used only to keep the fruit moist. The rolling pin wasn't invented until the nineteenth century, so cooks would have used their hands or a smooth stone to spread the dough.

Sugar was available during the Renaissance, but it was expensive and difficult to find. Even the wealthy lords and ladies did without most of the time. Honey was used as a sweetener, but in the case of apple pie, cooks would have relied on the sweetness of the fruit to make the pie taste good. Spices such as cloves, nutmeg, cinnamon, and even saffron were heavily utilized by cooks of that era.

Filling

8 large apples, peeled, cored, and sliced
2 teaspoons cinnamon
1 teaspoon nutmeg
1 teaspoon ginger
¼ teaspoon cloves

Pie Shell (Coffin)

2 cups flour
1 teaspoon salt
1 cup butter
½ cup milk
1 egg, beaten, to brush on crust

Combine all the filling ingredients in a large bowl and set aside.

In a separate bowl, work together flour, salt, butter, and milk until it forms a ball. Divide the dough ball in half. Flatten each half with your hand, and then roll out each one gently until it is the size needed for the pie shell. Line a pie plate with one of the shells. Pour the apple mixture into the shell, and then cover it with the second flour shell. Bake for one hour at 375 degrees. Remove tart from oven and brush egg on the shell; place the tart back in oven until the top crust has browned. Serve hot or cold.

Renaissance Terminology

It's a good idea to know some Ren words to get you through a festival or faire. They can be even more important than minding your manners at the king's table!

Peace-tied weapon: Peace tying a sword, knife, dagger, or any other weapon means tying it so that it can't be removed from the sheath. There are many different ways to do this, including using twine, tape, rags, and even belts. Most Ren Faires require weapons to be peace-tied if you want to bring them on the grounds.

Troubadour: Writers of music who often wandered the countryside and sang their songs.

Turret: A small tower rising above and resting on one of the main towers of a castle, usually used as a lookout to scout for enemies.

Chain mail: A type of armor made of small metal rings linked together to form a mesh that protected the wearer.

Riposte: An offensive action with the intent of hitting one's opponent who has just attacked.

See you next time. Huzzah!

—Jessie

Penguin Group (USA) Online

What will you be reading tomorrow?

Patricia Cornwell, Nora Roberts, Catherine Coulter,
Ken Follett, John Sandford, Clive Cussler,
Tom Clancy, Laurell K. Hamilton, Charlaine Harris,
J. R. Ward, W.E.B. Griffin, William Gibson,
Robin Cook, Brian Jacques, Stephen King,
Dean Koontz, Eric Jerome Dickey, Terry McMillan,
Sue Monk Kidd, Amy Tan, Jayne Ann Krentz,
Daniel Silva, Kate Jacobs...

You'll find them all at
penguin.com

Read excerpts and newsletters,
find tour schedules and reading group guides,
and enter contests.

Subscribe to Penguin Group (USA) newsletters
and get an exclusive inside look
at exciting new titles and the authors you love
long before everyone else does.

PENGUIN GROUP (USA)
penguin.com